MW00608474

THE DAGGER MAN

by Glenn Starkey

The Daggerman

Copyright 2019 by Glenn Starkey

Cover designs by Jake Starkey, www.BattleCryRevival.com

All rights reserved. No part of this book may be reproduced (transmitted in any form by any means, electrical or mechanical, including photography, cording, or by any information or retrieval system without written permission of the aut or, except for the inclusion of brief quotations in reviews.

Scriptures from the Holy Bible are KJV, public domain, and fi m multiple public sources.

This is a work of fiction. All of the characters, places, organiz ions, and events portrayed in this novel are either products of the author's imagination o are used fictitiously.

ISBN (print) 978-1-54397-077-7

ISBN (E-book) 978-1-54397-078-4

Books by Glenn Starkey

BLACK SUN

"Gold Medal 2016 Historical Fiction Award" —
Military Writers Society of America

"…It was Glenn Starkey's ability to capture humanity at its worst and at its very best that touched me so deeply… Where some authors write a great story you can't put down, Glenn Starkey weaves a richly coloured tapestry and breathes life into every thread of the story. Every sentence, every paragraph, every description, and every character matters…"

"2016 Readers Favorite 5 Star Review" —*Readers Favorite.com*

SOLOMON'S MEN

"… genuinely suspenseful… a cascade of power struggles… Exciting and unpredictable, Solomon's Men is highly rec-ommended as an original action/adventure thriller."
—*The Midwest Book Review*

"Silver Medal 2012 Mystery/Thriller Award"
—*Military Writers Society of America*

"... one thing I can say with certainty is that if Glenn Starkey's name is on a book, I'm reading it!" —"2017 Readers Favorite 5 Star Review" —*Readers Favorite.Com*

THE HONJO

Sequel to *SOLOMON'S MEN*. New Release!

THE COUNCILMAN

New Release!

AMAZON MOON

"Notable Indie Book of 2013 Award" —*Shelf Unbound Magazine*

"Bronze Medal 2014 Thriller/Mystery Award"
—*Military Writers Society of America*

"... This would be one incredible action movie for sure!
'Amazon Moon' is deeply layered in emotions and themes of
both revenge and redemption. The human elements of his
characters are sharply focused but layered as well..."
—*W. H. McDonald Jr., American Authors Association*

"Amazon Moon is the sort of novel that grabs you by the throat
on the first page and doesn't let go until the last. It is an exciting story and, at the same time, something more. It is a fable
about one man's redemption, his rediscovery of innocence."
—*Nicholas Guild – New York Times Best selling Author
The Spartan Dagger, The Ironsmith, Blood Ties,
The Assyrian, Blood Star...and more.*

MR. CHARON

"One of the evident appeals of Mr. Charon is Starkey's descriptive prose. It gives vivid pictures of the surroundings and moves
the story flawlessly, which also contributes to the plot's deft execution. The classic good versus evil theme mixed with love,
hate, and redemption makes Mr. Charon a great read."
"2016 Readers Favorite 5 Star Review" —*Readers Favorite.Com*

YEAR OF THE RAM

"... it felt as if a hand had made its way out of the novel, gently grabbed
me around the neck and pulled me into its story until such time as

what was being told had come to an end. After accomplishing what it set out to do, the hand would then draw me out of the world I was in, pat my cheek, and disappear leaving me sitting there in wonder..."

—*Sandra Valente, Novel Review Café*

THE COBRA AND SCARAB: A NOVEL OF ANCIENT EGYPT

"… Rich, vibrant, descriptive language. Characters with depth, imbued with loyalty, courage and strength or touched with madness for power and evincing raw brutality. Treachery, betrayal, intrigue at every turn…"

– *Amazon.com - Five Star Review*

STEEL JUNGLE

"…Terrific read. Talented writer. Recommending it to my friends. So easy to understand how this could happen. Scary…"

—*Amazon.com – Five Star Review*

Non-Fiction:

THROUGH THE STORMS: THE JOHN G. SLOVER DIARY
Edited by Glenn Starkey for the Alvin Museum Society

"…An important and valuable work…genuinely impressed with the completeness of the manuscript, as well as its organization…a work that, in my view, combines both the best of first-person observations and conventional historical narrative to understand Slover's experiences as part of the larger sweep of American history during that period."

—*Andrew W. Hall, author, historian, DeadConfederates. com - Civil War Blog, and regional Marine Archaeological Steward for the Texas Historical Commission*

Dedicated to

Donna, Jake, Cindy, and Caleb whom are
God's daily blessings upon me.

Tony and Ludwig for safeguarding and educating so many pilgrims.

Pastor Tim and Pastor Howard—true men of faith, guided by God...

"... If anyone thirsts, let him come to me and drink. He that believeth in me, as the scripture hath said, out of his innermost being shall flow rivers of living water..."

John 7:37-38

"... Be strong in the Lord, and in his might. Put on the whole armor of God, that ye may be able to stand against the wiles of the devil..."

Ephesians 6:10-11

CHAPTER ONE

5 B.C.
Near Bethlehem, District of Judea

A full moon painted the cold, desolate landscape with ample light to see the slopes of surrounding hills. As the three magi, each an esteemed astrologer from the eastern Babylonian school, traveled with their servants and watched the sky, they debated their divinations and calculations until the moment a star rose with a brilliance never witnessed by man. They had charted the coming of a magnificent star that would mark great change, a shift in mankind, and announce the birth of a new king. Now, sitting upon their camels, gazing at its wonder, there were no longer doubts as to the accuracy of their foretelling.

Consulting his counselors about the prophecies, Herod the Great at his Jerusalem palace had directed the magi toward Bethlehem when they spoke of the star and asked where the newborn 'King of the Jews' lives. Their audience with Herod had left them ill-at-ease when he requested to be told of the newborn's whereabouts so he too may go pay homage to the child. But in the nights that followed their dreams warned them against such an action, and they agreed as one not to advise him.

Resting for the night the magi Belshazusur, Melchior, and Gadaspar sat wrapped in thick wool cloaks about their campfire, observing the star's trek across the sky. When it appeared to halt over the next city ahead, they knew then that by the next morning their search for the newborn king would draw to an end.

* * *

Walking and riding a donkey the ninety miles from Nazareth in the district of Galilee to Bethlehem, the city of David in Judea, had worn heavily upon Miriam, Josef's young wife. The child she carried was due any day. Every jarring step taken upon the rocky, unlevel landscapes, worried Josef that the baby would be born in the wilderness. But they safely arrived at his relative's home yet with little time to spare for her.

The Emperor Augustus' decree for all within Roman rule to be registered had forced the trip upon Josef and his fourteen-year-old wife. Without such an order he would never have attempted the hazardous journey with her. The mass influx of people for registration took every available room in the city. The *kataluma*, the second-floor chamber of his cousin's stone and mud-brick home on the outskirts of Bethlehem was far too small for Miriam when her hour came. Yet no relative turned another away in need, especially a pregnant woman. Yigael, Josef's cousin, gave them use of the first floor's room that served the family by day and sheltered their few livestock in the adjoining sheepfold at night from predators and thieves.

Face growing pale, Miriam held her stomach. A wet spot appeared on her tunic and spread along her legs. She winced and although frightened, struggled to be brave for her nervous husband. Reaching out, she squeezed Josef's hands, faintly smiled, and gave a partial nod.

"I believe it's time." Bottom lip curling inward, she flinched and laid her hands once more upon her stomach. Drawing a deep breath, she exhaled and tried to calm.

Josef had piled fresh hay for the animals in their pen and cleaned their manger to use the stone feeding trough as the newborn's cradle. Hearing her labored breathing, he hurriedly spread blankets over a thick bed of hay for Miriam's comfort and eased her down onto them.

"She is young and strong, Josef," Leah said to bolster his spirit as she walked down the narrow steps from the second floor. The older woman went about lighting more oil lamps until satisfied. "Our God, *Elohim*, will help her through tonight. With His blessing, your son or daughter will be born by dawn."

Gaze drifting from Miriam to his cousin's wife, Josef stood silent. *But the child is not mine... and will be a boy—the Messiah. Gabriel, Elohim's messenger told me so in a dream... Miriam's still a virgin and conceived through the Holy Spirit,* he thought, wanting to tell Leah. He knew, though, if he did, only confusion and endless questions would rise—and he himself was still overwhelmed by the revelations.

On the blankets Miriam grimaced and clenched her teeth. Her face flushed as she clutched her stomach. Beads of sweat dotted her forehead and when the contraction passed, she gasped for breath and looked at Josef. Tears rimmed her dark eyes and fear painted her youthful face. The front door opened. A shawl wrapped woman walked in and went to Miriam's side.

"I sent for my neighbor to help me," Leah said, glancing over her shoulder at Josef as she knelt by Miriam. "Go outside. Wait until I call you. There's nothing more you can do here."

Josef lightly nodded in acknowledgment but stood a moment longer to watch. Leah moved to between Miriam's legs, bent them and eased the hem of the girl's robe over her knees and back onto her stomach. Pausing, Leah gave him a stern look and swung a hand toward the door.

"Go," she ordered and returned her attention to the young woman.

With a last look about the makeshift stable, Josef shook his head in exasperation and walked out. *Is this how the Anointed One is to be born—among beasts of the field and upon hay spread over a dirt floor?* Stepping out into the cold night's bright moonlight, his gaze swept the crowd that was silently gathering before Yigael's house.

"Has He arrived?" a bent-postured old man gently asked, holding his tattered gray cloak tight at the chest to keep it about his head and body. The people around the elder pressed forward to listen to Josef's reply.

Dumbfounded, Josef scanned the anxious faces staring at him then raised his gaze to the sky. Directly above was a mysterious, shimmering star with resplendent streaks of light radiating from it.

"No, not yet, but He is coming," Josef softly said, peace consuming his heart for the first time in weeks.

Back and away from the gathering stood a solitary, ominous figure draped in a thick, dark cloak, the hood on his head masking moonlight from his face. Over the heads of the people Josef saw the man standing off to himself, looking at him. In time the man lifted his face toward the star, scowled, and gradually lowered his gaze to

4

stare at Josef once more. The cloak's hood slipped from his bald head and the moon's light displayed a hardened, wrinkled face with deep-set, penetrating eyes of a murky yellowish tint. Two bony hands rose and long, slender fingers eased the hood back onto his head. The hideous face vanished within the cowl's black shadow again.

Two hours passed before a woman's anguished cry carried from within the house. Turning to the door Josef recognized Miriam's voice quickly followed by the wail of a newborn. His first impulse was to rush to her, but he restrained himself knowing Leah would summon him when the time was right. He raised his gaze to the brilliant star and let it drift to the crowd of anxious people. The dark cloaked figure was gone.

When Josef felt as if time had drawn to a halt, the door opened slightly.

Leah stood smiling. "Come, Josef, see your son."

Wheeling to face the crowd, Josef proudly raised his arms into the air.

"Praise *Elohim!* He is born!" he jubilantly shouted then burst into the room.

* * *

5 B.C.
Caesarea Maritima, District of Samaria

The hour was long past the mid of night and the moonlit streets of Caesarea Maritima were barren at every turn. Even the Roman legionnaires had grown weary of whoring and drinking and returned to their barracks. The city was uncommonly quiet except for an occasional bark of a dog.

"Why do babies never come during the day?" Johanna asked, grumbling as she walked, pulling her faded blue cloak tighter about her to ward off the penetrating chill in the night air. Before turning into a shadow-filled, stone paved alley, she gazed at the rare star shining in the distant sky.

"My old eyes have witnessed many things both good and bad, yet I've never seen a star such as that before," she whispered to herself. "What sign could it be?"

Shrugging at her thoughts, Johanna started along the narrow alley lined with decrepit doors. A soft clatter carried through the night, making her turn to look. The black silhouette of a cloaked man could be seen standing at the street corner she had come from. Fearing he was a robber, she hurried along the alley, her sandals clacking on the stones with each quick step. Glancing back, she no longer saw the man and slowed her pace. Relieved, she ran her right hand over the wall by a door. Her fingers found the deep cut, identifying marks of the brothel she sought. Within two knocks upon its door, a dirty-faced woman of thirty in a threadbare tunic and ragged robe, opened it and ushered her to the rear of the building.

Johanna entered a dimly lit storage room. The stench of stale wine and musty, soiled cloths struck her. She ordered her escort to light more lamps. The cramped room brightened, and the elderly mid-wife recognized the sweat drenched Jewish girl laying atop filthy blankets on the dirt floor. Enough room for the young woman to lay was cleared among broken baskets, cracked pottery dishes, a pile of blotch stained blankets and empty wine jars. In her mouth was a strip of leather she'd been biting to hold back her screams of pain to avoid waking the other prostitutes, *sinners* as the townspeople named them. Kneeling beside her, Johanna gently laid her right hand upon the pregnant woman's stomach and rubbed it, feeling the movement within.

"Your time has finally come, Mira," Johanna kindly said, looking at the girl of seventeen years. "How many hours has it been since your water broke and the contractions began?"

"Four, maybe five," the girl answered between gasping breaths. "Get this whelp out of me. It's burdened me long enough." Mira's face was a mask of resentment as she gazed at her rotund stomach.

"The price is a silver coin for difficult births such as this. The baby has turned. I will have to reach in to guide the child out."

Mira grimaced at the pain engulfing her. "And what is the price to take it out into the desert and leave it for the jackals?" she asked when the agony subsided.

"Because of the late hour and danger I must undergo—."

"I don't care about your danger. What price do you demand?"

Years of performing her services for the *sinners* had hardened Johanna, but Mira's heart was colder than the desert's worst winter night.

"Four silver coins."

Reaching beneath her blanket, Mira pulled the coins out and tossed them onto Johanna's lap. "Do it," she ordered, replacing the leather in her mouth as she laid back.

The mid-wife positioned herself between Mira's legs, cast the girl's tattered robe back onto her stomach and probed for the baby with her right hand. Muffled cries of misery came from Mira as the mid-wife worked. Unable to stand the sight of blood oozing from Mira onto Johanna's arm, the dirty-faced escort fled the room.

Johanna coached Mira along then when all was ready, ordered her to push the baby out. The minutes passed like hours but soon a baby's cry came. The mid-wife swiped the excess blood from the infant's face and lifted it into the air.

"Hold your son while I cut and tie the mother-child cord."

Mira opened her mouth and spit the leather away. She breathed in deep panting blasts and turned her head to avoid seeing the infant. Hair soaked from sweat, strands stuck to Mira's face. "I want nothing to do with him—and make him be silent before he wakes the entire house."

The mid-wife roughly cut the cord, tied it and wrapped the child with a filthy, stained blanket laying near. "Here," she said, placing the baby on his mother's stomach. "Your breasts are swollen with milk. Let him suckle while I finish with you." In the lamp light Johanna could see glistening blood trickle from between the girl's legs.

Mira let the child nurse but still refused to look at him. "How long must I wait before working again?" she asked, staring at a wall.

The blood flow had slowed, but the mid-wife shook her head, believing more would come. She glanced at the young girl. "At least two weeks, possibly more because of the problems you had with the birthing." She washed her hands in a bowl of dirty water and wiped them dry with a nearby rag.

A look of disgust swept Mira's face. She handed the baby back to Johanna.

"Do you know who the father is?" the mid-wife asked in a low voice, letting her gaze drift from the sleeping baby to the young girl.

A sarcastic laugh came. "Of course, he's one of several hundred Roman soldiers." Mira paused, then turned her face away. "I've paid you. Now take the whelp and leave."

Johanna rose to her feet, wrapped the child in a stained blanket and eased him within her thick cloak. She glanced at Mira and left the room. Mira refused to look at her and kept her gaze on the dirt floor.

* * *

Josef stood before Miriam's blanket, watching his wife lovingly rock the sleeping newborn in her arms. She'd wrapped the child in clean swaddling clothes and only his angelic face was visible. Miriam raised her gaze to Josef, faintly smiled and closed her eyes to rest, exhausted from the night's ordeal. There was a sense of tranquility within the room. Even the animals acted differently, remaining still and silent as they looked at the infant. Easing the baby from Miriam's arms, Josef gently laid the child in the manger and set blankets about him for warmth. Leah stood nearby to help if needed.

"So, you are the Immanuel... the fulfillment of the prophecies," Josef said, brushing his fingertips over the outline of the baby's arm. Tears rimmed Josef's eyes from the overpowering joy that warmed his soul.

Walking to the door for a breath of fresh air, Leah saw a growing crowd outside. She glanced back at Josef in confusion. "They wish to see the child, but how did they know?"

Josef motioned her to let the people in. A faint smile formed on his lips as he stroked his beard. "They've been waiting. I believe angels summoned them."

* * *

Johanna clutched the baby to her chest and felt it lightly squirm beneath her wool cloak. The moon still shone bright and formed a perfect white orb in the sky. The odd star remained glimmering in the distant night with the same brilliance as when she had first seen it. It disturbed her. She began to have doubts over what she was about to do with the child.

The moonlight lit the path she walked along the dirt road, yet also allowed her to see the pack of desert wolves that followed. *They smell fresh blood on the child*, she thought, wishing she had better cleaned the infant before leaving the brothel.

Having walked a mile from Caesarea Maritima, she turned onto a path leading toward the desolate region where other infants of *sinners* had been abandoned. The wolves howled as they tracked her for their next meal. They were drawing closer, ringing her, and their calls into the night to one another grew more frequent and louder. She nervously glanced about the land, increased her pace but abruptly stopped at the sight of the dark-cloaked figure ten steps ahead.

A growling wolf appeared to her left, teeth bared, edging closer with head hung low. When the animal was within range of attacking, the cloaked man raised his bony right hand and pointed a long, almost skeletal finger at the animal. The black-furred wolf yelped as if violently struck by a sword then spun with tail tucked between its legs and raced away. Hearing their leader's cry of agony, the pack chased after him into the desert.

"Show me the child," the man ordered in a voice as hard as a smith's anvil. He stepped forward.

The mid-wife edged the front of her cloak open and moved so the stranger would have to turn into the moonlight. A cruel smile appeared on his leathery, wrinkled face when he looked at her, knowing she wanted to see him. He cast his hood back and Johanna's eyes widened at the sight of his bald head. Foul breath flowed from him as he leaned to the infant. He smiled in satisfaction, his teeth stained and rotted along the gum line. Yet it was the dark, yellowish tint of his eyes that startled her most, making her back a step from him. He moved forward and extended a bony hand. With one of the flesh covered, skeletal fingers he eased Johanna's cloak further aside to study the infant. It was then she observed how long, sharp, and darkly blemished his nails were.

Dragging a fingernail along the child's left forearm he sliced the skin, drawing blood. The baby cried out but drew silent when the unknown man raised a finger. The bleeding stopped, and the child's wound closed, leaving only a scar.

Pulling the cowl of his cloak back onto his head, the man stared at Johanna.

"Tell me, old woman, have you given him a name?"

Without hesitation or knowing why, the mid-wife blurted, "Hanan."

The man shrugged. "It's really of no consequence. I shall find him when the time comes."

"When the time comes?" Johanna's eyebrows drew together as her eyes narrowed.

Ignoring her question, the man glanced at the distant gleaming star and sneered. He turned to face Johanna. "The child is not to die. Take him to raise as your own. Nurse him on goat's milk."

"Why not his mother's milk? I could—."

"The whore is dying as we speak—bleeding to death," the man bluntly stated. Without a further word he turned to leave.

Johanna was speechless then her senses returned. "Tell me your name?"

He paused and looked back at her.

"Abaddon," he said, renewing his walk.

Staring at his cloaked back, Johanna whispered, "The angel that rules the abyss?"

He nodded but never slowed his pace as he walked away.

A shiver raced through the mid-wife. Whether from the cold desert air or the evil permeating from the man she tugged her cloak closed and watched Abaddon leave. Within ten steps he melted into the night. Backing cautiously, she glanced about her then started toward the city.

CHAPTER TWO

I t had been a long night of shepherds and townspeople streaming through Yigael and Leah's home. They wanted a glimpse of the infant or to kneel and pray before him, while others sought only to touch his blanket. Leah had halted the endless procession of worshipers for the family to sleep, but dawn's faint light was already tinting the interior of the rooms, growing brighter by the minute. A neighbor's rooster crowed. The clamor of the awakening city and incessant chatter of the crowds in the street carried through her open, second-floor window. All attempts to rest were useless.

Donkeys brayed while goats and sheep bleated in defiance of their herdsmen's boisterous urgings as the animals passed by the home. Yet it was the deep grunting, rumbling growls outside the front door that forced Leah wearily from her bed. Confused, she listened to the growls as she dressed. Such sounds didn't match the common morning commotions.

Once Yigael properly belted his tunic, he slipped his robe and sandals on to follow his wife down the narrow stone stairs to the first floor. Leah glanced at Josef who sat asleep beside his wife, leaning against the wall with chin lowered to his chest. A light snore passed his lips. Miriam finished nursing the infant and adjusted her robe when Leah approached.

"Did you get any rest?" Leah took the baby from Miriam and gently rocked the infant before laying him in the manger. The child squirmed slightly then fell asleep once warmed by the blankets placed about him.

Miriam shook her head and yawned. She touched her husband's arm to awaken him. Stirring groggily, he glanced about the room, rubbed his face with both hands and stiffly rose from the floor. His thick eyebrows lowered as he looked about trying to comprehend the strange noises. Again, deep grunting, rumbling growls came from outside the front door.

"Yigael, see what that racket is." Leah knelt to help Miriam move into a more comfortable position upon her blanket. Before her husband could walk to the door, a light knocking came upon its wood. "If it's more worshippers, tell them to wait until we break our fast," she said in an irritated tone.

Running a hand over his graying hair and beard, Yigael paused at the door, yawned deeply then partially opened it. About to speak, he froze at the sight of a short, well-dressed man, his head wrapped in white cloth that matched his flowing robes. Looking over the man's shoulder, Yigael's gaze swept the sunlit gathering of people. But it was the twenty feet of clear pathway behind the short man that captured Yigael's attention.

At the end of the path knelt three camels, one emitting a deep grunting, rumbling growl. Their jeweled harnesses and expensive saddlery announced that their riders were of great wealth and station. Servants held the animals' reins while three bronze-faced men, attired in the finest silk robes and headdresses of assorted bright colors, stood beside the camels retrieving articles from their saddle packs.

Leah called out to Yigael, but he was too awestruck by the distinguished visitors to do little more than stand and stare. Opening the door further, Leah was about to speak again then drew silent at the sight of the camels and unknown men.

"Peace be upon you. My masters have traveled far to pay respect to an extraordinary child born under the sign of the magnificent star. Is this the residence? Is He here?" the short man asked, eyebrows rising as his black eyes flared in anticipation. He looked past the stunned man and woman into the house. Seeing the newborn in the manger, the little man excitedly spun and nodded to his masters.

Shocked by the approach of three tall men dressed in royal attire and long, pointed cloth boots, Leah bowed her head as she opened the door wide for them to enter. Yigael stepped aside and bowed his head, but Josef defiantly stood before his wife and the baby, ready to protect them.

The first man, gaunt faced and stern eyed, was the tallest of the three. His ocean blue robe shimmered in the morning sun and the precious gems of his peaked cap sparkled as he walked. Behind him came a hawk-nosed, thickly bearded man in a purple flowing robe with an equally jeweled headdress to match his robe. The last man, a slender, clean shaven magus, strode toward the home with head held high, gaze fixed on the interior ahead. His crimson robes and peaked cap displayed a dancing sheen of sunlight as he walked, and behind him, the camels released more grunts and rumbling growls.

Silence fell across the gathered crowd as they watched the royal visitors enter Yigael's home carrying small chests.

"Peace be upon you and all in this house. am Belsharusur, and this is Gadaspar and Melchior," the gaunt-faced man said to Josef as he halted before him. "We have come from Persia to honor the newborn King of the Jews. May we present our gifts of gold, frankincense, and myrrh to him and kneel in homage at his feet?"

Josef nervously brushed his moustache and beard with the fingers of his right hand then nodded and moved aside. When the stately visitors saw the sleeping infant in the manger, their faces displayed the wonderment rising from within themselves. Stepping forward, each man knelt at the manger and raised their small wooden chests to their foreheads. Closing their eyes, they lightly spoke in their native tongue and gently set the chests next to the manger. They remained upon their knees in silence, gazing at the infant for thirty minutes before rising and stepping back.

The hawk-nosed Melchior adjusted his purple robe about him and studied Josef a moment before speaking.

"Has the Anointed One received a name so all may know him across the lands?"

"In eight days he will be circumcised under my people's covenant with *Elohim*. Then he will be known by his Hebrew name—*Yeshua*."

Turning and whispering among themselves, the three men nodded.

Josef's gaze drifted across their faces. "Is something wrong?"

Gadaspar lightly smiled. "No. We were only discussing the name. The Gentiles will translate his name to Greek since it is a language spoken across nations."

"And what name will that be?" Miriam asked from her blanket.

"*Jesus*," Belsharusur replied.

* * *

The room was dark except for the small oil lamp Miriam kept lit near the baby's manger to be able to check on him through the night. Josef tossed about on his blanket in a fretful sleep, mumbling unintelligibly until his fear laden dream forced him awake. He bolted upright and apprehensively glanced about the quiet room believing danger to be within arm's reach. A clammy sweat stuck his sleep shirt to his chest. Running a hand over his face, he wiped sweat away and tried to slow his heavy breathing.

"What's wrong?" Miriam asked in a whispering voice beside him.

"A man in gleaming battle armor came and stood by my feet... His sword was like none I've ever seen."

Miriam looked about the room but saw no one. She shook her head lightly. "We are alone, Josef. No one is here."

Turning to his wife, Josef's eyes grew wide. "After our son is circumcised at the temple and your purification has been performed, we must leave for Egypt."

"*Egypt?*"

Josef nodded. "*Elohim's* messenger said we must take the child there in secret and remain until I am told the danger has passed."

"*Danger? What danger?*"

Gazing at the front door, expecting soldiers to burst through any moment, Josef turned to his wife and gravely nodded.

"Death is coming for Yeshua."

* * *

5 B.C.
Jerusalem, District of Judea

Herod shuffled about the sunlit throne room, sipping wine from a gem-encrusted goblet. He scowled and restlessly tugged at his regal robes as if they were slipping from his shoulders even though they were not. It had become one of many strange habits he had acquired in the past months. His downcast, somber gaze gave the impression he was studying the designs of the mosaic tiles crafted into the marble floor. The scribes, astrologers, counselors and the king's personal physician standing to one side of the massive room knew different. This was merely the calm before a volcanic eruption. The diseases settling within Herod were steadily destroying him. With each passing month his once obese frame was shrinking to little more than sagging flesh over bone. His dark eyes and cheeks were sunken, and his hands had begun to tremble. Each footstep came slow and measured as if he were unsure of himself, and though he had a reputation for murderous rages, now they arose more frequently, infused with unbridled savagery.

"Do those three believe me to be a fool? Bethlehem is only six miles away. A beggar could crawl there and back since they've been gone. But no, not one returned as I instructed. I tell you they have fled to Babylon!" Herod's voice was low and seethed with anger. He threw the wine goblet through the air, but his strength and balance were weak. The golden chalice fell less than ten feet away, spilling wine across the floor as it struck the marble with a sharp clank, bounced and rolled to a halt.

Three burly soldiers and a frail appearing physician rushed forward to carry the wavering king to his gilded throne on the wide dais. The young scribes lowered their faces to gaze at the floor, yet the aged astrologers cast guarded glances at one another while Herod was being seated. The star gazers agreed that the unknown diseases were devouring his mind and body.

"Get away from me—get away," Herod shouted, swinging his arms free of the soldiers. Easing back into his throne, the king ordered the physician to leave. He pointed the trembling forefinger of his right hand at the curly-haired, strong framed Greek of forty years who stood quietly at the edge of the dais.

Lucius, his court advisor, walked to him and bowed. "Yes, my lord?"

"Bethlehem is hiding this newborn from me. They've become treasonous if they believe the child is their new king. I want the city destroyed," Herod said in a growling tone. His dark eyes within their sunken hollows rose from gazing at the floor to stare at his advisor. Madness painted them.

"My lord, allow me to send spies to find the child and have him brought to you. Eliminating the entire city means eliminating the taxes you receive from it." Lucius always had a way of tempering Herod's blood thirsty side to bring about some sanity, but this was not to be one of those moments.

Herod nodded. "You're right... Well, send soldiers to Bethlehem. Kill every male child under the age of two. Let their blood flow like a river so the people will know there will be no other king but me."

The Greek stood stunned. There would be no changing the king's mind. The fury now in Herod's eyes had been present when he ordered his beloved second wife, Mariamme the Hasmonean, and later several of their sons, to be killed because he believed they were plotting against him.

"As you have ordered, my lord." Lucius gazed at the slump-shoul-
dered king sitting upon the throne. Bowing, he left to find the commander of Herod's army and assemble the required butchers.

* * *

Caesarea Maritima, District of Samaria

For the past ten days Johanna had done little more than remain
home to watch over her new ward and think about Abaddon's strange
words and actions—especially scarring the baby as he had on the left
arm. Everything about the man had reeked of evil. Even recalling
his yellowish eyes still sent a shiver up her spine. And what of the
odd star with its brilliant light? Within a day after Hanan's birth it
had vanished from the sky, leaving her troubled that the star might
have been some portend of ill omen. But at sixty-two years old she
realized there was little hope of living long enough to see what his
destiny held.

Standing in the doorway of her small home, she watched the
passersby and waved to several she recognized that lived in the
immediate area. Everyone knew of her work as a mid-wife, but none
suspected her association with the *sinners* and disposals of their
unwanted. A twinge of guilt swept through her but the thought of
the minor fortune she had amassed over the years from the brothels
eased her conscience.

The noon day sun had reached its zenith in a cloudless sky.
People crowded her narrow street, coming and going from the shops
and markets, but shepherds taking their herds to sale only added to
the congestion. Her home had once been far outside of Caesarea's
realm, yet with Herod the Great's endless construction of pagan

temples, an amphitheater, the massive hippodrome for chariot races, and opulent buildings to entertain the constant influx of Gentiles, her neighborhood now laid within the city's boundaries. Those boundaries were always extending, though, as the need arose for more land to build Roman styled palatial estates.

Herod loved the Romans, although, they treated him with inconsequence, merely as another conquered ruler of a conquered land. Jews thought him to be more Roman than Idumean the way he constantly catered to them and their hedonistic ways. He'd built Caesarea Maritima and its major port to honor Caesar Augustus and win favor by making the Mediterranean seaside community a playland for the Romans and other Gentiles—and he had succeeded. Foreigners came in droves by caravans and ships, and over half of the city's population was believed to be Gentile. Yet with a detachment of legionnaires from Caesar's *Legio X Fretensis* garrisoned in the city, the Romans' love of slaves, wine shops and decadent parties their masters loved to host, also came a flourishing flesh trade. Though, mostly out of sight in alleys and particular business districts, brothels prospered by fulfilling Roman needs.

Herod's passion for exorbitant construction projects throughout his realm had added 'The Great' to his name. In Jerusalem he had built more palaces for himself, a sprawling hippodrome, and an amphitheater for gladiatorial contests which the Jews detested. But as a conciliatory gesture to his Jewish subjects, he was expanding Jerusalem's *second* temple and sparing no expense in the project. The first holy temple, Solomon's Temple, had been destroyed by the Babylonian general Nebuchadnezzar II five-hundred-ninety-one years earlier.

"Elisha, come here, my dear," Johanna called out, waving a hand to the girl of twelve walking across the dirt street.

The short, slender youth ran to her, holding onto her shawl to keep it from slipping from her head. Her cute face beamed as she smiled, and her big, wide, light brown eyes shined like polished jewels. Elisha wrapped her arms about the grandmotherly woman, hugged her affectionately then stepped back.

"Would you watch over Hanan while I go to the market? I shouldn't be long. When I return, I'll have you go bring us more goat's milk from your father's herd. Would a *shekel* for watching over the baby and the milk be enough for your help?" Johanna asked. Her eyebrows rose, head canting with innocence. Several days before, she had explained the baby's presence to Elisha as the orphaned child of a family relation who had fallen upon misfortune.

Nodding eagerly, the young girl entered Johanna's home, removed the shawl from her head and took a seat by Hanan's cradle. She rocked it slowly and cooed to the infant. He smiled at Elisha and her own warm smile grew.

"I won't be long, only enough to buy what Hanan and I need. After I return, we'll get the goat's milk and you can feed him if you wish." The mid-wife was already wrapping her long scarf about her head and neck as she spoke. Brushing the front of her tunic and robe a last time, she paused at the door and glanced back at Hanan playfully squeezing Elisha's finger.

* * *

Little breeze flowed through the dusty, overcrowded market. The air was stifling and held a stench of musty bodies, animal manure, produce, and acrid textile dyes. Bleating sheep and a constant din of people's chatter mingled with the merchants standing at their awning covered stalls, crying out for passersby to inspect their wares for the best prices in all of Caesarea. Shawl draped women with baskets in hand haggled with vendors over the outrageous food prices while slaves in all manners of dress squeezed melons and examined other produce to purchase the best for their Gentile masters. Children raced in play through the crowds, attempting to steal fruit where ever possible, and pick the pockets of the unsuspecting.

"Tell me again, Akiba, why I should buy inferior dates and figs from you rather than the fresh ones at Simon's stall down the street," Johanna said, feigning dislike for the merchant's produce on display.

The leathery-faced Syrian, several years younger than Johanna, eyed her carefully as he leaned back, crossing muscled arms over a brawny chest. He raised a hand and slowly stroked his long, thick beard as he considered her words. His brows edged downward, almost forming a solid line across his forehead.

"How can a woman of such beauty like you have such a viperous tongue? You know well that my fruits come from distant lands and I select only the best for patrons as yourself. May Ishtar grant you wisdom and compassion to allow me to serve you," the Syrian said, a fragment of a smile breaking on his lips. He humbly bowed then rose with a roguish gleam in his eyes.

Johanna smiled and lightly shook her head. "Oh, look who now has a serpent's tongue. You invoke your goddess of love for reasons more than selling me fruit!" She laughed and winked at her friend. They'd had an on and off amorous relationship for years which suited them for neither wanted marriage, only to share an occasional night's companionship upon soft blankets.

The merchant watched as she carefully chose an assortment of fruits and set them aside to purchase.

"I see that your appetite has increased- or has another man taken my place in your heart?" Akiba said, lightly laughing as he placed the fruits in her shoulder bag.

Handing him a coin, her expression grew stolid, then she leaned forward.

"I now have a baby to raise. A boy-child born only a few weeks ago..." Johanna felt relief at being able to talk to Akiba about Hanan. Her friend of many years would hold his tongue and safeguard her secrets as he always had. But after she finished telling him all, especially about Abaddon, instead of nodding his head in understanding, his face grew ashen and he nervously glanced about them.

"Is the newborn the one Herod searched for? The child born under the star?" Akiba asked, visibly shaken.

"Herod? *King Herod?* What would he want with the child?" Johanna asked in a whispering voice.

"You haven't heard about the *massacre of the innocents* in Bethlehem? It was only a few days ago when he sent soldiers to Bethlehem to slaughter every male child under the age of two. They were searching for a child born under the sign of the star that everyone saw in the heavens."

Covering her mouth with a hand, the mid-wife stood shocked at the news. Her eyes narrowed as if a harsh pain raced through her. At last she garnered the courage to speak.

"How many were killed?"

Akiba shrugged his shoulders and frowned. "There are people that say less than twenty, yet others speak of greater numbers. Soldiers ran them through with swords and left them to die in the streets. Someone overheard a soldier saying that Herod believed one may be the 'King of the Jews'—marked by birth under a glorious star to replace him."

Johanna's gaze drifted across the marketplace as she stood deep in thought. *Then the star was a true ill omen? Abaddon had reeked of evil and his words of finding Hanan when the time was right had made no sense...but was the child destined to replace the king?* Her thoughts rambled and grew more confusing. She glanced at Akiba and found him staring at her with a puzzled look upon his face.

"Do you believe the soldiers will come here in search of the child?" she asked her old friend in a strained voice.

The Syrian shook his head. "If they were, they would have already been here. I doubt if Herod would risk upsetting his Roman masters with such a spectacle of bloodshed because his butchers might mistakenly kill a child of the Gentiles."

Tightening her grip on her shoulder bag, she forced a smile. "I had better be getting home. I have much to think about concerning Hanan."

Akiba reached out and laid his right hand upon hers, squeezing lightly.

"Keep the boy out of sight for another two weeks then if Herod's soldiers do not arrive here in Caesarea, all may be well for him. The king may believe the child he sought is now among Bethlehem's dead."

"Thank you," she said in a gentle voice. "I trust your counsel." A warm smile appeared on her lips as she turned to leave.

"If I learn more, I can always come by your house late one night so we may *talk*." Mischief painted the Syrian's dark eyes.

"My door is always open to you, but having the newborn there means you cannot stay. The way you snore in the early morning hours would only frighten him." She smiled and waved goodbye.

The Syrian watched her leave. He plucked a fig from his produce and held it ready to eat. "By Ishtar, she can bake my bread in her oven any day," he whispered, grinning as he bit into the fruit.

CHAPTER THREE

6 A.D.
Nazareth, District of Galilee

The setting sun painted the horizon with a fine orange, reddish tint leaving the dim light of dusk to spread gray and black shadows along Nazareth's dirt roads and between houses. Josef stood in his open-sided carpenter's shop, stretching his weary back from having remained bent over too long, sanding the roughhewn wood of a table, his latest project. He saw Miriam wave from the door of their stone walled home. Dinner was prepared. Acknowledging with a nod, he cleaned his work area.

"Time to halt for the day, son. Your mother calls us to dinner." He brushed sawdust from his robe. "Put your tools away. We must wash before we eat."

Josef started toward the large water bowls on a bench by their home's front door. He glanced at Yeshua and watched his nine-year-old son lay a small maul and chisel in their kept locations on a shelf.

The dark-haired, willowy boy dusted his tunic and raced after him to walk side by side to the washbowls. Shaking his sore right arm, Yeshua remained silent but Josef had seen the movement and laughed.

"Swinging a maul and chiseling boards all day will build your strength. A sharp mind requires a strong body." The father smiled. "To be a master carpenter requires full knowledge of wood and masonry so you may find employment wherever you travel when you are older."

"Will I ever be as good as you, Father?" the boy asked, tilting his head back to look up with wonder in his deep brown eyes.

"No," Josef replied kindly, his expression growing solemn. Ruffling his son's thick hair, he grinned. "You will be better than I ever was."

Hearing their approach, Miriam walked out of the house and met them at the wash bowls.

Josef lightly kissed her forehead, glanced at their son, and carried his gaze back to his wife. "Someone told me today that Antipas is rebuilding the town of Sepphoris, a few miles north of Nazareth. It's to be his first capital since taking over the rulership from his father, Herod the Great. Tomorrow I will take Yeshua with me to see if they are hiring carpenters. I'm sure the wages are good, and the experience will benefit our son."

"You've done well for us all these years since we returned from Egypt," she said, tenderly smiling as she touched her husband's arm. "I remember how worried you were when El him's messenger told you to bring us to Nazareth. You were so nervous about finding enough work here but now you have more than you can handle."

Reaching out, he gently patted his wife's lightly bulging stomach and proudly smiled. "Yes, it's difficult to forget those days. I'm still nervous about taking care of my family, especially since we will have more mouths to feed."

Turning to his mother, Yeshua grinned. "I think *James* would be a good name for my brother."

The sun had set and black blanketed the land. Only the oil lamps shining from within their home broke the night. Josef washed his face and hands then looked at his son.

"And how did you come upon that name? Or know you will have a brother?"

"I don't know. I may have heard it while talking with *my Father*." The boy spoke casually as he walked past them into their home.

Josef remained still. He gazed at Miriam with sadness in his eyes. Josef knew he wasn't Yeshua's father by blood relation, yet he had always attempted to be a true father to the boy. But though Yeshua loved him as if he were, the boy called *Elohim 'my Father'* and Josef *'father'* in a tone of voice that always left Josef with a sense of dejection.

* * *

6 A.D.
Caesarea Maritima, District of Samaria

The two men sat among the upper classed patrons of the city beneath the wide scarlet blue and crimson awning of Aharon's wine shop. They sipped fine Damascus wine from polished marble cups kept only for the more affluent and ate honey flavored figs while enjoying a reprieve from the broiling mid-afternoon sun. Though it was late spring, the oven heat of summer was already being felt.

From their vantage point they watched Caesarea's international cast of people walk by in all manners of dress and listened to the variety of languages spoken. The wine shop sat on the edge of the largest marketplace in the city. Like every day, Roman bureaucrats were among Aharon's regulars, discussing their losses at the hippodrome's chariot races and complaining about the lack of quality slaves to serve them.

Micah ben Netzer leaned back in his chair and casually adjusted the folds of his dark blue robe. He was taller than most men, lean in frame with a deeper tan than normal from his extensive travels. Black, collar-length hair flowed back over his head and matched his well-trimmed beard and black pearl eyes. Mindlessly tracing the rim of his wine cup with a fingertip, he watched the sea of passersby, studying their mannerisms with amusement.

At twenty-seven years of age he was known as one of the shrewdest and most wealthy merchants throughout the land, a station inherited from his father, a merchant with trade contracts in surrounding countries and across the Mediterranean Sea. But the inheritance hadn't been a gift. Micah had labored many a long day at his father's side since youth, learning the art of commerce and negotiations. Now, with his father in failing health and unable to travel, Micah ruled the family's trading empire with the help of his father's aide and bodyguard, Yosef ben Hagkol.

They were an odd pairing in appearance, yet both had the cunning minds of wolves and eyes as sharp as eagles. While Micah's handsome features and smooth-talking ways easily won over women's hearts, Yosef's barreled chest, shorter height, and bearded, rough face with thick, wild brows made women back away at first glance.

But they were a worthy team and Yosef's ten years of senior age provided mature counsel to the often overly ardent younger man.

A bellowing belch made Micah turn. He glanced across two
tables to see an obese Roman administrator dressed in stylish robes
wipe his mouth with the back of a hand. Shaking his head in disdain,
Micah turned to Yosef.

"Have our people strayed so far from the Laws of Moses that
Elohim punishes us by letting these *dogs* govern our lands? Their
pagan ways and increasing taxation will be the ruin of our country if
we do not take action," Micah whispered, cold rage in his eyes. "I tell
you, they are our enemy."

"Yet you go to their feasts, break bread with them, and mount
their wives like a rutting ram. Is that the action you speak of?" Yosef's
right brow rose as he benignly grinned. He drank his wine and held
the empty cup aloft for the shopkeeper's servant girl to fill.

"You well know why I go," Micah said with a tinge of anger. He
straightened in his chair. "If it were not for my gold and connections
abroad, the Romans would have nothing to do with me. They believe
they are using me to achieve their goals of political expansion and
commerce for their emperor, all while I use them to gain knowledge
of how to defeat them—and make a profit."

Micah paused when the servant approached to refill Yosef's
cup. No sooner had the girl left than the merchant renewed his talk.

"I do not enter their homes because doing so would make me
unclean. They hold their feasts on wide patios out of doors, and I
remain outside when they later enter the homes for what they call
the evening's entertainment," he said, nodding in confirmation.
"My discussions with them are about trade to further my father's
businesses...but laying with their wives—if you can call them wives

31

because they care nothing about the sanctity of their marriages—affords me valuable information about the secret plans their husbands are making with Caesar to control us."

"And this valuable information you learn from them... How can we best use it against them? Go to the Sanhedrin? Only a fool trusts the Temple priests. They've grown as corrupt as the Gentiles, feeding off of our people by pocketing portions of their money offerings. And why do you think they want unblemished sheep? Because they take most of the sheep sacrifices home for their families to eat." Yosef swung his hands through the air as he shook his head in contempt.

"We strike them all—the Romans, the Sanhedrin, and any Jew who sympathizes with them." Micah spoke with such a casual air that it made Yosef pause in his drinking. He waited for Yosef's shock to pass then continued.

"Surely, other than Judas of Gamala and his *Zealots*, we are not the only men troubled by this Roman occupation, their taxations, and the corruption within the priesthood. It was an insult to our people to be ruled by Herod the Great, an appointed 'King of the Jews', when he was only an Idumaean convert to Judaism with no Jewish blood in him! His sons are no better. The squabbles of Archelaus and Antipas made Caesar Augustus divide the kingdom. He gave the tetrarchy of Judea to Archelaus and Galilee to Antipas. But now that the Romans govern Judea, Archelaus has been pushed from power." Micah paused to let his anger settle. He tapped a finger several times against the table and spoke again.

"Our people are ready for the coming of the Messiah who will be a political leader and rally us against the Romans. The scriptures have foretold it in the prophecies. We have spies for our businesses. I say we use them properly across this land to extract the information we need and recruit the best clandestine operatives. Organize men willing to revolt against the Romans, yet not do so openly as Judas of Gamala did or become involved in a direct fight with the soldiers. The legionnaires are better equipped and trained for such confrontations—but eliminating key political figures and corrupt priests one by one. Assassinating them with a secret organization will strike fear in their hearts as they've never known."

"What secret organization?" Yosef asked, finishing his wine in a single drink. "Does one exist that I haven't heard of?"

Micah lightly shook his head. "No, not yet, but soon there will be when we make it. One that will surpass even Zealotism. It will take time—possibly years. With the right planning and training, though, I believe we can do it. We can draw on men from across the country and..."

Eyes narrowing, Yosef waited for Micah to finish speaking but the younger man's attention was focused on a disturbance in the marketplace. Yosef turned in time to see vendors and residents swinging their arms through the air and angrily shouting. The two men rose from their chairs and walked out into the dirt street.

Two sturdy, darker skinned, black-headed boys of about twelve years rushed out from an alley chasing after a much shorter boy. The lithe, brown-haired younger boy, appearing to be no more than nine or ten, raced through the marketplace, weaving through the crowd with a cloth-wrapped bundle clutched to his chest, never looking back at his pursuers. But sweat streamed down his flushed face and his breathing was labored. He must have realized further evasion was useless and slid to a dust rising halt, turning about to confront them.

The older boys stumbled as they tried to slow their speed, unprepared for their prey's sudden stop. They crashed into the light-skinned, smaller boy and all three tumbled to the ground in a rolling heap of flying dust. The crowd about them formed a large ring and while there were women who cried out for the boys to stop, the men shouted encouragement and laughed at the fight, enjoying the spectacle.

When the three came to a halt in the dirt, the smaller boy lay on his back still clutching his bundle while one of the larger boys climbed astride his chest. Backing and yelling encouragement the other boy watched his friend pummel the younger boy with balled fists and try to rip the bundle from his hands.

Yosef started forward through the crowd to halt the fight, but Micah caught his arm and lightly shook his head. The merchant kept watching the younger boy with interest. It was then, as if it were all part of a plan, that the smaller boy turned the tide of the battle.

Smashing his bundle into the face of the boy atop him, he knocked him aside, into the dirt, and nimbly jumped to his feet. No sooner had the brown-haired boy risen than he planted his sandaled right foot between the taller boy's legs. A sickening expression spread over the taller boy's face as he writhed on the ground and twisted into a ball, crying out in agony as he pressed both hands against his groin.

The smaller boy spun to confront the remaining older boy but froze.

The dark-haired boy had drawn a short, curved knife from within his robe and clumsily launched an attack. Like a mongoose fighting a cobra, the younger boy deftly moved past the gleaming blade and unleashed his own attack. He blocked the knife arm, and his balled hand smashed the nose of the older boy, momentarily stunning him when blood flowed. The young boy struck again, grabbing his attacker's knife hand. He twisted the wrist and crossed beneath the arm, sending the older boy flying forward, flipping head over heel onto the dirt.

A cloud of dust rose but there was no hesitation in the brown-haired boy. Teeth clenched, breathing hard, he grabbed the knife in his right hand and with his left, wrapped fingers in his opponent's thick hair. He yanked the older boy's head back to bare his throat. Bystanders shouted and raised their arms in panic of what was about to happen. The smaller boy was oblivious to the crowd and drove the knife toward the older boy's throat. But a man's hand clamped about the wrist of the young boy's knife hand with an iron grip and held fast.

Micah didn't release his hold and with his free hand took the knife from the boy. Chest heaving like a smith's bellows, the brown-haired boy stared at Micah with fire in his dark green eyes. Pulled away, it forced him to release his hold of the older boy's hair.

Walking to the two boys on the ground, one still rubbing his groin as he moaned, Yosef jerked them to their feet and held them by the rear of their necks with his own hard grip.

The younger boy quickly lifted the bundle from the ground and after dusting dirt from its cloth stood protectively holding it against his chest.

Micah studied the youths. Dirt and dust had mingled with their rivers of sweat to make splotches and streaks of mud over their faces, hair, and clothes. But the heat of the day was already drying the mud into thin, crusty cakes.

The knife's owner waited with trepidation in his eyes while his friend appeared on the verge of crying as he held his groin. Yet it was the rage still burning wildly in the younger boy that captured Micah's attention.

Turning the knife in his hands, Micah examined its wide, strong blade that tapered down into a slight curve. Well-worn leather wrapped the slender wooden handle and from tip to hilt, the knife was the length of a man's forearm. Its weight and balance were exceptional and made him smile inwardly. *A Sica... Made with a Damascus blade... The best weapon for close quarters fighting,* he thought.

Letting his gaze drift about the ring of onlookers, Micah shook his head as his brows drew downward. Annoyance flashed across his face.

"Move along," he growled. "There will be no blood shed today for you to gawk at."

After the crowd dispersed, he let his gaze drift to the older boys.

"Why were you chasing him? Does it take two of you to bully one boy?"

Slowly rising from his bent stance, the larger of the two pursuers stopped rubbing himself and pointed to the bundle held against the younger boy's chest.

"He's a thief. He stole that loaf of bread from my father's stall."

"What is your name?" Micah asked the brown-haired boy. He motioned Yosef to release his hold on the two older boys but kept the knife.

"Hanan."

"Did you steal the bread?"

At first no answer came then Hanan gradually raised his gaze to meet Micah's.

"I left a coin to pay for the bread. It was all I had."

"Why would you take it without paying the full amount?"

Silence followed for several seconds as Hanan stood defiantly staring off into the distance. "I have not eaten for two days and needed food. His father laughed and shoved me away when I asked to buy anything with my only coin. So, I left the coin and took the bread."

Yosef gave Micah a slight nod of approval and raised his eyebrows.

Lips pursed, Micah's eyes narrowed. He nodded agreement, appreciating that the boy had first attempted to be honest with the merchant, and truthfully answered Micah's questions.

"Give me the bread," Micah ordered, looking into Hanan's eyes.

The boy stood motionless then reluctantly handed the bundle to him.

Still holding the knife, Micah opened the bundle to examine it. Half of the large loaf of bread was crushed and broken from Hanan smashing it into his attacker's face. Micah tore the bread in two, handed the damaged half to the merchant's son and the good half to Hanan.

"He will keep the portion he paid for," Micah said, looking at the merchant's son who stood with eyes wide and mouth agape. "Return the other half to your father. If he has problems with my decision, tell him Micah ben Netzer is at Aharon's wine shop ready to discuss his displeasure."

The friend of the merchant's son spoke out. "What about my knife? It's my father's."

Micah carried his unsympathetic gaze to the dirt stained boy and leaned toward him.

"I should take a stick to your back for stealing your father's knife and trying to use it on someone over a loaf of bread! And after I beat you, I should beat your father for not teaching you better... No, the knife is now mine and will remain so." Micah straightened and crossed his arms as he stared down at the ashen-faced boy. "Leave my sight before I change my mind and beat you both with a stick. Go!"

The two older boys raced away, arguing over who was to blame for the damaged bread and loss of the Sica.

"I'm hungry. Are you, Yosef?" Micah asked, his voice carrying a light, casual tone. He glanced at Hanan and nodded. "Come along, I'm sure you're hungry too."

The two men started toward Aharon's wine shop without looking back at the boy. They grinned at one another when they heard him running to catch up.

Making their way through the crowded marketplace, they returned to their table. Micah ordered wine, more honey flavored figs, slices of spit-cooked lamb, and two bowls of water.

Within minutes the servant girl arrived with the water. Micah looked at Hanan and pointed to the bowls.

"You're filthy. Wash your face and hands as best you can. You know our laws about being clean before eating."

Laying his bread on the table, Hanan appeared confused about the laws but obeyed. He washed his face in one bowl and cleaned his hands in the other. Finishing, he sat back in his chair to await the food. Neither of the two men spoke as they sat drinking their wine and looking about the street, unconcerned with the boy's presence.

The food had barely been set before them when Hanan began to eat like a starving wolf pup. Micah poured a cup of wine for him and watched the boy wash down pieces of lamb with it. Yosef shook his head and glanced at Micah.

"Easy, boy. You'll make yourself sick eating so fast. No one will take your food away," the burly aide said. He exhaled in relief as Hanan nodded while eating a fig.

Micah sat in deep thought turning the Sica in his hands, examining it with a gaze that told of his interest in the knife being more than about its construction. He laid it before him on the table and crossed his arms as he studied the boy. Hanan reached out for a fig with his left arm.

"That is quite a scar on your forearm. Is it from another knife fight?" Micah asked, watching Hanan's green eyes for signs of deception.

"Johanna told me I received it the night I was born, but she would never speak of how it happened," the boy said, selecting another slice of lamb.

"Who is Johanna? Your mother?" Yosef asked, elbows resting on the table as he listened.

"No, the woman who raised me."

"Where is she now? You said you haven't eaten in two days. Did she abandon you?" Micah glanced at the passersby and let his gaze drift to across the street. An aged, gray-bearded man in the ragged tan robes of a shepherd, stood leaning against a stone wall, gazing in their direction. The shepherd lowered his head when Micah stared at him.

"She died a year ago when Akiba discovered the money she had been hiding. He killed her and left me on the streets," the boy answered.

"*Akiba?* Her husband killed her and left you on the streets?"

Shaking his head, Hanan frowned. "Akiba was her lover. He's a Syrian."

"Who taught you to fight?" Micah asked sipping his wine. He glanced across the street, but the shepherd had left. He turned to face the boy again.

"I learned from Akiba and..." Hanan replied, voice growing hard. "... and living on the streets. There are more bullies in this city than those two boys. I would have beaten them if you hadn't stopped me. They were slow and stupid."

Yosef shot a quick look at Micah and gave a piecemeal grin.

"You would have killed that boy if I hadn't stopped you," Micah said, tapping the Sica on the table.

Hanan glanced at it and shrugged with indifference. He returned to his food but paused. "May I have the knife?"

"Why?"

"One day I might find Akiba. He's a vendor sometimes in this market."

"You seek revenge for him killing the woman?" Yosef asked, straightening in his chair.

"For killing her, stealing her money, and leaving me to starve on the street," Hanan said in a matter-of-fact tone.

Micah liked the boy's courage. "You are rather small to be hunting a man that is, I'm sure, much bigger than you. And if he taught you to fight, then he already knows your tactics."

Hanan had eaten his fill and leaned back in his chair. He looked at Micah. "My size doesn't matter if he doesn't see me."

Nodding agreement, Micah smiled. "But tell me, how will you know where to strike him? One chance to attack may be all you have."

"Johanna taught me about the body. She was a mid-wife and I helped her... with the *sinners* in the brothels." Hanan abruptly grew glum. "Thank you for the food. May I go now?"

Micah glanced at his aide. "Do you remember our earlier conversation, Yosef?" He let his gaze drift to the Sica. Lifting it off the table, he held the knife up for his companion to see. "I believe we have the seed that will grow to become the tree I want." Micah looked over the knife to Yosef and saw him smile.

There were fewer patrons in the wine shop now, but none paid heed to the two men and young boy sitting in the center of all the tables. Casting a quick look about the area, Micah thought he saw the shepherd again, standing across the street watching them. But in the next moment the old man vanished behind a vendor's stall. Micah returned his attention to the boy.

"Tell me, Hanan. Do you wish to live on the streets as a beggar or come to work for me and learn a special trade? I will raise you as if you were of my blood, let you live with us at my home in Nazareth, and teach you to read, write, and learn the scriptures. If you say *yes*, I promise to resolve your problem with Akiba. If you say *no*, well, you are free to leave and return to the streets, stealing food to exist."

"I can read."

"Oh? Can you read Greek, Latin, or any other language than Aramaic?"

The boy shook his head.

"Then you will learn if you accept my offer?"

Hanan sat staring at the slices of lamb remaining on the table as he considered his two options. One held promise for the future while the other led to starvation and death. In time he nodded to Micah.

Laying several coins on the table to pay for their food and wine, Micah stood and motioned Hanan to rise. "Wait for us over there until we return." He tucked the Sica into his belt and pointed to a location along the wine shop's wall.

With Yosef close behind him, Micah crossed the busy market street and walked to the stall where he had last seen the old shepherd.

"I'll check the right side and you go left. An old shepherd should be behind the stall curtains. He's been watching us while we were talking to the boy."

Yosef nodded and moved to the left side of the stall. He waited until Micah was in place then they both swung behind the stall's curtain to look. All they found was a clean-shaven man in his thirties, dressed in a fine knee-length, gray tunic and long robe, girdled with a golden braided rope and wearing a *keffiyeh* headdress of quality make. A jeweled necklace with a large, deep red, polished stone hung down onto his chest. The man's yellowish tinted eyes flared at Yosef's sudden approach from the front and Micah from the rear.

Raising his long, slender hands in a surrendering motion, the unknown man shook his head. "If you are robbers, I have no money."

"No, we are not robbers. Our apologies for startling you."

Micah and Yosef returned to Hanan at the wine shop, but the stranger lightly grinned and watched them walk away.

CHAPTER FOUR

8 A.D.
Nazareth, District of Galilee

The horizon was embracing the setting sun when Hanan walked across the ancient olive orchard to rest against the gnarled bark of his favorite tree. He waved to Micah's men in the round, stone watchtower at the edge of the large field who ensured the valuable crops remained untouched until harvest time. The trees were known to be the oldest and finest producers of olives throughout the country. When the watchmen acknowledged him, he continued his walk.

A light, spring breeze swept the field and only the occasional, distant bleat of goats being herded home broke the quiet. It was the best time of day for Hanan, allowing him to think about Micah's exhaustive daily lessons and rest from Yosef's grueling physical training. Micah insisted upon at least three hours of study every morning whether it be learning numbers for contracts, reading from Greek and Latin texts or discussing the Mosaic Law. The one thing Hanan realized most about Micah over their two years together was that his new uncle's abhorrence of the Romans matched Johanna's. After having seen legionnaires cruelly crucify Jews along the roads, Hanan was coming to understand Micah's aversion.

Hanan stretched his weary back and shoulders before sitting beneath the wide-spread branches of his favorite olive tree. Today's training had been one of Yosef's preferred afternoon exercises; rock lifting. With a countryside of unlimited stone resources, Hanan would lift and carry the largest he could manage to different mounds in a field while Yosef sat in any available shade relating tales of the endurance training Spartan warriors underwent. But Hanan enjoyed the house courtyard exercises the most, dodging swinging sandbags as he deftly approached straw dummies draped in Roman armor to stab them with his Sica.

All that Micah had promised him in Caesarea Maritima were being fulfilled. He ate well, wore good clothes, had been educated and was treated as if he were of Micah's blood. The Syrian, Akiba, had vanished from the face of the earth, and money stolen from Johanna was returned to Hanan as if it were his inheritance. He was growing taller and 'filling out' as Yosef often stated. Soon Hanan's training would expand to the art of spying on selected people in the crowded markets, but only after successfully completing his education in numbers and languages.

Resting his head back on the wide girthed olive tree, Hanan closed his eyes and relaxed. He was almost asleep when the sound of a rock bumping another rock came from his right side. Hurling himself away from the base of the tree, Hanan swung onto his feet and crouched ready to defend himself as Yosef had taught him.

A dark-haired boy stood facing him dressed in a clean but old tunic. They appeared to both be the same age, but the newcomer stood slightly shorter.

"I'm sorry... I didn't see you until I walked around the tree." The unknown boy backed several steps before halting.

Hanan calmed but felt his heart still pounding against his chest. He glanced in the watchtower's direction and realized the men may have seen him jump and would come to ensure his safety.

"Here," Hanan said, motioning to the far side of the tree. "Sit with me so the watchmen don't see you."

The sun had set further on the horizon and pale shadows were spreading across the field.

"Thank you," the boy said, seemingly unconcerned about the men as he took a seat against the olive tree. "My name is Yeshua. Is this your orchard?"

Shaking his head, Hanan grinned as he sat beside him. "I wish I owned these trees, but they belong to my *uncle*. Don't you know there are men in the watchtower who will chase you away if they see you in this field?"

"I meant no harm. I was talking with *my Father* and turned the wrong way to go home."

A puzzled look crossed Hanan's face as he glanced about the orchard. No one else was in sight. He shrugged it off, believing Yeshua may have kept walking after earlier leaving his father.

They talked as boys of twelve do, discussing their lives, likes and dislikes, exchanging information which seemed of no true importance. But to Hanan, though, everything his new friend said was important. Micah had taught him well to pay heed to the slightest detail that composed a larger story about a person, information that may later be used to obtain a future business contract or protection from them. Hanan realized they were of separate worlds. Yeshua held a purity of thought, a wisdom of sorts yet seemed innocent to life's harsh realities while it had forced Hanan to grow old working with Johanna in the brothels.

Shame raced through him at having been with her the times she left the *sinners'* unwanted in the wilderness. Few nights passed without Hanan recalling the newborns' frantic cries that only summoned wolves, jackals, and hyenas. Regardless of Johanna's explanations about death being better for them than starving on the street, in time he refused to accompany her past the city's limits.

Hanan sat wrapped within his thoughts when Yeshua abruptly said goodbye and left. A minute passed before Hanan's mind cleared. He glanced about the orchard and saw how dim the dusk had become. Rising from his tree, he walked toward the watchtower and the path leading home.

* * *

Men's voices carried from the courtyard of the palatial house as Hanan washed himself clean in preparation to eat. In the cooking room he lit several oil lamps and found food the servants, Elizabeth and Benjamin, had left for him. He sat by a window that allowed him to listen to Micah and the unknown visitors while he ate.

"What's his name again?" Micah asked, his tone flat and stern.

"Elias ben Nagar, a minor Sanhedrin priest of the temple in the twentieth course of Jehezkel. We confirmed that he is retained by the Roman Prefect Coponius as a spy. Passes along information about other priests and any Jews he believes that may rebel against Roman rule," a deep-voiced man replied. "If someone wrongs him, he doesn't mind reporting them as Zealots for the Romans to *question*."

Other men said more, but they kept their voices low and Hanan couldn't fully understand all of their conversation.

"And the woman?" Hanan recognized Yosef's voice.

"The Romans have a prostitute in Jerusalem they pay for Elias' use. We've heard he wants to marry her, but temple laws prohibit such marriages," a new man answered; his voice light in tone with a slight northern country accent.

"What are you thinking, Micah?" Yosef asked. "Wait and kill him when he goes to the woman?"

A long silence passed before Hanan heard Micah speak.

"No, she would have to be killed if we waited. She could identify our men. We may later use her against the Romans. I think it's best to take the priest during the Passover Festival. Kill him while he's in the middle of the crowd then blend with the masses to escape. The woman can't expose us, and the Romans will have no one in particular to suspect."

More talk passed in low voices then the visitors left. Hanan finished his meal, washed his cup and bowl, and put them away.

Micah and Yosef entered the cooking area. "Did you hear?" Micah asked, gazing at Hanan.

The boy nodded impassively.

"We will go to the Passover Festival in Jerusalem next week. While we are there, you will assist Yosef while I attend to several contracts. After the festival we may stay an additional week."

Hanan let his gaze drift from Micah to Yosef. "Yes, sir."

Micah warmly smiled. "Your studies have been going well. Yosef believes you are ready to expand your training with him. I agree. We'll talk more tomorrow, but for now, prepare for bed. Be sure your prayers are given."

Hanan was elated at Micah's compliment and the coming opportunity to begin his next level of training. He couldn't restrain his smile.

"Yes, sir... Thank you."

CHAPTER FIVE

Settled in the Judean Mountains between the Mediterranean Sea and the Dead Sea, Jerusalem was an old city, actually older that many in surrounding countries. Considered a holy site, Jerusalem had endured the ages, although, every conquering army renamed it to their pleasure. Canaanites, Egyptians, Assyrians, Persians, Macedonian's, and Jewish kings had at one time dictated its fate. But now with the Roman empire occupying the country, and like all past victors of war, they chose their own name; *Jerusalem*, transliterated from the Greek and Latin name of *Hierosolyma*.

Previous wars had destroyed Jerusalem, yet through different political turn of events the city had always been rebuilt. Herod the Great, to appease the Jews for his having constructed gladiatorial rings and pagan temples, was having the Second Temple erected and expanded over the original site of King Solomon's destroyed temple. Almost complete, the Second Temple was an architectural marvel both inside and out, declaring itself once again to be the true religious center for the Hebrew faith, one the Sadducees attempted to govern through the Sanhedrin priesthood. The temple's massive stone walls rose high into the air and stretched its sprawling rectangular shape across the land, devouring a majority of the city. Within the walls lived workers to clean the temple, and Levites who acted as priestly assistants. More than a thousand priests divided into courses, the divisions to daily maintain the temple's religious needs, were housed there. Attached to the temple's northwest corner by parapet walkways was the *Antonia Fortress*, an equally large Roman fort with a residence for the Prefect, the governor if he wished during the major festivals, and a regular garrison of legionnaires assigned to Jerusalem.

The city's population throughout the year was no less than forty thousand, yet during the days of festival, especially Passover, the streets overflowed with thousands more from across the country. In the congested streets the faithful brushed and bumped shoulders with one another as they walked. Upon arrival Hanan, Micah, and Yosef were thrust into the masses and struggled to make their way to the small house Micah owned near the temple.

"Tomorrow will be worse with even more people arriving," Micah had said before they retired for the night.

Hanan had never seen such maddening crowds and high levels of activity even in Caesarea during the Gentile's pagan holidays and temple worship. Laying on his bed in the second-floor room, he listened to the din of laughter, talk and boisterous singing out in the city. The hour was late yet Hanan's mind refused to allow him to sleep, running rampant with thoughts of all he'd seen that day, and the important mission to come. The last thing Hanan wanted to do was fail and disappoint his uncles.

"The man we seek is a corrupt Sanhedrin priest," Micah had said during their journey to Jerusalem. "He has grown evil and hurts our people. He's turned from the Laws of Moses and defiles the house of *Elohim*. For these things he must feel the blade of our Sica and know *Elohim's* justice."

"Will it be my blade?" Hanan asked, reaching beneath his robe to the small of his back where Yosef taught him to carry his Sica.

"No, another man will act. Your time will come. For now, you're only to be my eyes and ears when we serve justice. I must know the mission is complete and the priest is dead."

Hanan turned on his bed and pulled a blanket over him. With Micah's words replaying in his mind, the twelve-year-old boy closed his eyes.

* * *

The rooster crowed mere seconds before the first trumpet blast blared across the city with the strength of the voice of *Elohim*.

Hanan leaped from his bed and stood in his loincloth, anxiously looking about the room. At the window Yosef leaned on the sill, watching the crowds in the street. He glanced back at Hanan and grinned.

"Did you believe the world was ending?" He laughed. "It's only the temple priests awakening the city for the start of the day," he said, turning back to gaze at the people in the street below that rose from their blankets. "They sound three blasts from long, silver trumpets every morning."

Walking to him, Hanan leaned on the windowsill to stare out at the faint blush of dawn's light.

"See the man standing atop the temple wall? He signals the trumpeters when to sound their horns," Yosef said, watching the priest slowly raise his arms twice more.

The trumpets sounded with clarity, each forceful blast cutting the morning air. When they silenced, the clamor of the street people rose and settled into a consistent level of noise.

"Is that all the priests do to begin the day?" Hanan's question came with such blamelessness that Yosef chuckled.

"No. Right now several hundred workers and Sanhedrin priests of all ranks are hurrying about performing different tasks. Before the massive temple doors swing open, the temple is inspected, cleaned, and prepared to receive the travelers. Large fire pits will be lit, and a lamb is placed on the north side of one of the many altars, watered from a golden bowl then laid upon the altar. As tradition described the binding of Isaac with its face to the west. The priests stand on the east side and once they slash its throat, the manner in which the lamb's blood flows marks the difference between whether the lamb will be an ordinary sacrifice or one to be wholly consumed."

"Why is there a difference?"

Yosef shook his head and laughed. "I suppose it depends on how hungry the priests' families are... In time you will understand how corruption within the Sanhedrin comes in many forms." He straightened from the windowsill and ruffled the boy's brown hair. "The servants are waiting for you. Wash and break your fast. We have much to do today."

Hanan walked to his bed to dress in his normal tunic and robe made of good quality, but Yosef stopped him.

"No, today you are to be a poor shepherd boy and must dress accordingly." Having spoken, Yosef walked to pile of old, but clean clothes folded in a corner. "Wear these."

* * *

While Micah and Yosef waited for Hanan to finish eating, they stood outside the house discussing their plans for the day. Micah wore quality sandals and a fine, knee-length blue tunic girdled with a wide rope belt. An expensive white robe covered the tunic, and a large leather bag draped from his left shoulder. Yosef stood dressed in old sandals, rough cloth tunic, and a patched, long, cream-colored robe of a shepherd. They appeared no different from any other master and servant within the throng of passersby.

"Well, boy, where are your sheep? Have you lost your flock?" Micah asked as if not recognizing his young ward wearing the ragged sandals, tunic and tan robe of a shepherd boy.

Hanan walked out of the house and stood by them, smiling at Yosef's slow nod of approval. Yosef settled a *keffiyeh* on his head and made adjustments to let the cloth hang about his shoulders.

Holding his own out to Yosef, Hanan shook his head. "I need your help to put this on."

Micah smiled, glad to see how close the two had become. He reached out before Yosef did, took the headdress and eased it onto Hanan, covering his brown hair, wrapping the cloth, and curling parts into rolls about the boy's head. The excess length draped from his neck and hung freely. Gazing at the boy, Micah reached down and scooped dirt into his hand and smeared it over the top of Hanan's headdress and robe, then dusted the excess off.

"There. Now you look like a thousand other boys here in Jerusalem," Micah said. "Listen well, Hanan. I will conduct business today in the wine shop of Mohamed al Ibrahim while I wait for your report. This mission may take all day or be delayed. We cannot hurry such things. Pay attention to Yosef and do as he orders. Whatever the outcome may be, find me at the wine shop. If I am talking to someone and the mission is successful, ask me or a coin for the temple. If the mission is unsuccessful, ask me if I wish to buy a lamb for the temple. After that, make your way home. Do you understand?"

Hanan's eyes narrowed as he placed the words into memory. "Yes, sir."

Patting the boy's shoulder, Micah nodded confidently to Yosef and walked out into the street to join the flow of people.

"When we get to the temple, find a spot along the edge of the steps to sit and watch the area. I'm to meet a man there who will tell me if the priest Elias is coming out of the temple today. If the priest does, I will point him out. All you are to do is follow him and be observant. Don't worry, I'll never be far from you. When the assassin strikes, just stay back and watch to see if the priest lives or dies. Then go report to Micah as he told you."

"Are you supposed to—"

Yosef adamantly shook his head. "Never ask such questions. In this organization, people only know what they need to know and nothing more. The assassin will strike when the time is best. Your job is only to be Micah's eyes and ears and report all to him."

The boy's green eyes displayed a mixture of excitement and apprehension. He tried to speak but his mouth was parched. All he could manage was a nod.

* * *

At the temple Hanan found a location along its front steps and sat waiting while Yosef went to the far side of the wide steps. The stream of people in and out of the temple made it difficult to keep watch on Yosef so Hanan rose to his feet.

Looking up the boy observed Roman archers patrolling the tops of the temple walls, monitoring the movement of the massive crowds in the streets. He returned his attention to Yosef and watched a beggar hold a bowl out then they talked. After the beggar left, Yosef nodded across the way to Hanan. An hour passed, then another.

As Hanan was thinking the corrupt priest wouldn't appear today, a priest in a simple gray robe and cloth draped headdress bearing no designs to denote rank, strode out of the temple, eyes squinting against the sunlight. From his left shoulder hung a large pouch as most men wore of varying design. Yosef raised a hand for Hanan to see, then motioned to the priest Elias. Receiving an acknowledgement, Yosef backed away to blend into the crowd.

Elias was short compared to the others about him. A narrow streak of black beard along his jaws outlined his gaunt face. He walked down the temple steps and into the flowing crowd like an angry man. It was as if the people were fierce waves crashing onto a beach and he was fighting the strong tide to enter the sea. At first, he fell back. Frustration appeared on his face, but he edged his way into the mass of festival goers. The deeper the priest walked into the crowd, the more he was enveloped by the bodies pressed about him.

Hanan was tall for his age, but the festival goers blocked his view of the priest for several seconds until he could draw near. He struggled to keep pace with the agitated man who shoved people back when they bumped against him. There were moments when a gap appeared, large enough to see Elias' gray robe that contrasted dramatically against the desert-colored robes of the poor. Then the next second, the priest was out of sight. Hanan never looked back for Yosef. He was afraid if he did, when he turned again, the priest would vanish forever.

Movement along the street was slow but steady. Hanan caught sight of a skinny, dirty-faced boy move closer and attempt to reach into the priest's bag. The priest felt the pull and spun, knocking the boy's hand away. When the crowd pressed forward again, the boy bent and slipped between the bodies.

Keeping pace with the priest as best Hanan could, they continued down the street. Another boy, his head loosely draped with a ragged shawl, tried to reach into the priest's shoulder bag but again, the priest felt the pull and grabbed at the would-be thief. The head covering came off into the priest's hand. The boy fled, bent and moving between the people, leaving the priest holding only the shawl. Anger painted Elias' face. He threw the shawl to the ground, shook his head and started back along the street.

Hanan felt himself being shoved closer to the priest and tried to move aside to avoid contact. His effort was useless and as the throng ebbed toward Elias, Hanan was almost picked up and carried forward. He lost balance and stumbled toward the priest's left side, bumping the handbag.

Primed for action, Elias waited for the next person's attempt to steal from his shoulder bag. He spun, eyes wide with fury, lips curled as he spoke. But the surrounding people's din of talk made the priest's words difficult to understand. The priest bent forward and grabbed the stunned shepherd boy by both shoulders, fingers digging deep into flesh. He shook him hard then released his hold of the shepherd boy's right arm to raise a hand and strike him.

Instinctively, Hanan's right hand shot beneath his robe, fingers wrapping about the leather handle of his knife at the small of his back. Time felt as if it were slowing to a halt. He was no longer shocked by the priest's actions. Like a morning fog rising within his mind, Hanan knew what should be done, yet he paused.

"Kill him, Hanan. Kill him," came the cold, haunting voice of a tall, clean-shaven man in a noble tunic and robe standing beside Elias. A dream like world existed where no one bumped against them and Hanan could only hear the man's voice.

"Kill him," the man growled, his yellowish eyes flaring with delight of the moment. A malevolent smile displayed rotted teeth. A hand of long, slender fingers with sharp nails rose, closed into a tight fist, and swung before him.

"Kill him now!" the man yelled, casting his head back as he cried out in ecstasy. Time sped up, gradually returning to normal.

The priest leaned forward to Hanan then his face transformed from an angry mask to one of astonishment. Eyes flared wide, mouth agape, Elias shuddered and tried to speak but nothing passed his lips. He lowered his head and gazed at the crimson stain spreading across his chest, and the Sica buried to the hilt in him.

Hanan's training took control. Leaving the knife in the priest's chest, Hanan twisted the handle about to carve a circular path within the man, feeling its curved tip hook and slice through vital internal organs. With the crowd so close about them, no one could see what was happening. The shepherd boy withdrew the knife, wiped the blade across the priest's chest, then returned the Sica to beneath his robe.

He glanced at the tall man beside him whose yellowish eyes gleamed in approval.

"Good, now go! Have no fear, the priest will die... Good work, Hanan."

The last thing Hanan saw before turning to dive between people to escape was the large, deep red, polished jewel hanging from a necklace about the unknown man's neck.

Abaddon watched the priest crumble to his knees, hands futilely pressed against chest to halt his death. Elias fell forward, smashing face first into the dirt street. Looking up at the Roman archers atop the wall, Abaddon saw them staring further down the street. They had witnessed nothing of the disturbance. A malicious smile formed on his lips. Abaddon stepped over the body and left with the maddening throng parting a wide path for him without looking his way.

* * *

Hanan wasn't sure how far he had traveled before stopping. He glanced about the crowd but couldn't see Yosef. People blocked his view at every turn. Working through the wall of festival goers he made his way to the vendors along the side of the road. Asking directions to Mohamed al Ibrahim's wine shop, Hanan flowed with the people until the shop came into sight. He paused, gaze drifting over the patrons then saw Micah resting in a chair sipping wine. Across from him sat a white bearded, aged man dressed in a purple robe and white headdress of a rich Bedouin chieftan, nodding slowly to their conversation.

Sweating profusely and breathing hard, Hanan walked between the tables and stopped at Micah. He stood quietly until Micah turned his attention from the chieftain to him. Micah's eyes widened as he glanced over the shepherd boy, then self composure returned. For the first time since killing the priest, Hanan lowered his gaze and observed dried blood on his hands, and his robe speckled with dark stains.

Hanan breathed deep, tried to speak but his mouth was as dry as the desert, and Micah could barely hear him.

"Here, boy, have a drink of wine then tell me what you want," Micah said kindly, his gaze anxiously racing over Hanan for signs of injury.

The shepherd boy emptied the cup and handed it back to Micah.

"May I have a coin for the temple, sir?"

Sighing in relief, Micah lifted a coin from the tabletop and gave it to him. "Here, now run along—and may *Elohim* bless you."

"Thank you, sir." Hanan wearily turned and walked away.

Micah's gaze followed the boy. He looked for Yosef but didn't see him and turned back to the Bedouin.

"May *Allah*, the merciful and benevolent, bestow blessings upon you for your kindness to the poor," the chieftain said, nodding in admiration.

* * *

Two hours passed before Micah rushed through the door and raced up the narrow stairs of his home. At the room Hanan used, Micah found him sitting beneath the window, cross-legged on the floor, with his *keffiyeh* rolled into a ball in his hands resting on his lap. The boy gazed downtrodden at the floor, washed and dressed in a fresh tunic.

Beside Hanan sat Yosef, face calm yet with a look of concern in his eyes. Micah was about to speak but Yosef raised a hand for him to wait.

"Rest for now, Hanan. You did well today. We will talk more later," Yosef said, his wild brows drawing together. After the boy eased onto his bed, Yosef pulled a light blanket over him and motioned Micah to follow downstairs.

Yosef and Micah sat facing one another on blankets spread over the dirt floor. Pulling his headdress from his head and running rows through his thick black hair with his fingers, Micah had wine brought for them. They sat in silence collecting their thoughts until a servant brought the wine and cups, yet even then they didn't know where to begin.

"The priest is dead, right?" Micah asked in a low voice.

"Yes, Hanan killed him."

Micah was sipping wine but stopped. "Why the boy? What went wrong? He was only to observe."

Yosef shrugged his shoulders and glared about the stone-walled room. He let his gaze settle on Micah and explained that the crowd of festival goers was far larger and stronger than they expected in the mission's planning. The boy had followed as best he could, staying back, but for a boy his size and age to keep proper pace was almost too difficult in such a jostling crowd. The assassin could never act because a gang of street children kept attempting to steal from Elias' bag, alerting the priest to be on guard. The mission was cancelled but by the time Yosef reached Hanan to call him off, the throng pushed the boy into the priest. When the priest spun and grabbed Hanan, the boy took action as if he were a professional assassin then blended into the thousands of festival goers.

Micah exhaled in a long blast. "When he came, blood was on his tunic and I thought someone had hurt him. I must tell you it worried me..."

Yosef sat solemn, making Micah stare at him in wonder of what else was involved.

"As you suspect, there's more. Hanan believes he has disappointed you because he killed the man and you had told him to only observe. He thinks he failed you," Yosef said with a light smile. "He doesn't understand that he performed well under the conditions."

"I will talk with him and let him know he didn't fail me," Micah replied, shaking his head as he grinned.

But Yosef's expression turned as stern as a granite statue. He leaned forward and in a whispering voice explained about the unknown man and the order given to Hanan.

"I made it through the crowd just as Hanan was escaping. There was no clean-shaven, well-dressed man as Hanan described standing beside the priest." Yosef paused. "One thing Hanan told me about the man was his yellowish eyes, rotting teeth, long bony hands—and a large, well-polished red stone on a necklace."

Micah straightened his posture and remained motionless. He was about to speak but Yosef interrupted him.

"The day we brought Hanan from Caesarea to live with us... Do you recall the man we found behind the vendor's stall—the man with the large red stone necklace? I've never forgotten his yellowish eyes. I believe Hanan about the man who gave the kill order today. The boy has *never* lied to either of us," Yosef said.

Tapping a finger lightly on his wine cup, Micah gazed out the front door in deep thought at the passing people. In time he turned back to face his aide.

"Yosef, do you remember the night we took Akiba into the desert after we retrieved Hanan's money?"

A slow nod and frown answered Micah. "How could I forget? The Syrian babbled like a hysterical child."

"Do you remember the story he told us about what the woman Johanna said concerning Hanan? The odd star that appeared the night of his birth? He was born in a brothel and to be abandoned in the wilderness by Johanna to die except that some evil man stopped her? The same man who marked Hanan with a scar on his left forearm."

"Those are things Hanan doesn't know about," Yosef whispered, not wanting the boy upstairs to hear them talking.

"Let's keep an eye out for this strange man. If he's been following Hanan all this time and was present today, there must be a reason. I'm curious how he knew about today. Meanwhile, I'll talk with the boy and let him know he has not failed us," Micah said, his worried gaze flowing across the floor.

CHAPTER SIX

T he spring sun was descending from its zenith on the third day after Passover as Hanan wandered the streets of Jerusalem. There were no more struggles to walk where ever he wished. The suffocating crowds had gone; the streets appeared deserted compared to only days before, and everyone in the city seemed to breathe easier in the absence of the masses of pilgrims.

As Micah had said would occur, he remained away from dawn to dusk, completing negotiations for new contracts. In his absence, though, Yosef had strolled the city with Hanan, pointing out the various buildings Herod the Great ordered rebuilt before his death, telling the young man tales of their ancient destructions by foreign invaders.

"Only the eastern boundary line out of the entire temple complex has not changed," Yosef said the day they stood gazing at the towering, white stone wall. "For a man who never spared money with his constructions, the king refused to change this wall due to the expense. All else was rebuilt, but the eastern wall was not touched."

The two had walked the streets as historian and student though no one would have ever suspected the depth of their discussions by their appearances; Yosef with his barreled chest, short height, and bearded, rough face with wild brows, and Hanan beside him, slender and youthful with wind-ruffled brown hair and alert dark green eyes.

Today there were no history lessons or training of any sort. Hanan was free to go where he pleased and enjoy himself as a reward for the mission he had performed for his uncles. Yet as odd as it would seem to others having such a choice, Hanan walked along the street bordering the temple. The immense stones that comprised the walls, some weighing sixty tons Yosef had said, fascinated the boy. *How were they moved, lifted and stacked upon one another so high? And the arched gates? What keeps the stones in place above the colossal Corinthian brass, double gates plated with gold and silver that requires more than a dozen priests to open them each day?* A hundred questions about the architecture raced through Hanan's mind as he gazed at the wonder of the temple.

Glancing at the top of its southern wall, he saw no Roman archers and walked on until arriving at the wide steps of the Hulda Gate that led into the temple. Never having seen the temple's interior and not knowing what to expect, he followed worshippers that appeared to know their way.

Once through a wide tunnel that angled upward, he walked out into the sunlight again. Behind him, running the length of the southern wall, stood a huge colonnaded structure. He left his sandals with others, studied the shaded area of the structure and the large courtyard before him, and listened to the robust calls of temple merchants. Dressed in his plain gray tunic and robe of rough wool, Hanan looked no different from all the other faithful of Jerusalem in the Court of Gentiles. Stones of various colors paved the massive court and its activity was lively with bearded, shawl-covered men who sat grumbling at tables stacked with coin, passing money back and forth to people who approached their tables, exchanging one coin for another, which made no sense to Hanan. To the far end of the Court of Gentiles walked two Sanhedrin priests along small pens of bleating sheep and goats, inspecting the animals for blemishes, approving them for sale to the rich making offerings and sacrifices. Doves and pigeons flapped their wings and cooed in cages as the poor eyed them to purchase for offerings and the women's purification ceremonies.

Hanan eased his shawl over his head as everyone in the court had done. He strolled among the merchants' tables of money, pens and cages, confused by such activity being permitted in the temple. Observing a short balustrade behind the Court of Gentiles that no one seemed to dare pass, Hanan was staring at the open space beyond the wall when a voice came from behind him. The young man turned to find a solemn-faced elder in the white tunic and robe of a mid-level priest gazing at him.

"All may enter the Court of Gentiles but upon penalty of death, no one that is uncircumcised may cross into that area which leads to the Holy of Holies and other courts such as the Court of Women."

Thinking as he glanced back at the sizeable crowd in the Court of Gentiles, Hanan shook his head. His first thought was of Johanna never having taken him to a rabbi for the procedure. "Do you mean that all of these men are uncircumcised?"

The priest laughed aloud at the innocence of Hanan's question. "No, they probably all are—but they don't want to lift their tunics and prove it in front of everyone." The priest continued to laugh as he ambled away.

Hanan moved through the people of the court toward the temple's eastern wall where at ground level stood the sixty-foot wide, magnificent 'Gate Beautiful' used for morning and evening sacrifices and as a place of public worship. The gate's stairs also led up to the Court of Women, where no woman could go beyond, and where the temple housed its treasury. Seven treasure chests sat in front of towering columns near the Court of Women. These were for the voluntary offerings of money as well as the mandatory half-shekel tax the Sanhedrin priesthood used for temple maintenance. Once a chest filled, temple soldiers carried it away to the treasury, leaving an empty one in its place.

Signs posted on several columns and interior walls provided directions to the faithful in Greek, Latin and Hebrew. Leaving the Court of Gentiles, Hanan paused to regain his bearings. Men's voices carried from further down a walkway, rising and falling as they debated scriptures with someone Hanan could not see. A nearby sign written in Greek displayed 'Solomon's Porch' noting the area where the men gathered.

Eight elderly Sanhedrin priests in flowing white robes of quality material and square headdresses with black striped shawls draped over their priestly hats stood in a semi-circle around a young man who calmly sat listening on a stone bench fifteen feet before them. The priests turned to one another, pulled at their long gray beards in thought, spoke and anxiously waved their hands through the air in emphasis of their words. Their ornate jeweled necklaces gleamed when sunlight splashed across them. Hanan assumed the men were of high rank, teachers or Rabbis of the temple, but knew nothing more. He remained behind them and off to the side, listening, not wanting to interrupt their discussions.

Hanan leaned against the wall and canted his head to look around them. A stream of sunlight shined upon a young man in a simple tan tunic and robe with a time-worn *tallit gadol*, a prayer shawl, over his head. When the young man turned his face to glance across the priests, Hanan's mouth went agape and his eyes widened. *Yeshua*, he thought, catching himself before speaking the name aloud.

"But what distinguishes a hypocrite among men?" a priest cautiously asked. His tone of voice and narrowed eyes conveyed a belief that the young man would finally be lost for words.

For a young man of twelve engaged in a scholarly discussion with learned men at least five times his age, Yeshua appeared as relaxed as the day he sat with Hanan in the olive orchard. Gently stroking a *tzitzit* of his shawl, one of the twined and knotted fringes attached to its four corners, Yeshua softly smiled and gazed at the priests.

"A swine doesn't chew its cud, yet has hoofs which are cleft through," he said, pausing for the men to digest his words. "When the pig stretches itself out to rest, its legs are out for all to see the cleft hoofs. The pig seems to be saying, 'I am kosher, am I not?' yet fails to mention that he does not chew the cud. He parades his virtues and conceals his faults. Such an action symbolizes the hypocrite."

The priests stood stunned, unable to think of a response. They nervously glanced at one another, their eyes displaying hope that one among them would speak. But silence hung heavy in the air and several of the priests shook their heads in dismay.

"*Yeshua!*" The woman's terrified voice carried from the far end of the hall nearest the Court of Gentiles. "Yeshua, we've been searching for you for three days." She ran with tears trailing down her youthful face toward Yeshua, clutching her shawl at the throat to keep it on her head. Her bare feet lightly slapped the smooth stones of the long hall. Close behind her walked a slender, bearded man in a tunic, robe, and head shawl of a quality slightly better than a shepherd's clothes. Concern painted his dark eyes.

The priests breathed sighs of relief and stepped back to permit the woman to hug the boy. She kissed her son's forehead and squeezed him to her, unable to speak.

"My name is Josef, and this is my wife, Miriam. We apologize if Yeshua has disturbed anyone. Our son has been missing for three days and we had grown frantic, searching everywhere for him," Josef said, bowing respectfully to the esteemed Sanhedrins.

"The boy has been here from dawn to dusk the last three days, asking questions and discussing the scriptures," stated a priest whose wrinkled face displayed delight that the boy would soon be leaving. "Tell me, who is his Rabbi? His teacher is to be commended for having instructed him so well."

Hanan stood unnoticed behind them, still leaning against a wall. He listened to Yeshua's father explain how the boy learned from many sources, yet Hanan's attentive ear told him Josef's reply was as sound as a reed basket filled with water.

The priests left, shaking their heads and talking in low voices.

Yeshua's mother brought her weeping under control and stood with an arm wrapped about her son's shoulders. Josef stood with arms crossed over his chest, sternly staring at his son.

"Why were you worried, mother? You know I would be in *my* Father's house."

Miriam's gaze drifted to her husband, knowing how such words hurt him. Josef's eyes briefly closed. His shoulders slumped. He drew a breath, glanced about them and returned his gaze to Yeshua.

"Son, *Elohim* is your heavenly father. I am your father on earth and love you. It is my responsibility to watch over you and your mother and ensure no harm comes to either of you. For three days we worried about you until we grew sick... You know the scriptures better than me and what do they say about a mother and father?"

Lowering his face in shame, Yeshua nodded. He raised his eyes to gaze at his father. "*Honor thy mother and father...* I'm sorry. I will never disobey you again."

Josef smiled and let his gaze carry from Yeshua to Miriam. "Let's go home," he said, reaching out to embrace his wife and son.

They walked from Solomon's Porch but Yeshua abruptly halted at seeing Hanan. "Mother, there is my *friend* from Nazareth!"

Hanan stood surprised by Yeshua calling him a *friend.* He'd never had a friend or even thought of anyone as a friend. But hearing Yeshua call him such spread warmth through Hanan's soul and left him with a sense of confusion.

I like him... He's smart, but odd, Hanan thought, watching the family walk away. *Why would he say the temple was 'my Father's house?* Questions rose in his mind for which he had no answers, yet he knew one thing—he had enjoyed being called Yeshua's *friend.*

CHAPTER SEVEN

15 A.D.
Nazareth, District of Galilee

The slightest wind caught the frayed gashes in the linen canopy of Uriah's wine shop and made it flap like the sail of a Galilean fishing boat. The rips had grown through the years guaranteeing that as the sun trekked across the sky, patrons at the stone tables would have sunlight upon them.

The young man of nineteen bent his head to walk beneath the ragged awning and take a seat at a table that allowed his muscled back to rest against a wall. He laid a large, square bundle on the table's stone top and as Yosef's training had engrained into him through the years, let his green eyes casually sweep the surrounding area for anyone following him.

"Uriah," Hanan bellowed as if irritated. "Must a man die of thirst in the noon sun before he is served in this shop?"

A willowy built man in his mid-thirties slowly walked out of the wine shop and stood with hands on the hips of his knee-length, cotton tunic, his haggard face turning left and right in search of whoever had called him. He kept his gaze focused on the street although he grinned, knowing Hanan sat at the table near him.

"What son of a motherless camel shouts my name?"

"This son of a motherless camel," Hanan replied, smiling wide. "I have something for you—if I can ever get a decent cup of wine."

Feigning surprise at Hanan's presence, Uriah spun, his grin spreading into a wide smile. He flung his arms out into the air then bowed. Rising, he snapped a finger and ordered a servant to bring wine.

"Where have you been these last weeks? I talked with your uncles the other day and they said you were in Caesarea Maritima," Uriah said, bushy eyebrows rising.

"Business for Micah," Hanan replied. He shrugged his shoulders. "A minor problem he wanted me to address, but let's not discuss such boring things. Here, this is a gift for you, so your patrons do not get burnt from the sun as they attempt to enjoy their wine."

Uriah's eyes sprang wide. He eagerly opened the bundle and lifted the bulk of a new cloth canopy into the air. Lowering it, he softly brushed his fingers along the wide, royal blue stripes decorating the beige cloth.

"A beautiful awning like this is only found at the finest shops of great cities. It's of the best weave and far more expensive than I can afford. It—."

Raising a hand to stop the shopkeeper, Hanan warmly smiled and shook his head.

"A gift is a gift, not something you pay for. My uncles and I have come here since I was a boy. We've seen you give food and drink to those that were in need. Now, take this and let's speak no more of payment. Anyway, I can't return it to the wine shop I stole it from."

Hanan gave a sharp nod, grinned and glance about him. "But if I don't get a cup of wine soon, I may die of thirs."

Uriah's eyes were wet as he gazed at th generous gift. "May *Elohim* bless you and your family." Having s oken, he carried the new awning into his shop, shouting orders fo his servant to hurry with Hanan's wine.

Nazareth was a small community an few strangers ever entered the town without being reported to M ah. It was one reason Micah lived here even though his vast wealth llowed him to have a palace wherever he wished. The solitude of th countryside and his expanses of vineyards, olive and fruit orchard provided tranquility when he sought refuge from the world of con merce. But now, with hooded men arriving at his home on moonl ss nights to speak in whispers with Micah then leaving like stars n elting into the dawn's light, there was a need for isolation.

Waiting for his wine, Hanan sat thinkin of the faceless spies who came, and once they left, a new *mission* a aited him. While the Zealots burned carts at random and harassed ie Gentiles with protests and minor disturbances, the *Sicarii, the agger men,* as Micah said his assassins were named because of their icas, didn't play such games. They attacked cruel soldiers, corrupt a lministrators, priests that dishonored the Laws of Moses, and Rom in sympathizers with the lethal stealth of a desert cobra, all in the op n at religious festivals under the eyes of legionnaires.

Some missions took the assassins into guarded homes, but those were few and only to show everyone t at no one was safe if the Sicarii wanted them dead. Such had been ie reason for Hanan's recent trip to Caesarea Maritima. He had left thieving Roman tax collector in bed, throat sliced through, for the nan's Jewish mistress to find when she returned minutes later to his bed. The mission was two-fold; stop the Gentile from pocketing the people's money and leave the woman a warning about her choice of lovers.

Absorbed in thought, Hanan reached beneath his robe and adjusted the grip of his Sica at the small of his back so it didn't rub against the wine shop's stone wall. He never kept count of the missions he had undertaken with the knife since the first one at age twelve. Micah justified each as cleansings of the poison Gentiles were spreading with their occupation. But after each assassination, Hanan returned home to purge his mind and body of any slivers of guilt through Yosef's rigorous training.

The innocent faced boy of nine, standing with arms full holding a bowl of water, a cup of wine and a small platter of freshly grilled lamb, bread and olive oil, broke Hanan from his thoughts.

"Here, sir. My master hopes you will enjoy the meal. He says it is a gift." The dark-skinned boy nodded and was about to leave when Hanan touched his arm.

"If the meal is a gift, then this coin must be yours," Hanan said, dropping the money into the boy's palm. A beaming smile spread across the servant's face. He bowed and raced away.

"You realize, my friend, that is more money than the boy will receive from Uriah in a year."

Hanan recognized the voice before ever raising his gaze to see who spoke. He smiled inwardly. There was only one man who called him 'my friend' with heartfelt sincerity.

Yeshua stood out in the sun, his dark, thick hair brushing his neck. He was as slender and plainly dressed in a one-piece, cream colored, linen tunic, sandals and tattered shoulder bag as the last time Hanan saw him. Only now, the faint shade of a beard tinted his jaw and chin.

"Yeshua! Come sit with me," Hanan said, standing as he eagerly motioned to a chair. "Would you break bread with me and share my wine?" He smiled warmly when Yeshua walked to him. They hugged and washed their hands in the bowl of water before sitting at the stone table.

Seeing Yeshua pray, Hanan laid aside the bread he had taken from the plate and lightly closed his eyes until he heard 'Amen.' Before Hanan could call Uriah, the shopkeeper had seen Yeshua's approach and sent the servant boy out with a full jar of wine and an additional cup to the young men.

"Your mother and father? Are they well?" Hanan asked, pouring wine for his friend.

Nodding his head as he dipped bread into the olive oil, Yeshua grinned. "Yes, mother is fine... Always busy, though, circling about my brothers and sister like a hawk. Father has more work than ever. He complains of always being tired but would have it no other way. Antipas' palace in Sepphoris has kept us busy for years. The king always wants some change made which only pays father more and extends its completion date." Eating the bread, Yeshua closed his eyes and lightly moaned in delight before washing it down with a sip of wine. "This oil must have come from your uncle's orchards. Only his trees produce such a delicious flavor."

Hanan slid the plate of grilled lamb closer to Yeshua, took a slice and leisurely sat back to eat it.

"And what of your uncles?" Yeshua asked. "Business must be good. You're never home. I always say a prayer for your safe journeys."

Hanan made a nod of gratitude. "Micah still mourns the passing of his parents four years ago but is doing well. He too has more work than hours in the day but would want nothing else. As for Yosef, well, Yosef is Yosef, and I doubt if he will ever change. He's a good man but takes delight in finding some new torture for me to endure during our training sessions."

Yeshua used his cup to motion toward Hanan. "Whatever he does appears to suit you. Your arms are as big as my thighs and your muscles look like rocks. Your tunic is stretched tight like a man who works in a quarry lifting boulders."

"I *have* been working in a quarry. If you saw the boulders that Yosef makes me move from our fields, you would understand!"

They laughed and drank their wine, talking as old friends do who have been apart too long. But Hanan drew serious at the thought of how opposite they were and the separate paths they followed in their lives. He was about to speak when a rising dust cloud to the south caught his attention.

Yeshua followed his friend's gaze, and both sat staring until a centurion riding a tall, prancing black horse came into view. Behind the granite-faced centurion who eyed the town with contempt marched a lengthy column of fierce appearing legionnaires with large, curved rectangular shields on their left arms and spears clutched in their right hands. Their rhythmic cadence as they marched grew louder, more defined, and the dull clack of swords bumping shields became stronger. Dust rose like a pale fog about them and carried through the town.

Hanan recognized them by their chest armors and transverse, the horsehair crested helmets, as a detachment of blooded warriors from the Tenth Legion in Caesarea Maritima. *Are they here to arrest me or have they come for Micah? Has an opera ve been captured and tortured until he told all? No, Micah only all wed me and Yosef to know who others were among the Sicarii, Hana i thought* as his right hand eased along his thigh to his hip in prepa ation of drawing the Sica. *I'll kill the first filthy dog that lays a hand n me.*

The centurion raised his vine stick cud el, the symbol of his rank, and harshly reined his sweat drenched orse to a halt. Seeing the cudgel, a soldier behind the prancing ani nal shouted an order and the column of soldiers abruptly stopped. hen the dust cleared, the commander sat upon his horse staring a the two men seated beneath the torn canopy.

Hanan let his gaze drift over the beautifu nimal and to the soldiers standing with eyes looking forward, aw iting their next command. Beige dust blanketed their dark maro n armor and shields. Like the centurion's horse whose frothy sweat aptured the dust and turned it brown, a mixture of dust, dirt and s veat streaked the soldiers' faces and dripped from their jaws.

At the wine shop's doorway, Uriah groa ed as he stepped out and observed the elongated line of soldiers. eshua glanced from Uriah to Hanan who sat poised, ready to leap om the table. Taking up the half-filled jar of wine, Yeshua rose and v lked to the man who glared at them from atop his horse.

"Centurion, you must be thirsty. We ha e little, but offer you what we have," Yeshua said in a kind voice. Le raised the wine to the officer.

At first the stern commander didn't mov then leaned from his saddle to take the jar. He curtly nodded and af er straightening himself on the horse, drank deep from the jar. W ping his mouth with the back of his right hand, he turned and looked at the soldier stand-ing behind his horse. "Varus, here, clean the dust from your throat."

The soldier walked forward, took the jar and drank in loud gulps. When empty, he handed it to Yeshua and returned to his for-mer position.

"Have you come far?" Yeshua asked.

"From Jerusalem and we still have forty miles to go before reaching Tyre," the centurion replied, his gaze drifting about the town.

At hearing their destination, Hanan relaxed and sat listening.

"We don't have enough wine to share with all of your men, but we will give what we have if that will help," Yeshua said, pat-ting the horse's neck. He paused and squinted against the glare of the afternoon sun as he looked up at the centurion. "Ahead you will find water for your horse and enough area for your men to rest if you wish."

Glancing at Hanan, the centurion's gaze remained on him sev-eral seconds, studying the muscular man, but he returned his atten-tion to Yeshua.

"Thank you for the wine and information," the commander said in a courteous tone. Before he gave the order to march, he glanced a final time at Hanan as if trying to remember where he had seen him.

Uriah removed the dishes from Hanan's table. "I'll bring fresh wine," he whispered, disappearing into his shop.

Sitting once more near Hanan, Yeshua scratched his thin beard and watched the legionnaires until the last man was gone from sight.

"You were friendly with that *dog*." Hanan's words slipped from him more confrontational than he realized.

Yeshua didn't appear disturbed by his friend's tone or usage of the Hebrew's derogatory nickname for the Romans. He kindly smiled.

"It is better to pet a dog and become friends than to strike a dog and suffer its bites." Yeshua gazed at Hanan for several seconds. "What bothers you? That they are soldiers—or *Gentiles?*"

"Both. They occupy our land and leave it stained with their pagan ways. Have you ever witnessed a man scourged or crucified by the Romans? If you had, it would make you reconsider extending any benevolence to them, my friend. The scriptures tell us of a Messiah that is coming to deliver us from evil. When He arrives to fulfill the prophecies, I will be ready to march with Him and run those *dogs* from our land."

Walking out of the wine shop with cups and a jar of wine in hand, Uriah glanced down the road where the soldiers had gone. "Good riddance," he mumbled and poured the two men's cups full. Yeshua thanked him and turned to Hanan.

"What if the Messiah comes but brings a different message of deliverance, one other than the war you wish? Would you still be so eager to march with him?"

Hanan shook his head in dismay. "I wish I could see good like you do where there is evil, but I can't. The day you leave this quiet town, you'll see how badly our people suffer." Frustration mounted and steadily became an all-consuming rage. Not toward his friend, but at himself for the way his life began and the mixed blood that coursed his veins. He'd overheard Micah and Yosef talking. Truth was a bitter morsel to digest. But now, as an assassin, through one mission at a time, he was righting wrongs in his land—and serving vengeance whenever he slew a Gentile... especially if they were a Roman soldier as his unknown father had been.

They spoke nothing more between them for several minutes as Yeshua sipped his wine and watched Hanan. He set his cup aside and leaned forward, resting his weight on his forearms, fingertips touching fingertips.

"Each morning in prayer I ask *my Father* to show me the way to follow. I receive glimpses of the future which make no sense and are often frightening, yet I must trust that His will be done in me. In time our God, *Elohim*, will make all clear." Yeshua slid back in his chair and let his hands rest on his lap. He lowered his gaze as if saddened by something deeply personal. Eventually, he looked up at Hanan and spoke.

"How can I blame the Romans for bringing their pagan ways and cruelties with them to our country when the scriptures tell of our own people having done worse? At the end of Solomon's life, civil war divided our nation into the northern kingdom of Israel and the southern kingdom of Judah. The monarchs of those kingdoms were far more wicked than the Romans. The Gentiles haven't forced our people to worship their gods, but the kings of old did. They planted the seeds of idolatry and watered them to maturity. They murdered without conscience and appointed priests to worship false gods. Ahab and his wife, Jezebel, raised sinful temples to Baal and our land became one of unbelievers and ungodliness by the hands of our own kings—abominations to *my Father*."

A mask of confusion covered Hanan's face. He glanced at the sunbaked street and let his gaze drift back to Yeshua. He raised a hand to stop his friend from speaking further.

"I've heard you say '*my Father*' several times, but whom do you mean? Your father, Josef, or—*Elohim*?"

A serene expression flowed over Yeshua's face as his dark eyes locked upon Hanan.

Uriah's canopy flapped from a light breeze and a stream of sunlight shone on Yeshua through a gash.

Hanan shook his head. His green eyes narrowed. "No... No, don't answer that. You've already given me too much to consider."

"As you wish," Yeshua replied and softly nodded. He exhaled deeply, stretched his back and tapped the table with his right hand. "Thank you for the food, drink, and conversation, but I must be going. Father will wonder why I haven't returned from a simple errand. Peace be upon you, my friend."

They rose from their chairs, hugged, and Yeshua left. Hanan watched him. His heart grew heavy, confusing him.

"Yeshua?" Hanan called out. His friend paused at the edge of the canopy and looked back.

"Pray for me—please."

A sincere smile formed on Yeshua's lips. "I always do."

CHAPTER EIGHT

24 A.D.
Caesarea Maritima, District of Samaria

The transition from winter to spring gave the days warmth but left the nights with sufficient chill to warrant a thick robe for late hour travels. Hanan adjusted the hood of his brown robe and glanced skyward as he walked, glad to have a moonless evening. It made trailing his prey easier.

For the last four evenings Basim ben Haim had followed the same path home, walking along major streets until arriving at a dark, fifty feet long alley that cut between buildings. From there he was only minutes from home, a residence that wasn't palatial yet envious to own in Caesarea.

Hanan kept his distance from the Jewish merchant until nearing the narrow passageway, then increased his pace to be close behind when Basim made the final turn. Following him wasn't difficult. The stubby built, squatty man had a rather odd waddle as he made his way along the street, making him easy to distinguish from within any crowd.

Collaborators should know better than to walk through dark alleys, Hanan thought, steadily gaining on his quarry. With practiced ease he ran through a mental checklist of how he would approach, and the best part of the body to strike since Basim had little neck and wore a thick outer robe. *No, it will have to be the heart to ensure death. He's ignored our warnings about helping Gentiles steal prized land from Jewish families. There will be no more empty threats.*

Basim turned and entered the black alley. His sandals clacked against the stone pavement, and he shivered as the night's breeze funneled between the buildings. Within fifteen steps of walking into the alley, he heard his name whispered. Startled, he spun, looking about him. The figure of a wide-shouldered, cloaked man silhouetted against the street he had come from, stood mere feet away. A strong hand clamped over Basim's mouth, muting his scream, and next came the feel of metal driving deep into his chest. Eyes flared, body shuddering as the blade twisted within him, Basim rose onto his toes from the pain and the ruthless thrust. His legs failed him, and his knees buckled. Life began to drain from him. No screams passed his lips, only choking, gurgling mutters came. The last thing he felt was his body falling, sliding off the blade. Basim ben Haim, traitor to his own people, died within a minute of striking the stone pavement.

Hanan wiped his Sica clean on Basim's robe, stepped over him and started toward the end of the alley.

* * *

Abaddon stood in the black shadows of the passageway, intently watching the assassin. He nodded approval of Hanan's deftness with the knife and grinned as the twenty-eight-year-old moved quickly past him.

Oh, Hanan... You've become a perfect executioner...No conscience, the strength of an ox, the stealth of a lion, and able to flow through the night like a desert wind, the demon thought with glee. *You are ready for what I need.* His yellowish eyes narrowed, lips parting into a smile of rotted teeth. Long bony fingers rose and pulled his cloak's hood tighter about his bald head as he unhurriedly turned to follow his protégé. There was no need to rush. He knew Hanan's destination; the same place he regularly went to for the last five years after every mission—the only difference was the city.

* * *

Three hours after the mid of night, Abaddon watched the last Roman soldier leave the brothel in a drunken stumble. The owner of the *sinners'* house shook his head as he stood holding the door, observing the legionnaire, helmet tucked under his arm, stagger from one side of the street to the other. Rising from the bench seat after five hours of sitting motionless as a marble statue, Abaddon walked across the street and entered the brothel as the owner eased the door closed.

Abaddon let the hood of his cloak slide off his bald head as he glanced left and right at the small rooms he moved past. Their linen curtain doors were drawn back, open to see within. Prostitutes lay sprawled on their beds, wrapped in cloaks as blankets, snoring loudly, exhausted from their night's work. He paused at a wooden door, looked to both ends of the long hallway, then eased it open. This was a more private room, one which only higher paying clientele used—one which Hanan always favored.

An oil lamp burned low in a corner, leaving the room dimly lit with wavering shadows. The odor of strong wine permeated the air, mixed with the dismal stench of unwashed bodies. In the middle of the dirt floor room, atop the wood-framed bed with rows of wide leather straps to support a sleeping mat lay Hanan on his back between two olive-skinned, black-haired women draped over his torso. Their scattered clothes lay across the floor and the three slept, covered by the assassin's dark brown cloak. A Sica lay within reach near Hanan's head.

Walking to a stool, Abaddon carried it back to the bed, positioning it close to the sleeping man's head. He settled his weight upon the stool as his yellowish eyes glanced over the outline of the prostitutes' bodies beneath the thick wool cloak. Abaddon grinned when his gaze drifted to the four large, empty wine jugs beside the crowded bed.

"Hear my words as you rest, Hanan. Listen well so you will remember them tomorrow after you awake," the demon whispered close to the assassin's ear. "You've done well today and earned tonight... But there is a man in Nazareth who speaks to you as a friend yet is not. He spreads sedition with his talks of peace toward all men, especially the Romans... There will never be peace with the likes of them as long as one legionnaire remains in this country. They spawn children and abandon them as happened with you. They murder and butcher Jews regardless of age... Don't allow yourself to be deceived by the one who calls you *friend*. You've been misled by his words and naïve manner. The day will come when Yeshua must be eliminated for the good of the people—and you cannot turn away from that duty when the time arrives."

Hanan groaned in his sleep and shifted his weight upon the bed. The nude women wrapped themselves about him like constricting serpents, adjusting to his movement but never waking. Abaddon wickedly grinned as he gazed at Hanan's muscled shoulders and thick, rock-like arms draped across the *sinners*. The sight of the long scar along Hanan's left forearm brought a wide smile to the demon's lips.

All of my children bear the same mark as you, Hanan, Abaddon thought.

* * *

Jerusalem, District of Judea

The mid-day heat baked the land. Dust choked the people as a gust of wind swirled through the marketplace in a spiraling pillar the height of a man. Micah sat at his usual table beneath the porch awning of Mohamed al Ibrahim's wine shop. He squinted against the thick dust in the air then his cough came, fiercer than all the times before. His chest hurt, feeling as if it were about to explode, and his throat grew raw from the harsh coughing. The dust devil passed, but he covered his mouth with the sleeve of his robe to mask the coughing. Lowering his arm, he saw sizeable specks of blood dotting the cloth. As the coughing spell dwindled, he breathed deeply to recover from his chest pain then drank his remaining wine mixed with honey to ease the ache in his throat. He'd been adding honey for the last three months as a physician in Cyprus had advised. But the honey did less each week to soothe the rawness, and as his physician warned, the disease had spread within him beyond anyone's control.

"Don't turn around," a man said in a stern, whispering voice from close behind Micah.

Micah stiffened, not knowing what to expect next. He heard a chair being dragged on the half stone and dirt floor. The unknown man was at the table directly behind him.

"That's a bad cough you have. I knew a man once that had such a cough. He died within a year of contracting it. No appetite, sweating profusely at night...a cough that only grew worse each day."

"You didn't come to discuss my health. What do you want?" Micah asked, wondering if the stranger poised a knife at his back.

Micah heard a low, dispassionate laugh then silence followed for several seconds.

"I am told you are the leader of the Sicarii. Your assassins have performed well all across the land and driven fear into the minds of the Sanhedrin and Gentiles."

"You must have me confused with another man. I'm a simple merchant that trades in everything from olive to textiles and—."

"And murder."

The mysterious man's haunting laughter sent shivers up Micah's spine.

"Now, let's quit playing this foolish game of words and move on to business."

"I'm listening."

Sharp fingernails clicked against the table's top in drumming manner then stopped when the man spoke. "In Nazareth is a young man named Yeshua. Have you heard of him?"

Micah tensed and stared at his empty wine cup. *The young man that's the same age as Hanan,* Micah thought. *The one everybody in Nazareth, except for Hanan, considers strange because of his continual debates with the Rabbis.*

"I may know of him. Why do you ask?"

"He must die. Rather than incite the people to rise against the Gentiles, he speaks of living in peace with one another. He stands in the way of revolts against the Roman oppressors."

"I've heard all of that. But Yeshua has no followers and only a handful of Nazarenes' believe what he says."

The guttural growl of a wolf came from behind Micah.

"The cough must have weakened your spine. I'd been told you were a dauntless man, wanting to do what's right for your country." The man spoke with a hint of condescension.

Micah didn't reply immediately to the stranger. He needed a moment to control his anger.

"I can pass your request along to the right people."

"You do that, Micah ben Netzer. And for your efforts I'm leaving a small token of my appreciation to ensure the Sicarii make this a priority mission."

Micah felt a coughing spell coming and fought to suppress it. "You know my name, but what is yours?"

No reply came.

"Your name? What is it?" Micah asked once more, turning upon his chair to look behind him.

No one was there. Micah glanced at the other tables and about the area. He saw the back of man dressed in a long black robe with its hood pulled over his head, passing beneath the edge of the wine shop's awning and out into the sun. Returning his attention to the table behind him, Micah lifted a large leather pouch. It was heavy and gave muffled clinks as he sat the pouch in his lap and opened it. A king's treasure in silver coins and precious jewels shined at him.

"That's a tidy sum. Did someone pay their contract?" Yosef asked, his bushy eyebrows rising as he approached the table.

Micah raised his worried gaze to Yosef before letting it drift to the street in the direction the cloaked man had gone. "Did you see the man sitting at the table behind me? You would have seen him stand and walk away."

Yosef glanced about the area and shook his head. "I saw you from the street and have seen no one sitting behind you. Are you sure someone was there?"

Micah slowly nodded but kept staring at the street. Turning to face Yosef as his aide was taking a seat at the table, Micah paused then explained what had happened. When Micah finished, Yosef looked about the wine shop and the street before leaning close.

"How did the man know who you were—or about the *organization?*" Yosef's dark eyes narrowed. His stare grew intense. He motioned to the leather pouch. "That's a great deal of money to pay for an unknown young man in a small town who does nothing more than debate the Torah with Rabbis."

Micah nodded and remained silent.

"Do you intend to fulfill the request? If so, expect problems from Hanan. Yeshua's his friend—*good* friend."

Gaze rising from the table's top, Micah barely shook his head. "Hanan confides in you more than he does with me. Talk with him. See if there is something about Yeshua we don't know. I won't make a decision about Yeshua until after you've talked with Hanan."

Yosef was about to reply when another severe coughing spell struck Micah. He motioned Mohamed's servant to bring more wine mixed with honey. The servant brought a jar rather than a cup. When Micah recovered from the brutal coughing session, he drank deep gulps straight from the jar and sat back in his chair, exhausted, one hand resting on his chest.

"You need to talk with Hanan about your sickness. He's seen your health steadily decline and told me he's worried about you," Yosef said in a gentle tone. "I'm concerned about you."

"Listen, old friend, when I die, you and Hanan will have more money than you both can spend for the rest of your lives—you more so than him because you served my father and served me with equal trust and loyalty." Micah paused, his eyes taking on a despondent look. "Yosef, there're times when I feel as if I've done a great injustice to Hanan these last sixteen years he's been with us. In my haste to drive the Romans out, I've created a merciless, cunning beast with the intelligence of a philosopher. Reports I've received about him going to the brothels after every mission makes me wonder if I've pushed him too hard, if he's now at war with himself. It's one reason I'm not leaning toward a mission involving his friend. Yeshua's death might push him over the edge and turn him against us. I'd rather pull him from the organization for a year then gradually allow him to return."

Nodding his head, Yosef toyed with an empty wine cup. "We've both grown attached to him. I've learned the same thing about his visits to the brothels. He doesn't go to the houses where Jewish women are, only to those that use foreign women. That alone tells me he may be in conflict about his mother's heritage. Let me talk with him about Yeshua."

"Good... And don't worry, Yeshua is safe from the Sicarii for now. I'm not eager to start a private war with our nephew unless there is truly a definite reason." Micah wearily rubbed his face with his right hand and let his gaze drift to Yosef. "When you talk with Hanan, don't speak of my illness. I need to tell him myself."

* * *

Nazareth, District of Galilee

Dawn's serene tiers of the retreating black night atop faded blue and golden yellow stretched across the horizon. With each passing minute the colors were dissolving into the bright light of day as the sun readied to break over the distant mountains.

Sitting on the terrace in his favorite chair, wrapped in a wool blanket against the slight morning chill, Micah stared at the sunrise. The morning air was crisp and clear, permitting him to breathe without coughing. Entrenched in thought, he never heard Hanan approach.

"Micah?" The tone held an uneasiness in it.

Micah slowly turned his head and looked up at his stout built, young ward dressed in a linen tunic and tattered outer robe. He gazed at Hanan for several seconds then let his eyes drift back to the sunrise. "You're up early."

"I'm sorry to disturb your prayers, but you were sitting so still I was afraid you might be—."

"Dead? No. I wasn't in prayer, only watching the arrival of another day."

Glancing across the land, Hanan stood enjoying the moment with Micah.

"Why are you wearing those old clothes?" Micah asked in a fatigued voice.

Hanan looked over Micah's frail features. His uncle no longer resembled the handsome business man that once turned women's heads and made hearts beat faster. Since the coughing had come, more gray painted his hair, and his pale cheeks and eyes kept a sunken appearance. With Micah's loss of appetite came a deterioration in his weight, and lately, he had grown quieter, never indicating why.

"Yosef wants me to meet him in the pomegranate orchard. I don't know why because I've already carried all the big rocks out of that field and every other field on the entire estate." Hanan chuckled but Micah only smiled and nodded.

"After you have finished with Yosef for the day, I would like to talk with you about several matters."

"Yes, sir," Hanan replied uneasily. "I'll be back as soon as Yosef releases me."

* * *

The rays of the morning sun were shining through the branches as Yosef walked among the pomegranate trees, examining them and touching their fist-sized fruits. He saw Hanan strolling toward him along the dirt road and quickly pulled two from a tree. When Hanan drew close, Yosef tossed a fruit to him. With cat-like reflexes Hanan caught it with a single hand.

"We will break our fast with these and enjoy a morning walk," Yosef said. "There will be no training today because we need to talk."

Hanan had broken his pomegranate open to get at the delicious red beads within it but stopped. A curious look spread across his face. "What's wrong? I saw Micah earlier. He wants to talk with me after I leave you."

Motioning to Hanan's fruit, Yosef returned his attention to his own. "Eat then we will talk." He broke the palm-sized pomegranate open further and used a finger to hook and scoop the red beads into his mouth.

Hanan did the same, only faster. He was more eager to hear what his uncle wanted to talk about than eat.

Both men tossed the empty rinds to the ground. Yosef turned and walked toward the road with Hanan following.

"One thing I admire most about you, Hanan, is that you've always spoken the truth to us regardless of what we asked. The other thing I've always liked is that no matter how hard I trained you through the years, you never complained. You are a remarkable man."

"That may well be the first time you've ever complimented me," Hanan replied with a soft laugh.

"Probably so. I'm not one for flowery words to swell your head." Yosef nodded and kicked a small stone off the path as they walked. "After every mission you head to the brothels, drink heavily and— well, do what a man does with two or three women."

Hanan's pace slowed. A stunned look filled his eyes. "You had me followed? I completed my missions and—

Hand rising to interrupt Hanan, Yosef came to a halt and stared at him. "No, you've not been followed. We pay women in those houses to keep us informed of what they see and hear while with their lovers. With the money you spend each time on wine and multiple women to lie with, you've become well known—especially since they learned you are our nephew. Other than the obvious reasons for going to a brothel, is there any reason you've been drinking so heavily?"

Yosef's words were upsetting to Hanan but logical. He hadn't considered spies working in the houses or that he would become so prominently known. Yet Hanan couldn't truthfully answer Yosef's question as to the reason for washing away the missions with jugs of wine and flesh. He was still trying to understand what bothered him.

"I've found that the brothels help close out my missions... a cleansing of sorts that leaves me ready for the next."

Staring at Hanan for several seconds as if judging his honesty, Yosef renewed their walk. "Are you having second thoughts about what we do?"

A long pause passed between them before Hanan answered.

"Not about eliminating traitors and unethical priests, but I wonder with as many assassinations I've performed, if it's doing any good... I kill one and a dozen more still await me. That's about the best I can answer. Is Micah upset with me over the drinking and women?"

Yosef shook his head. "No, he admires you as I do and is thinking about having you work more in the family business than the organization. But I'll let him talk to you about that."

"Yes, sir."

"I need to ask you about another matter." Again, Yosef kicked a small rock with his sandal as they walked. "Tell me about Yeshua."

Hanan halted. "If you're going to make him my next mission, I won't do it." His hands clenched into hard knots and his jaw tightened as he gritted his teeth. "He's my friend."

"I asked you to tell me about him." Yosef's voice was calm yet firm.

"He's peculiar but has always been that way. He cares nothing about material things and only speaks of peace and quotes passages from the Torah. He's nothing like the people I've killed." Hanan thought a moment then decided it was best not to mention Yeshua's references to 'my Father.'"

"Does he suspect you are a member of the Sicarii?"

Hanan shook his head. "If he knows, he said nothing. We've never discussed the organization. I doubt if he even knows of it."

"Do you know of any reason why someone would want him dead? Does he have enemies?"

"He's a carpenter like his father, Josef. They work together and I'm probably Yeshua's only true friend. Why would anyone want him dead?"

Yosef gazed at the ground as if looking for another stone to kick. He raised his eyes to Hanan. "Someone wants him dead," Yosef said, his bushy eyebrows rising. "A man approached Micah in Jerusalem and gave him enough money to pay for the assassination of three kings. But all the person wanted was Yeshua's life."

"Nothing makes sense. Why Yeshua of all people—and so much money?" Hanan grew aggravated. He shook his head and glanced about the surrounding orchards. His brows drew downward. But a disturbing dream came to mind, one which warned him of Yeshua's deceptive friendship, his talks of peace, and the day to come when Hanan couldn't turn away from his duty as a Sicarii.

"We don't know why. Matter-of-fact, we don't know who wants him killed because the unknown man remained behind Micah as they talked and left without being seen. Now you understand why I wish to know more about your friend. As you said, 'Nothing makes sense.' But Micah has given it all thought and doesn't intend to fulfill the request regardless of the money he received."

＊ ＊ ＊

Micah still sat on the veranda, blanket tucked about him with a cup of wine and honey within arm's reach. He appeared no healthier in the morning sunlight than he had in the shadows of dawn. His gaze followed the young man walking up the road to their home. It was clear by Hanan's downtrodden look and slow pace he had discussed Yeshua with Yosef. *Or have they talked of Hanan's involvement with the organization and a problem exists*, Micah asked himself.

"Your training finished early," Micah said, watching Hanan walk up the veranda's steps. He motioned to a stool beside him.

"Yosef gave me a day off," Hanan replied, sitting on the stool. "He wanted to talk instead, but I believe you already knew that."

A slow nod came in answer. "Did he mention that I am pulling you from the missions to work with the family business? It's nothing to do with your performance of the missions, but I've reached a point where I need help. Our trades have grown beyond my control. Never thought this day would come, but it's true. Anyway, your health is good, and most of our contracts require travel, so this works best for both of us."

The coughing began, light at first before increasing until the severity of pain painted Micah's flushed face and his hands pressed against his chest to ease the ache. Wiping specks of blood from his lips, he gulped down the cup of wine and honey, and sat breathing heavily. His eyes softly closed as he rested, then he opened them and looked at Hanan. Lightly shaking his head, Micah tried to smile. "I believe you understand the reason why I need help."

"Is there no cure?"

Staring at Hanan, Micah weakly shook his head. He set his empty wine cup on the table. "Death, but *Elohim* will decide when that time comes."

"I'll do as you wish, Micah, but tell me... Is Yeshua safe from the Sicarii?"

"Whatever harm comes to him will not be of my doing."

* * *

Micah's words, *'will not be of my doing,'* kept replaying in Hanan's mind after leaving Yeshua's home. The threat to his friend still existed, and the two most important questions remained unanswered; why was Yeshua targeted, and who wanted him dead? Hanan had intended to warn his good-hearted friend to be cautious, although, he knew it would serve no purpose. Yeshua never saw the worst in people, only their best. But Hanan had experienced the worst and grew more worried at learning his friend had left for Jericho two days ago through the Wadi Qelt— *the Valley of Death.*

"A man summoned us for work in Jericho, but his message was confusing. Yeshua thought it best he go talk with him since my old bones don't allow me too many long journeys anymore," Josef had said. "If I know Yeshua, he'll go through the Wadi Qelt to stop and pray by every pool."

The Wadi Qelt was a seven mile, heavily traveled route from Jerusalem to Jericho. Cut deep in a winding serpentine path through steep sloped canyons of the Judean desert mountains and hills, the route was called a valley because of its vegetation yet was only a hundred feet wide in few parts. On the western half of the route were soothing waterfalls of varying sizes, scattered pools of clear, cool water, tall palm trees, wild growing fruit trees and vines of vibrant red and yellow flowers hanging from the cracks of the rock-lined walls. The eastern half of the trek through the valley was more rugged, narrower and lacking in water until it reached Jericho and the Jordan River. But the constant shade along the entire route, provided by the sheer height of the walls to both sides, was what made the path highly favored by travelers. Regardless of the hour of the day, except for noon when the sun was at its zenith, shade and deep shadows protected the people from the baking rays.

Water and shade were its allure, but robbers infested the route and validated its name—the Valley of Death. With severe turns and dark shadows throughout the route, bands of robbers laid in waiting along its midway point, watching for travelers foolish enough to walk alone. Such was the thought raging through Hanan as he envisioned his nonviolent friend praying at the quiet pools.

Yosef was entering their home as Hanan rushed past him heading to the road.

"I'll be back in a few days," he called out, never looking back at his uncle. A goat-skinned water bag draped from his left shoulder.

CHAPTER NINE

Wadi Qelt
The Valley of the Shadow of Death
Judean Desert

Hanan knew the advantage of catching up with Yeshua was that his friend never hurried wherever he traveled. Walking at a grueling pace day and night the first two days, even trotting, Hanan pushed himself mentally and physically to cover the eighty-five miles to Jerusalem and draw closer to his friend. Reaching the junction of the path into the Wadi Qelt valley and the Roman road that lay parallel to it atop the hills, Hanan wiped dust from his face and drank from his water bag. He stared at the two routes, debating which to take.

If Yeshua is being followed, I may come up behind the assassin too fast... If he's waiting ahead of Yeshua, I could be too late, Hanan thought. He gazed at the Roman built road, knowing he could use it to race ahead of his friend. *But if I find the killer, there may not be a way to descend into the valley because of the canyons' severe sloping walls. Either route holds risks.*

The sun was within two hours of setting when Hanan started along the Wadi Qelt path. Traveling as far as he could until the dark canyons forced him to stop, Hanan bathed in a pool of water he came upon. He wrapped himself within his wool cloak, nestled his body among boulders and ate the meager food he had bought in Jerusalem. When exhaustion overcame him, he slept his first full night since leaving Nazareth.

* * *

Hanan awoke before sunrise, eager to leave but couldn't until enough sunlight shown in the valley to see where he walked. The majority of the path on this western end was easy to follow yet there were sporadic areas that required climbing stair-stepped rocks. One misstep could cause a twisted ankle or broken leg.

When faint light permitted him to see his surroundings, he found a mature fig tree and broke his fast with a handful of its delicious fruit. He ate while gazing at the north canyon wall and the three black spots gouged into it at different levels. As more light painted the valley, he recognized them as caves, similar to others dug into mountains and hills throughout Judea. While some were barely large enough to protect shepherd boys from the sun as they watched over their herds, other caves could house a Bedouin family during their travels across the desert. Religious sects often left relics and scrolls in large vases concealed in the backs of the caves as protection against plundering Roman soldiers. And always, Hanan realized, every cave was in the most obscure location with few means to get to them.

Filling his water bag, he waited another thirty minutes then set out again, walking eastward to Jericho.

Every rock that slid and clacked against another beneath his sandals seemed to reverberate through the valley as the least sound bounced off the canyon walls. The echoes were not as loud as he believed, but with his nerves growing more tense with each step, and his concern mounting of blundering upon a robber or unknown assassin that lay waiting, Hanan removed his sandals to continue bare-footed.

His green eyes swept the valley ahead in search of the least movement. Every twenty or thirty feet, he paused long enough to listen for the least click of rocks being stepped on, a cough, or the whisperings of hidden men. At such a sluggish pace he wondered if he would ever find Yeshua or an assassin in time to prevent a murder, but if he increased his speed, he might sound an alarm to robbers. Frustration set in yet Hanan knew all he could do was push ahead with the greatest caution. His taut nerves were taking a heavy toll on his energy. Never had he experienced such a problem on his missions, yet this was different. If his gut instincts proved true, his friend's life was at stake.

The ground grew warmer as the sun rose directly overhead, forcing him to wear his sandals again. Twenty feet ahead the valley twisted to the right. He found a rocky overhang to sit beneath and slip his sandals on but drank first from his water bag. Wiping beads of sweat from his face, his eyes were closed when he heard the faint click of rocks bumping rocks. The sound stopped, but it was enough for his keen ears to hear. Glancing at the dirt and shrubs about him, he realized he was nearing the midway point of the Wadi Qelt. Vegetation grew sparse; the valley path had becoming narrower, and small rocks littered the ground as if from an ancient riverbed.

Wrapping one end of his *keffiyeh* headdress across his nose and mouth until only his eyes were visible, he gently set his water bag on the ground and withdrew his dagger. His assassin's training took control, settling his nerves as he left the overhang and crept forward, walking on bare feet to mute his steps. At the turn in the valley's path, he remained near the canyon wall then sank behind a chest high boulder. The silence in the canyon was deafening and for a second, he wondered if the unknown man ahead could hear the beats of his heart. Rising to look over the boulder, Hanan saw the back of a gray-robed man of average height and slender frame, peering over a boulder, cautiously watching someone in front of him.

There was nothing to show whether the man was watching Yeshua or another innocent traveler. When the man withdrew a Sica dagger from beneath his robe and held it close with his left hand, Hanan couldn't wait any longer.

Twenty-five feet of open ground lay between the two men. Glancing at the ground, Hanan crept along a stretch of softer soil to come up within arm's reach of the unknown man's back. The man was so intent on watching his prey he never heard Hanan's approach.

Hanan's urge to kill him was overpowering yet he wanted information, and for that the man must live. The strength in Hanan's arm was greater than he realized. He struck the would-be assassin on top of the head with the brass hilt of his dagger. The man's knees buckled, dropping him like dead weight. Catching him with one hand before he crashed into the dirt, Hanan knocked the assassin's dagger away from the boulder to avoid it repeatedly clinking metal against rock as it fell. Only a single, light clink came as one dagger struck another.

Lowering the assassin to the ground, Hanan waited, listening for Yeshua or anyone's footsteps. He heard nothing, sheathed his Sica and waited. After a few minutes passed he stood and looked over the boulder. He smiled inwardly at seeing Yeshua walk toward Jericho as if he didn't have a care in the world. Returning his attention to his unconscious captive sprawled on the ground, Hanan pulled the man's *keffiyeh* from his face.

Moshav ben Ami, a professional temple beggar by trade and one of Micah's two hundred operatives, lay spread-eagled in the dirt with blood oozing from his head where the dagger struck him. He groaned and rubbed his head with a hand. His eyes gradually opened, and he groaned once more when he saw the blood on his fingertips.

Hanan found no additional weapons on the assassin but removed Moshav's dagger sheath and slid his Sica into it. Kneeling at Moshav's right side, Hanan was staring at him when the man regained his senses. The two men had never met but Hanan knew him. He knew a majority of the operatives by sight and name from being at Micah's house, passing along information they had learned in their respective areas.

Turning the dagger and sheath in his hands as he studied them, Hanan recognized the weapon as one of many special made in Damascus for Micah's operatives. The leather wrapped handle was its trademark.

Moshav attempted to sit upright, squinting against the sunlight but Hanan pushed him back onto the ground.

"Who ordered you to kill the Nazarene?"

Silence was the only reply Hanan received. He slowly withdrew Moshav's Sica from its sheath and let him see it.

"I am Hanan, nephew of Micah and Yosef, and next in line to lead the Sicarii. Who ordered you to kill the Nazarene?"

Again, no answer came. Hanan sniffed and rubbed his nose as if it itched. He let his gaze drift about the valley then looked down into Moshav's wide eyes. "I've told you who I am so you will know I speak the truth. Having such knowledge means you must die, but I can do nothing about that. What I *can* do for you is this—if you wish a quick death, answer my few questions. If you wish a long, lingering death, remain silent." Hanan shook his head in irritation. "If I were you, I'd take the quick death. The slow death involves fire, vipers, scorpions, and a second circumcision with your own dagger... And trust me, I know for a fact that being circumcised hurts more when you're older."

"Micah gave the order."

The words caught Hanan off guard. He never expected to hear his uncle's name. He stared at his captive with a puzzled look. "Were you told face-to-face?"

Moshav shook his head. "A man I never saw, came from behind me and said Micah ordered the assassination. He gave me information about the Nazarene and when I turned, he had gone."

"Do you remember anything else about this stranger?"

A slow nod answered Hanan. "The man's breath upon my neck smelled like a decayed corpse—and I kept hearing a low growl as if a wolf were near me."

Brows pulled down hard, eyes narrowed as he looked at Moshav, Hanan was deep in thought when he realized a long scar ran down the man's left forearm. He let his gaze drift to his own. Both scars were identical.

* * *

Abaddon stood at the edge of the canyo 's cliff, observing the two men in the valley below. He pulled at his c)ak's hood to keep his pale, leathery face protected from the sun. H ; dark yellowish eyes squinted against the harshness of the sunlight ; s he watched the men with idle curiosity.

Striking with the swiftness of a cobra, I man's hand rose and fell to Moshav's chest. Legs thrashed the air t en smashed into the dirt to never move again. Rising to his feet, Ha an dragged Moshav's body back up the trail to thicker brush and hi the corpse.

A scowl edged across Abaddon's face as a ger filled his eyes. He watched until Hanan vanished from sight aro nd a winding turn in the valley, heading back to Jerusalem.

Adjusting his cowl, Abaddon walked a ay from the edge of the cliff.

"Another day, Yeshua... Another day," he nuttered.

CHAPTER TEN

26 A.D.
Nazareth, District of Galilee

Hanan waved to the men in the watchtower as he and Yeshua turned off the dirt path to stroll between the orchard's olive trees. The sun was setting on the horizon and the evening air was cool.

"Your favorite tree," Yeshua said, motioning to the wide-girthed tree Hanan always walked to. "You were sitting here when we first met as boys. I was returning home and took a wrong turn."

Hanan grinned as he eased to the ground to lean against the gnarled bark. "Yes, and I was afraid the men in the watchtower would report you to my uncles and we would both be in trouble."

"Both? Why would you have been in trouble?" Yeshua took a seat beside his friend and glanced about the field. He closed his eyes a moment as he inhaled the scent of the orchard.

Hanan's laughter came louder than he expected. "Who knows what reasons boys of twelve have for what they think? As for us being in trouble, Yosef would have only given you a hard stare while Micah shook his finger in your face and ordered you to stay out of the orchard. Nothing more. They were good about such things." Hanan stared off at the horizon.

"Do you miss Micah? I know the coughing sickness was difficult on you and Yosef in his last months."

A long silence passed between the two men. "Seeing someone's health dwindle before your eyes, becoming unrecognizable each day from what they once were, is never easy. Yes I miss him and owe him much for all he did for me..." Hanan drew quiet a moment then smiled. "... But I still have my grumpy, old uncle Yosef to contend with, watching over me and assisting with Micah's trade businesses."

Yeshua made a soft nod. "I give thanks to *Elohim* for taking father in his sleep, without suffering. He worked hard all of his life, loved my mother, me, and my brothers and sisters, and taught me the scriptures and a craft. But father and Micah are now in *my Father's* house. One day we will see them again."

"Well, until that day arrives, I suppose I'll continue with Micah's businesses and you will continue in Josef's footsteps as a carpenter," Hanan said half-heartedly. But his thoughts were on the missions, the steady increase of taxes the Romans constantly demanded, the mounting dissension among the Jews toward their oppressors—and the newly arrived Prefect of Judea, Pontius Pilate, whose reputation for cruelty had preceded his arrival.

"No, I believe my time has come. *Elohim* told me so in my prayers. I'll be leaving."

Hanan turned to his friend, confused by Yeshua's words. "What *time* has come?"

Raising his gaze to the cloudless sky, Yeshua stared for several seconds then let his gaze drift to Hanan. "Tomorrow is the Sabbath, and I will go to the synagogue as is my custom. I will read from the scroll of the prophet Isaiah and the people will know me at last. Then I must leave for it to begin."

Eyes narrowed, Hanan looked at his friend. "*Know you at last?* The people of Nazareth already *know* you. You've lived here since you were a child nursing on your mother. What will you read from the prophet? Tell me, because you've left me thoroughly confused—and worried."

An expression of sincerity passed over Yeshua's face and his dark eyes burned with passion. "I will tell them that the Spirit of the *Elohim* is upon me. He has anointed me to bear good news to the poor, proclaim freedom for the prisoners, give sight to the blind, and set the oppressed free. This is the year of *Elohim's* favor."

Hanan sat stunned, his mouth agape. Words failed him.

A gentle smile formed on Yeshua's lips as he gazed at his friend. "Then I will tell them that the scripture is fulfilled by their hearing of my words."

"I must be with you tomorrow! You'll need protection from the people when you say these things. They will call you a blasphemer, shout threats, and want to stone you or throw you off the cliff. Yeshua, you're saying that you are *The Messiah.*"

A nod answered Hanan. "No one will believe me. That is to be expected. No prophet is accepted in his town. I must prove it through deeds as *my Father* directs me, and the fulfillment of the prophecies to their end." Having spoken, Yeshua drew solemn. He gazed at the ground and raised his eyes. "I have a request, my friend, one which greatly bothers me."

"There is nothing you can ask of me that I would turn away from. Now, tell me what is so disturbing to you?" Hanan asked, lightly shaking his head.

"After I speak in the synagogue, I must leave Nazareth. There are actions I must take to begin this path *Elohim* had chosen for me. My mother, Miriam, needs someone to watch over her and ensure her safety and welfare. I trust my siblings, but I trust you more. There will be dark days ahead and she will need someone with a lion's courage and a bull's strength to lean on. Please be that person for her when those days come."

"Your words are difficult to understand concerning all that is to come about, but one thing is clear between us—your mother will be safe. I have men to keep watch and see she is never harmed nor without food or shelter."

Yeshua warmly smiled. He nodded in gratitude and reached out to pat Hanan's knee. When Yeshua touched him, he startled as if struck by a fierce cold shiver.

"Are you hurt?" Hanan anxiously glanced about the ground expecting to see a scorpion or snake moving away from his friend.

"The image of a large curved dagger flashed in my mind," Yeshua said, leaving him muddled as to its meaning. "This happens... I see things which I do not understand and must wait for *Elohim* to make them clear in time."

Hanan's mouth was agape. He didn't know what to say. His first instinct was to reach beneath his robe to see if the Sica was still at the small of his back. "Fear for your mother's safety is playing tricks on you. I will see to her welfare and provide her with money."

"A man could not have a better friend," Yeshua replied. He glanced at the dim light in the orchard. "I must go now. Tomorrow will be a long day, and I have much to prepare for before leaving."

The two men stood, a blend of sorrow and confusion upon their faces as they struggled to find the words to say goodbye.

"Tomorrow at the synagogue, do not worry when the people grow angry at me. I will be protected by *Elohim*."

"When you leave, where will you go?"

"Galilee. There are several men I will ask to follow me as I do *my Father's* work," Yeshua replied.

"Of all places you're going to Galilee? They're fishermen! Everyone knows they are stubborn, zealous people who argue about the least thing. You would ask such men to help you with *Elohim's* plans?" Hanan was beginning to wonder if his friend had fully gone mad.

"*Elohim* doesn't choose perfect people to carry out His plans. Moses stuttered when he went before Pharaoh; Noah was a drunkard; David was a shepherd boy when he went before Goliath, and there are others who had weaknesses but chosen for greatness. I will be fine among the Galileans, in time you will see," Yeshua said. He slowly nodded to his friend. "Until we meet again."

Hanan stood in silence and watched Yeshua walk away.

* * *

It was mid-morning when Yeshua arrived at the synagogue. His sandals were as plain as his one-piece tunic and the *himatia* robe which he wore cast over the left shoulder and wrapped about his body. About his neck hung a cream-colored prayer shawl with a blue stripe he would wear over his head once he entered the synagogue. Yeshua never wore white or bright colored clothes because he believed it to be a sign of the rich, always preferring the gray, tan or cream colors the poor wore that came from the sheep of the fields.

The day was already warming the interior of the building, and the usual large crowd had taken most of the available seats. Hanan was glad to stand outside the front door wher air flowed, and from his position, he could jump into a crowd to rotect Yeshua if they demanded his blood.

Yeshua removed his sandals and eased is prayer shawl over his head, never glancing at Hanan. He appeare different, his expression far more solemn than Hanan could ever call seeing. Entering the synagogue, Yeshua moved through the bui ding until he took his seat near Rabbi Jacob ben Magen, the elder of Nazareth.

Straining to listen, Hanan heard the rabl reciting prayers and the people responding in order. There was a ge eral talk of scriptures then Rabbi Jacob announced that Yeshua wou l read from the scroll of the prophet Isaiah.

Yeshua spoke the words he'd told Han n he would say. All within the synagogue were silent until Yeshua nnounced, "I am the Anointed One."

An explosion of gasps, outcries, and ang y shouts came.

Hanan glanced around the door's corr r to look inside the building. As expected, he saw Rabbi Jacob pu ling at his vestments, tearing them open and furiously shouting, "Bl sphemer!"

The men within the synagogue leaped tc their feet and swung balled fists in the air as they surged forward t encircle Yeshua who had already started toward the door.

Pausing long enough to slip his sanda s on, Yeshua calmly walked out of the synagogue into the brig t sunlight with the incensed crowd swarmed about him. Hanan ollowed, pushing forward through the people to be near his friend.

"*Stone him... Take him to the cliffs nd cast him over... Blasphemer!*" came the irate cries of the towns eople.

But by the time the mob reached the street, everyone brusquely halted. Their shouts fell away to a stunned silence as they glanced about themselves. Yeshua disappeared before their eyes as they threatened him.

Hanan stopped. He'd been looking at his friend in the middle of the mob when the man vanished. Stepping away from the hushed crowd, shocked by the sudden disappearance, Hanan let his gaze drift to the road leading out of town.

In the distance Yeshua stood looking back at the townspeople for several seconds before turning and starting north along the road to the fishing town of Galilee.

CHAPTER ELEVEN

27 A.D.
The Jordan River

In the wilderness of Judea at Tel el-Kharr r, the Hill of Elijah, five miles upstream from the Dead Sea, a one man stood waist deep in a natural pool of the narrow river wit n arms held high and wide, and his bearded face cast back to gaze t the sun-bathed sky. His Aramaic name was Yokhanan, yet thousa ids knew him as the prophet, 'the voice of one crying out in the vilderness'—*John the Baptizer.*

Thick, untamed hair hung from his head down onto his shoulders. His beard grew bushy and equally unru y from neither being cut or trimmed in years. A long, camel hide oak draped from his left shoulder down his chest and back, belte only with a strip of leather to hold it in place. He was of average h ight, slender framed, and from his daily existence on the leaves of locust trees and wild honey, he kept an emaciated appearance. But was the passion raging in his lustrous black eyes and his deep, esounding voice that were so hypnotic to all in his presence.

John lowered his arms and let the river gently flow against the palms of his hands. His eyes swept the masses standing along the western bank and up the rising landscape. Many of the people had divided into separate groups, intentionally avoiding others because of their political or religious affiliations. Curious onlookers strolled the river banks, pausing to listen before renewing their walks. Sanhedrin temple priests with their soldier escorts stood near leaders of the Sadducee sect; a Roman patrol watched from horseback; Pharisees sat on the side of a hill, keeping their distance from the Sadducees, and a line of devout believers waiting to be baptized stretched from the river and back over the hill.

* * *

Halting atop the hill, Hanan gazed at the people spread about him and down to the water's edge. He studied everyone's clothes and easily spotted the Sadducees in their expensive robes, cloaks and finest headdresses. Of the six he counted one was Eleazar ben Makim, the man Hanan had tracked from Jerusalem. The Sadducees, among their other activities, regulated relations Jews had with the Gentiles, and it was Eleazar who had given approval to the sons of Annas, a former high priest, to establish the money-changers market within the temple. From their collection of *administrative fees*, Eleazar received his portion, and for this corruption and others, Hanan marked him as a Sicarii target.

Hanan stood assessing the gatherings of people, the manner in which they clumped together leaving wide, open gaps between the groups. *No, there's not enough of a crowd to conceal me if I strike and attempt an escape,* he thought. He glanced to his far left and saw the mounted Roman legionnaires. *Their horses would be upon me before*

I could reach the thickets of brush, reeds, trees and hermit caves further upstream. His gaze rose to the afternoon sun. *His death can wait until tonight when they make camp.*

With a final look at the Sadducees, Hanan walked down the hill, wandering between the people as they anxiously listened to the wild man who preached from the water. Except for his muscled body, Hanan's tattered, cream-colored tunic, robe, and *keffiyeh* of a herdsman, allowed him to blend with most of the onlookers and believers present. The closer he drew to the river, the better he could hear the angry prophet's words.

"You brood of vipers!" the baptizer shouted, pointing to the Sadducees and Pharisees along the hillside. "Are you fleeing from the wrath that is to come by seeking repentance in the water? You are no better than Herod Antipas, a wicked and egotistical ruler who violates the law and revels in sin. He divorced his wife and married his brother's wife, Herodias, while the man still lives. Antipas makes a harlot of her and openly lusts after his niece, Salome, before the eyes of our God, *Elohim.*"

Hanan had heard of John. Only a handful of people from Judea had not. He had immersed hundreds, if not thousands in the river, and more still came. No words were spared against anyone he believed had desecrated the Laws of Moses and the Word of *Elohim*. But the surprise of all came when Yeshua had told Hanan that *the voice in the wilderness* was his kinsman, related by some lineage through their mothers, Miriam and Elizabeth. Zachariah, John's father, was a former high priest of the temple in Jerusalem, chosen and placed into the authoritative position by the Sadducees, the very group John had accused of being a brood of vipers. Yet it was Herod Antipas who the baptizer berated most for his immoralities with Herodias and her daughter Salome.

Glancing at the Sadducees, Hanan saw them cringe and whisper among themselves at John's accusations. But the sight of a slender framed man walking toward the river, dressed in ragged sandals, a one-piece tunic, *himatia* robe, with a linen prayer shawl over his head, made Hanan pause. He'd seen that slow, strolling walk many times. As the man drew close to the water, he stopped, slid the shawl from his head and calmly gazed at the baptizer. Drawing a sharp breath, Hanan recognized Yeshua.

* * *

"I am not the promised Messiah, nor am I the reincarnated Elijah," John shouted. His gaze swept the crowds across the hillside. "But I am the fulfillment of Isaiah's prophecy, the voice of preparation for the arrival of our God, *Elohim*, in the flesh. I am unworthy to carry his sandals or even unloose their thongs. The Anointed One to come is the lamb of *Elohim* who will take away the sins of the world. Repent, for the kingdom of Heaven is at hand!"

John drew silent as he stared at the man slowly walking out into the water. Brow drawn down hard, John the Baptist kept watch until the man stopped less than an arm's length from him. Realizing who he was looking at, John's eyes widened, his mouth gradually opened, and he knelt before Yeshua in the water. But Yeshua warmly smiled, grabbed his kinsman by the shoulders and pulled him up to stand.

"You—You are him... The son of our God, *Elohim*. Are you here to baptize me?"

Yeshua slowly shook his head. "No, you are to baptize me. The prophecies must be fulfilled as my Father wants."

Hanan moved through the people to better hear what the wild-looking man and Yeshua were saying to one another. Confusion wracked his mind at listening to John name Yeshua *the Son of our God, Elohim.* A part of Hanan had always believed it was so yet hearing the Baptist confirm it sent the assassin's soul further into a maelstrom.

John the baptizer wept as a smile formed on his lips. He stepped to Yeshua's left side, placed his right hand at the base of the Anointed One's neck, prayed, and leaned him back into the water until he was fully immersed. Raising Yeshua from the river, John cried out to the masses.

"Behold the Lamb of our God, *Elohim!*"

The fluttering of wings forced Hanan from his dumbfounded state. He looked up and observed a white dove flying over the two men in the water. Yeshua stood with droplets of river water trailing down from his hair, onto his face and drenched tunic. A ray of sunshine painted the river where the men stood, and a voice came, not to Hanan's ears but as if it echoed through his mind:

"This is my beloved Son, in whom I am well pleased."

* * *

Abaddon had heard the voice as well and glanced skyward with a scowl. From behind the Sadducees, the demon shook his head and released a low growl of fury as he gazed at Yeshua and the Baptist. He edged closer to Eleazar ben Makim's shoulder and whispered in the Sadducee's right ear.

"You came for proof and now you have it. Blasphemers, both. You must tell the others that the time has come for their deaths. Those two are too dangerous to the temple to be allowed to live and spread such sacrilege. Listen to how they incite the people to rebel against you, the temple, and even Roman authority. Send word to Herodias how the Baptist ridicules her and calls her a harlot. She'll demand his imprisonment."

Eleazar stroked his long beard as he watched Yeshua leave the water and start along the river bank toward the Judean desert. Men fell in behind him. The Sadducee had heard of Yeshua's followers, the ones he called *his disciples*, but until now, Eleazar had never seen them. He turned to his companions and spoke in a voice so only they could hear.

A piecemeal grin formed on the demon's lips as he watched Eleazar and his priestly band talk and nod in agreement. He waited until Yeshua walked over the hill before trailing after him.

* * *

On the third day after Yeshua's baptism, the Sadducee, Eleazar ben Makim, was found with his throat slashed in an alley near the Jerusalem temple. Two months later, at the goading of Herodias, Antipas ordered his soldiers to arrest John the baptizer. They cast him into the tetrarch's dungeon cells at Machaerus in the District of Perea.

CHAPTER TWELVE

27 A.D.
Machaerus, District of Perea

He sat leaning on the right armrest of his gilded throne, lethargically watching his guests dressed in their finest robes and sparkling jewels as they entered the palace courtyard. They laid gifts on an elongated table then made their way to the dais to bow and pay homage to the tetrarch on his fiftieth or fifty-first birthday. No one was sure of which age, but none dared to ask. As each approached, Herod Antipas offered a partial nod and raised his right hand in limp manner to acknowledge their presence. There was only one gift he desired—one he was anxious to receive, and the minutes passed like hours as he awaited Salome's *Dance of the Seven Veils.*

Beside him sat his wife Herodias, regal as always in her sea blue silken robes and headdress adorned with rubies and emeralds. Her expression was impassive, yet her coal-black eyes were alert to everyone that drew near. For weeks she had prepared for this night, coaching her daughter Salome in the performance to give her step-father. Herodias knew her husband's thoughts; had caught him spying from behind curtains on the young girl as she bathed in the *mikveh*, the ritual pool, and seen the way his hungry eyes devoured Salome's body when she strolled past him. Tonight, though, Antipas would willingly give Herodias what she wanted in exchange for the hope of a moment's lust with the dancer.

The musicians played throughout the evening, but few people paid heed to their efforts. The din of talk and laughter blended with the strums of the zither, the beating of drums, clanging cymbals, and piercing flutes to create a deafening chaos in the lamplit courtyard.

Herodias glanced at her husband and struggled not to laugh at his anxious shifting upon the throne. As she had ordered, servants never let his chalice go empty, and a light rosiness highlighted his cheeks. His gem encrusted, gold crown had slipped slightly on his head and he nervously tugged at the front of his robe, a sign she knew meant his passion was rising. She glanced at the musicians, raised her hands into the air and clapped twice. By the time her hands lowered to her lap, a new song began, one more vibrant and flowing. The audience grew silent as the beat of a drum started, slow and light, building to a harder, primal throb.

Curtains parted to the left of Antipas and the slim, lithe figure of Salome slipped out into the flickering light cast from the flames of a dozen large oil lamps. Transparent veils of different colors shrouded her head and body, floating through the air with each step she took before the tetrarch. Herodias wickedly smiled as her husband leaned forward on his throne, eyes wide as he watched the undulating body flow left and right, then spin and bend before him.

The music's tempo increased, became intoxicating, and the pounding of the drums matched the hammering beats of his heart against his chest. Throwing herself to the marble floor, Salome thrashed about and rolled onto her hands and knees, pitching her magnificent body like a mating animal, swinging her long, raven-black hair in wide circles. She flung the veils away one by one as she swirled and caressed herself. With each crash to the floor, cymbals clanged as she spread her legs for the tetrarch's private view. Antipas' eyes were flared, and his mouth remained agape. His hands gripped the throne's armrests and squeezed until his knuckles were white. He was oblivious of everyone and everything in his palace except for the sinful flesh before him.

A black-robed man behind the throne edged closer to Antipas, his vile smile displaying rotted teeth as his yellowish eyes focused on the dancer writhing across the marble floor.

"She is yours to command. You are the tetrarch. Order her to your bed. Mount her. Take her. It's what she wants," Abaddon whispered in a low, guttural voice. "Think of the pleasures she will give you."

The demon glanced at Herodias who sat maliciously smiling, watching her husband's sanity shatter more with each beat of the drums and sway of her daughter.

"Offer her whatever she wants. Do it! Reap your rightful reward!" the demon whispered with urgency. Looking at Herodias, his mischievous smile grew before stepping back from the throne. He spread his black robe and vanished within its dark shadow.

The music reached its crescendo at the moment a drum was violently struck. The musicians stopped. Salome spun to a halt with arms opened wide before Antipas, her final transparent veil wrapping her sweating body as if it were her flesh, leaving nothing hidden from his sight. Her breasts rapidly rose and fell with each blast of air she took, and her vixen gaze locked with his wanton stare.

"Tell me what you want, Salome, and I will give it to you up to half of my kingdom. Tell me and I will grant it now," the tetrarch said, breathing as heavily as the dancer.

For Herodias, her moment of revenge had come, and she basked in it with spiteful pleasure. She glanced at her daughter and lightly nodded.

Salome lowered her arms and stepped close enough to Antipas to slide her right hand along his thigh.

"Bring me the head of John the Baptist on a plate," she said in a whispery voice.

* * *

28 A.D.
Caesarea Maritima, District of Samaria

Pontius Pilate, known in Rome by his Latin name Marcus Pontius Pilatus, was the fifth Roman Prefect of Judea. Lucius Sejanus, the chief administrator and favorite of Emperor Tiberius had appointed him to the post. Pilate was of the Equestrian Order of the Samnite clan of Pontii. From this order came political and military leaders from Roman citizens of wealth and station, yet not always of the highest heredity. But moving through the ranks and becoming a prefect afforded a military officer such as Pilate the opportunity to advance into the senate.

His career path weighed heavily on him this cool evening. He lay wrapped in thought, stretched upon his dining couch next to his wife's. Their arms and heads almost touched, and with the slightest turn, he could face her. Their evening meal of assorted fruits, fish, olives and olive oil, breads and wine were within arm's reach upon the short table before them. Slave servants scurried about their master and mistress, ensuring every need was met

Freshly bathed in scented water and clothed in a fine maroon robe with subtle designs in golden threads, Pilate wore his dark hair short and was clean shaven in the Roman style of the day. But it was his hard-set features of a furrowed brow over a penetrating gaze, a firm jaw, and cold demeanor which set him apart from all others. The muscles in his taut arms flexed as he reached out for food, his body kept strong by a daily regimen of sword training and strenuous exercise with his legionnaires. And his rulings with the Jews were as sharp, swift and merciless as his sword.

Holding a grape to his mouth, staring at the food on the table, Pilate's day-dreaming broke when he realized his wife was watching him. "What?" he asked, brows rising.

Claudia Procula faintly smiled and glanced at the servants in the room. Waving them away, she waited until they left before speaking.

"What bothers you, Pontius? Please, do not say 'nothing' because something is on your mind," she asked. "You've held that grape to your lips for five minutes without moving."

Amused, the prefect quickly ate the grape as he looked at her. "I must have been thinking about how the gods favored me with such a beautiful wife. How can a man consider food when a woman like you is near?"

Pilate's rare boyish moment was truthful. Claudia was an educated, stunningly attractive woman from a high born, wealthy family in Rome. Her self-confidence equaled her beauty, yet all knew her to be a ruthless lioness in the protection of her husband's career. Pilate was no fool though. He knew without her and her father's influence, he may never have been considered for the equestrian order.

Long black hair fell about her soft shoulders and bare arms as she rolled her head back in laughter. Returning her gaze to him, her golden honey-brown eyes were mesmerizing. Jewels gleamed in her earrings. A silver necklace hung low from her neck and laid atop her deep cut, emerald green robe. She lovingly smiled as his gaze drifted to her cleavage.

"First, tell me what bothers you then we may discuss *other* matters," Claudia said in a teasing tone.

Pilate reached out and lifted a wine cup from the table. He sighed hard and glanced about the lavish dining room of the palace that had once been Herod the Great's residence while in Caesarea Maritima.

"I was wondering how soon we may leave this wretched posting for one better suited to a prefect's wife. Not this barren land where dust constantly flies, and barren desert is at every turn. Each day the Jews grow more rebellious and the political environment becomes tenser. I could easily squash the problems by making examples of a few hundred troublemakers, but it would only push this forsaken country to the verge of a multi-sided revolt—and we both know how that would infuriate the Emperor. Every time one of these bickering Jewish factions writes a petition to him denouncing my orders, I receive a letter stating his displeasure and concern over my ability to control the land. He doesn't understand these people or their strange laws yet insists on me following *religo licita* which binds my hands."

The prefect paused long enough to empty his cup. His gaze remained fixed on the food table as he toyed with the alabaster cup. Julius Caesar had originally created the policy of *religo licita* allowing the Jews to follow their traditional religious practices in Rome, and the following emperor permitted it to continue. Now Judaism had such status throughout the empire, and every complaint from the various Jerusalem factions argued that Pilate had violated the policy.

"The Sadducees rule the Sanhedrin Council and can't stand the Pharisees and the Essenes. The Pharisees hate the Sadducees and the Essenes, and the Essenes loathe the Pharisees and Sadducees—then atop that, you have the Zealots who dislike them all for attempting to coexist with us and urge the people to rebel. Oh, and I can't overlook the dozen or more prophets that pop up at every turn claiming to be a messiah."

Taking her wine cup from the table, Claudia lightly sipped it. She lowered the cup to rest on her couch as she leaned closer to her husband. "How is Tiberius to know what the truth is when he's hidden himself away on an island fortress at Capri and left the empire in the hands of his chief administrator?" she whispered.

Pilate nodded once. "Sejanus' hands are tied in this mess. He's tried to explain our situation to Tiberius but now has too many wolves in Rome nipping at his heels and is busy defending his own self. The Senate may not like taking orders from the emperor, but they surely dislike taking orders from the emperor's chief administrator even more."

Sipping her wine again, Claudia paused. "Speaking of prophets, I understand that after Antipas cut the Baptist's head off, another named Yeshua replaced him. He supposedly has been traveling about performing miracles, curing the blind, healing the sick—even raising the dead."

"You never cease to amaze me. Between your dreams and your network of informants, I wish I had a dozen advisors as knowledgeable as you," Pilate said, smiling and shaking his head in admiration. "Antipas is a fool and should have his own head cut off. As for this new prophet you speak of, I'm sure his miracles are nothing more than magicians' tricks. My spies say he goes about in dirty clothes and relies upon handouts from people so he and his little group may eat. He preaches about the love of some invisible god they cannot even make an image of—but he speaks nothing of sedition. No, he's certainly not the kind to lead a revolt against the Roman Empire."

Claudia set her wine cup on the table and rose from her couch. "Still, my love, keep a watch on him. The numbers grow each day of those who believe in him," she said, moving to stand in front of her husband. Allowing her emerald robe to slip from her shoulders and fall about her ankles, she stood nude except for her earrings and necklaces. "Now, let us talk of *other* matters and forget your worries for the night."

From his dining couch Pilate looked up and let his gaze drift over her supple body.

"The goddess Venus has truly blessed you," he whispered, pulling her down onto his couch.

* * *

29 A.D.

Hanan and Yosef sat across from one another at their favorite table beneath the weathered awning of Uriah's wine shop in Nazareth. The afternoon sun was hot, yet a pleasant breeze flowed in the shade of the awning. With one man facing north and the other facing south, they could keep watch on the road for strangers entering the town as they talked.

The wine shop owner set a plate of g illed meat and honey-soaked dates on their table, refilled their c ps and stepped back, wiping his hands clean on a cloth hanging fro 1 his belt.

"It will soon be time to steal another a ning for you, Uriah," Hanan said with a wry grin, glancing at the f ded blue stripes decorating the beige covering. "It's held up g d, though, through the years."

Uriah squinted his eyes as he studied th awning. "That is the difference in quality between those made in J usalem and the ones you find around here. The colors may have f ded but there are no rips and tears from the wind like the one befo . This awning should last a few more years." The shop keeper smiled vide, politely nodded and returned into his shop.

"So, tell me, uncle. What is this talk yo say we must have?" Hanan gazed at the gray sprinkled throughou Yosef's hair, his wild growing brows and thick beard. His uncle's rou h features had grown haggard, and his once barrel chested, bullish frame had dwindled with age, yet Hanan knew immense strength 1 mained in the man.

"I've decided to retire from the organizati n, move to Jerusalem, and set up a little wine shop of my own. I've a ready secured a shop and made arrangements for my shares from Micah's businesses to become yours. Don't worry though, I've kep a sufficient amount. Aside from some thieving king, you are now he richest man in all the land." Yosef sat back, appearing relieved a finally telling Hanan of his plans.

Resting his muscled arms on the table, 1 anan took on a somber look. "I'll miss you. You and Micah have b en the only true family I've known since I was nine. When you lea , who will be around to badger me and make me move mountain of rocks?" A forced smile broke on Hanan's lips. "I would feel better if you kept your part of our trading business. You may need the money to open more wine shops someday."

Yosef adamantly shook his head. "No, it's yours. I have enough for what I want to do."

Hanan sat back slowly and gazed at his uncle. "You mean, like marrying the widow Sarah who bakes and sells bread in the Jerusalem markets?"

Bolting upright in his chair, Yosef's brows rose. He hammered the top of the table with a knotted fist. "Have you had your men following me?"

Hearty laughter poured from Hanan. He lightly slapped the table. "I've known for months. As you once told me, information about the activities of prominent rich men quickly spreads—and when I learned it was you always buying up all of her bread and giving it away to the poor, well, I knew there must be a reason."

Yosef groaned and appeared flustered. "I'll be sixty next year. I'm not getting any younger, not becoming better looking, and I'm tired of being alone. Oh, I'm not tired of being around you, but—."

"I understand, and you deserve to be happy. But let me ask a question. Would you mind if I sold our entire trading empire? I'd give you half and keep half."

"What of the organization?"

"One thing at a time, uncle," Hanan replied. "I'm still considering what I should do. We've grown to almost three hundred operatives spread out across the country and I can pay them from my money for years—and still do as I desire."

Yosef cast him a suspicious look. "Like going to the brothels and drinking heavily after a mission?"

"I haven't done that for a week or more."

Grinning, Yosef shook his head. "You've been home for a week or more."

The two men laughed, shook hands and returned to their food and wine.

"I've heard strange tales about your friend Yeshua," Yosef said between bites of goat meat. "People say he cured lepers, raised the dead, and has a dozen men that follow and call him *Teacher* and *Master*."

Hanan quickly downed another cup of wine and shook his head. His lips formed a thin line as his brow lowered into an intense stare. "What if he's the Messiah the scriptures say is coming?"

A light laugh came from Yosef as his eyebrows rose. "You don't seriously believe Yeshua is *The Anointed One*, do you? A carpenter's son?"

Silence passed between them for several seconds. Yosef's eyebrows gradually lowered. He leaned forward, resting his weight on his forearms on the table.

"You *do* believe it," he whispered.

"Since Yeshua and I were boys, I always thought he was odd, then everything about him fell into place and—." Hanan lowered his gaze to the table's top then raised his eyes to look at Yosef. "I was there the day the Baptist immersed him in the river and said Yeshua was the Lamb of our God, *Elohim*. The man is like an unblemished lamb—I've never known him to become angry, speak ill of anyone or become drunk and do reckless things. I doubt if he's ever had a woman. When we were twelve, I watched him in the temple arguing scriptures with the priests. Words, educated words, flowed from him without hesitation. There was a light on his face and about him I've never forgotten to this day."

"All that means little. So, he was a good boy growing up, smart, and has an excellent memory for our Laws. That doesn't make him the one we've been waiting for," Yosef said, keeping his voice low even though they were the only patrons of the afternoon in the wine shop. "Maybe he's had a woman you don't know about or maybe he likes—."

"No, sir," Hanan said, vigorously shaking his head. "No. From what he's said, it's something about his *destiny* that doesn't permit him to take a wife and have a family. He speaks in riddles about his life being short because of the prophecies—and that he's following the will of his father, *Elohim*."

Pouring himself more wine, Yosef emptied his cup in one continuous drink. He gazed at his adopted nephew and pursed his lips. Finally, he spoke. "What does his mother, Miriam, think of all this? I know you've been watching over her."

"Now who's been spying?" Hanan chuckled. "I know she's gone to him and asked for him to return home, but he refused. He calls her 'woman' rather than 'mother' as if they are not of the same blood. Says he has not finished his father's work." Letting his gaze drift to the street, Hanan sighed. "I've had men trailing Yeshua. When they come to report his doings, they are in awe and speak of him with reverence. Not just one man, but several returned and told me they witnessed the miracles he's performed. My men, trusted men in the Sicarii, have told me they believe *Elohim's* hand is upon Yeshua."

Hanan paused and stared into Yosef's eyes. "I believe them because I followed him in secret. With my own eyes I witnessed Yeshua lay his hand on a demon-possessed man who was also mute."

Raising his right hand up before Yosef, Han n gazed at it several seconds then solemnly looked at his uncle anc spoke in a calm, sincere voice.

"The man was lost within his mind, a razed creature, drool dripping from his mouth, eyes glazed over, n aking bizarre sounds as he fought and tried to bite those who held l im. Then without the least fear, Yeshua touched him, spoke—and the demon fled. The man became as normal as us, and he wept and cr ed out giving thanks to *Elohim*."

Yosef sat listening, staring at his nephew

"I questioned people about the man, cu ious whether he may have been acting, but everyone said the demo had afflicted him for over ten years. Later when I saw Yeshua, thou; 1, it was at a distance, I could tell he's different from when we last ta ed—I tell you truthfully, he is different. *Elohim's* hand is upon hin "

"I believe you," Yosef said with a soft nod gazing at his nephew.

CHAPTER THIRTEEN

30 A.D.
Caesarea Maritima, District of Samaria

The dawn was breaking when Hanan walked out of the brothel, his head muddled, mouth as dry as the Judean desert. His body still ached from the blows he had taken a day ago from the soldiers, and his steps were slow and wobbly from the jars of wine he'd drank last night.

A sharp chill hung in the air, yet it felt good and helped to clear the fog from his head. He wrapped his cloak about him and began the walk to Jerusalem, deciding to break his fast later at a shop further along the road. He coughed and a piercing pain shot through his left side, but he laughed inwardly knowing a squad of legionnaires had suffered worse.

Three days before, a Sicarii operative had botched his mission and was arrested. By the time Hanan received word, legionnaires were already on the road to Caesarea, escorting their prisoner to trial and execution. But before his death, Hanan knew the Romans would torture the operative, and the soldiers were experts at extracting information. Gathering fifty of his men, Hanan waited until the mid of night before ambushing the sleeping squad along the trail. Over half of the legionnaires had died swiftly from S carii archers, yet near the end of the short battle, the fighting had b come hand-to-hand. It was then two soldiers tackled and beat Hai in until they died by his dagger. Stripping the squad's bodies, they ere abandoned in the desert for the hyenas and vultures. But before Ianan's men left, they executed the captured assassin for failure to omplete his mission and allowing himself to be arrested. Wrappin his body in a cloak, they placed him in a cave along a mountainsi e. No matter that the man had failed, Hanan refused to leave him w h the Roman dogs.

Now, as Hanan walked in the crisp morning air toward Jerusalem, his thoughts shifted to surprising Y sef and Sarah at their wine shop and bakery. Unfortunately, his stay ould be short. Hanan had other matters to address yet seeing the ma ried couple so happy in their work and life together, always warme his soul when visiting. He was glad his uncle had at last found ace and a woman to love. Hanan envied him.

* * *

Jerusalem, District of Judea

The journey took longer than Hanan inte ded but stopping for several days to allow his side to further heal as necessary. If Yosef greeted him with a bear hug, his ribs would as uredly crack.

Wiping sweat from his face, he glanced t the position of the afternoon sun and let his gaze drift to the ho zon ahead. The towering walls of the city and temple were at last n view. He smiled at the thought of sitting with Yosef as they dippe Sarah's freshly baked bread into a plate of olive oil from Micha's o chards, and all while downing a jar of the finest Damascus wine to wash the day's dust from his throat.

His thoughts renewed his energy and lengthened his stride, and with each step, the walls rose higher.

* * *

By late afternoon Hanan had made his way through the congested city streets, burgeoning markets and around the temple to the former wine shop of Mohamed al Ibrahim. The shop was easy to remember. After his first mission, it had been the location where he met Micah to report the corrupt priest's death. But never did he imagine Yosef one day buying the well-known establishment for an outrageous amount to serve wine to patrons and have an outlet for his wife's baked goods.

Taking a seat with his back to a wall, he wearily rubbed his face and stretched the fatigue from his body. He glanced at the scattering of patrons beneath the shop's awning, saw no one that gave him grave concerns, and summoned a willowy servant to him.

The man's grayish tunic displayed several dots of wine stains across the chest and marks along his waist where he wiped his hands. He wore his headdress in the fashion of a desert dweller, but the long cloth ends were cast back over his shoulder to avoid falling into wine as he bent to fill cups. His face was weather-worn from days in the sun, as if he had at one time been a shepherd, and the carved wrinkles about his cheeks and light brown eyes set his age near Yosef's or a few years younger.

Approaching the brawny patron sitting by the wall, the servant's eyes widened in recognition of him. "Master Hanan, you've come at last. We've been expecting you."

Confused, Hanan leaned forward o to the table. "You know me?"

"I remember you from your last visit to e Master Yosef."

Hanan's green eyes narrowed. Confusion held him.

"What did you mean when you said, *me at last'* and that you've been *'expecting me'*? Where is my uncle and his wife, Sarah?"

The servant's eyes revealed sorrow. His gaze lowered to the table. "You do not know?"

Hanan leapt to his feet. "Speak up. What a e you talking about?"

Voice laden with remorse, the man rais d his eyes to Hanan. "Our master is dead, killed by the Temple gua ds in the market two days ago. His wife is injured too and remains at eir home to recover."

Hanan stood unable to move then rage gulfed him with the ferocity of a desert sandstorm. A maelstrom questions swirled in his mind yet all he could do was squeeze his nds into balled fists. Pressure built within him to the point he want to scream at the top of his lungs and smash something, anything u til he destroyed it. He glanced about the area, a fiery inferno blazing n his green eyes.

"I'm sorry to be the one to have told you. thought the messenger had reached you and you already knew bu —."

"Sarah's at their house now? Is she alone? Hanan asked, knowing his uncle had moved into Micah's home af r the wedding.

"She is with the servant Master Yosef g ve her," the old man replied in a weak voice. "She is in mourning, b t otherwise well. The broken arm will—."

"Broken?" Hanan shook his head in dis ay and drew a deep breath. "I'm going to her."

Before the servant could reply, Hanan le .

* * *

In his own insensibility, Hanan brushed, bumped, and pushed people out of his way as he hurried toward the house. A part of him wanted to deny Yosef's death, yet he knew the servant wouldn't tell such a lie. *Why would they kill him? How did Sarah's arm break?* Questions jumbled his mind.

At the home, he had walked partially through the open door before a young woman servant jumped to block his way.

"Who are you to enter this house without permission?" she adamantly asked, head canted far back to look up at Hanan's face. It was an odd sight, her slender frame against his wide-shouldered, stout body; her shawl covered head barely reaching his chest. She stood her ground with lips pressed into a thin line and black eyes in mere slits to show her defiance.

"I'm—I'm Hanan, nephew—nephew of..." Hanan stuttered, eyes spread wide as he lowered his chin to look down at her. His earlier rage left him when surprised by the diminutive lioness.

"He's Yosef's nephew, Jamila. You may let him in," a woman said, making her way down the narrow stairs from the second floor, cautiously watching each step she took. Her right hand brushed the wall to help her balance.

The servant respectfully bowed and moved out of Hanan's way. The pain in Hanan's heart returned as his gaze drifted to Sarah on the stairs. Seeing her left arm in splints and wrapped in a cloth sling that hung from about her neck, forced the reality of his uncle's death into Hanan's mind once more.

"I knew you would come, Hanan. Thank you," she said, stepping onto the level dirt floor and slowly making her way to him.

Her brown eyes were blood-shot, and a weariness was about her like someone who hasn't slept in days. Gray streaked the black hair free from her linen headdress, and though she was fair-skinned, the creases of time were growing more visible, especially from her sorrow. It was clear by her round face she bore a few additional pounds, but she carried herself well, her tunic and robes concealing her weight.

Removing his sandals, Hanan walked to Sarah and lightly kissed her cheek. She guided him to a stool and looked at the servant.

"Jamila, we have family visiting. Please bring some of Yosef's finest wine for our guest."

The servant rushed away as Sarah eased herself onto a chair, holding her left arm with the right to prevent it from moving too much. Her red eyes rose to look at Hanan and he could see a thin line of tears building on the rims. She wiped them dry with the sleeve of her right arm then bravely returned her gaze to him.

"Will your arm heal in time?" Hanan's voice held sincere concern as he motioned to the sling.

"My arm, yes, but my heart, no. I never thought I would love again after my husband died years ago... Then your crazy uncle came along, fumbling about me like a love-struck boy who has never been kissed, following me through the market while I tried to sell my bread. He would shout 'Come buy the best bread in all of Jerusalem!' and he would buy all of my loaves and pass them out to the poor so we could talk."

Hanan warmly smiled and gazed at the floor for several seconds. He lifted his eyes to her. "You saw a different side than I did," he said as he grinned. But the memory of sitting with his uncle in the orchard, Yosef providing encouragement to a small boy plunged into an abyss of depression and rage over being a bastard child with a mother who wanted him left in the desert—those memories and more flooded Hanan's hurt soul.

Jamila brought cups and a small jar of wine, but Sarah refused any when offered. Hanan observed the servant's disappointment and assumed Sarah had probably been turning away all food and drink.

"He talked about you often, telling me how you and Micah were the only family he'd known since he was an orphan," she said, her gaze gently drifting over the brawny man sitting across from her.

"*Orphan?*" Hanan's posture straightened and his brows rose.

"You didn't know?" she asked, appearing fearful she'd given away some secret. "Micah's father found him living on the streets, took him in, provided an education, and later kept Yosef on to work for him."

Hanan exhaled a long breath and lightly shook his head. "That explains why he was always so loyal to Micah's father and Micah," Hanan remarked, more to himself than to Sarah.

"One thing I remember well was Yosef saying how he always worried while you were away on *business* for the organization. I think he was referring to you overseeing Micah's trading contracts," she remarked.

Hanan stammered a moment then agreed, not wanting her to know about the Sicarii. He felt as if a burning sword had skewered his chest from hearing so much about his uncle he'd never known, especially how much he cared.

"Sarah, please... If you will, tell me what happened. Why did he die?"

Lowering her face, she covered it with her right hand and wept. In time she sniffed and wiped her nose and the tears from her eyes before raising her gaze to Hanan.

"He's dead because of me. We were in the market, the larger one on the east side of the temple. While Yosef was busy talking with a merchant, I looked back and saw two boys fighting with a smaller boy. Yosef didn't see me walk away, but all I intended to do was make them leave the younger boy alone."

Hanan nodded. The story sounded all too familiar.

"The crowd gathered about them encouraged the brawl. While I was trying to pull one of the bigger boys away, a temple guard appeared out of nowhere and shoved me aside to reach the boys. I fell, broke my arm, and the next moment saw Yosef bursting from the crowd like a madman. More guards arrived and all I could see in the cloud of dust was Yosef struggling with them. He pulled an odd knife from within his robe and stabbed several of the guards... that was when their captain drove a spear into him, and the others did too..." Sarah's voice trailed to silence. She lowered her face to her hand, crying once more. "We placed Yosef in a tomb near here as he wanted," she said, never lifting her head.

Hanan rose from the stool and stood as motionless as a bronze statue with only the fire burning in his eyes to show he was human. Quiet filled the room for several seconds, broken by the servant Jamila rushing to her matron's side to comfort her.

"Do you know the captain—his name?" Hanan asked in a cold voice.

"It was the pig Daimyan..." Jamila's tone held contempt. Her eyes narrowed.

Hanan acknowledged with a slow nod and reached out, gently laying his right hand on Sarah's shawl covered head. She took his hand and pressed it to her face. He could feel her tears on the back of his hand. When she released her hold, he sat back on his stool. Her shoulders shook from her sobbing. Feeling his heart rip apart, he rose from his stool and looked out into the street. Glancing at Jamila holding Sarah, comforting her, Hanan spoke in a gentle voice to the grief-stricken widow.

"I will see that this house and the wine shop will always be yours. Keep all the staff and servants you wish. You will never want for anything."

Sarah gradually raised her face to look at the mountainous man. Tears trailed down her cheeks.

"But I want Yosef..." she said, voice breaking as she wept.

Hanan stared at her, struggling to control his grief.

CHAPTER FOUR EEN

Jerusalem, District of Ju dea

E scorted by Captain Daimyan of the Tem le Guard, four elders of the Sanhedrin Council walked in sil nce through the cavernous grand hall, the Chamber of Hewn Ston. At the bronze-plated door of an adjacent room, they waited until D myan entered and lit large oil lamps before proceeding in. Compar d to the Chamber of Hewn Stone, the room was small. Ten oversiz d chairs sat in a wide arc for council members to face one another s they talked, and to have an unobstructed view of anyone addre ing them. From this secluded room the High Priest Joseph Caiapha discussed matters of the most sensitive nature to the priesthood an Judaism.

While the four priests took their seats, t e captain latched the door and turned to stand inside the room guar ing it. He would permit no one to enter or leave without Caiapha permission. Leaning his stout frame against the door, Daimyan a justed the sword on his belt, then crossed his hefty arms over th leather chest-armor covering his brown tunic. A thin scar trailed fr m beneath his round helmet, over his white-hazed, left eye and d wn his pock-marked cheek. As Captain of the Guard, only he could remain in the priests' presence while precarious discussions transpired.

Caiaphas sat in the curve's center with Nicodemus to his right, and Matthias, and the former High Priest Annas, often called the Great Hoarder of Money, to his left. From Daimyan's position at the door, the captain looked directly at Caiaphas, and had a clear view of all. The priests glanced at one another, stone-faced, waiting for someone to speak. Finally, Caiaphas broke the stalemate.

"I'm tired of hearing about Yeshua. Every day someone tells me of a new magician's trick he's performed, and the crowds this false prophet draws when speaking." The High Priest shot a look of frustration at the men about him. "I'm told his followers are mostly Galileans... Galileans of all people! Only ruffians and rebellious dissenters ever came from Galilee, which tells me he's preparing trouble for the temple."

Leaning forward in his chair, pulling at his long gray beard, Annas nodded. "I've heard he makes disparaging comments about the Court of Gentiles and the money-changers there. My sons control those tables and the sacrificial animal sellers. They're concerned this diviner will disrupt business."

Shadows danced along the walls from the wavering flames of the oil lamps. Caiaphas watched the shadows as he listened to his father-in-law speak. Although, Annas' sons were Caiaphas' brothers-in-law, he held little pity for their greed. For years without the slightest remorse, they had milked their wealth from the money-changers who in turn milked the poor with no regrets.

Matthias straightened the pleats of his fine white robe and brushed a wrinkle from the cloth covering his left leg. His murky brown eyes rose to gaze at Caiaphas. "There's more at stake than his sons' profits. If the people turn away from us to follow Yeshua and his teachings of the Law, our treasury will be destabilized by the loss of offerings."

"Losing offerings is not the concern here today. We have sufficient funds in the treasury to maintain us for several years, even with the loans we make to the wealthy." Caiaphas took his head slowly and let his gaze drift to each man. "Yeshua is undermining our rule of the people and control of Judaism. His blasphemous statements of being *The Chosen One* are turning people away from our temple, not drawing them closer. He is a threat, one we should eliminate before it's too late to save our faith."

"You mean, *save yourselves*," Nicodemus said, raising a wrinkled hand to point at each man. The elder's grey eyes narrowed, and the lines across his face deepened. He twitched his nose as if a fly had landed upon him and gradually lowered his hand to stroke his silver beard.

"You've become a *zaken mamre* in your dotage," Annas said, shaking his head in disdain.

"Better to be a *rebellious elder* than a greedy thief, Annas!" Nicodemus shook from his anger and rose from his chair. But Caiaphas intervened by holding an arm out to prevent the furious priest from leaving.

"Please, Nicodemus, take your seat." Caiaphas let his gaze drift over the men. "Let's have no more bickering amongst us. I summoned each of you to this meeting because of your wise counsel." The High Priest turned to face the aged man on his right. "You do not see this false-prophet as a threat to the temple?"

Slowly rubbing his right hand with his left, Nicodemus sadly looked at his fellow priests.

"I will not be a part of *eliminating* Yeshua. Who here but me has heard him speak? Who here but me has witnessed his miracles such as letting the blind man see again or healing the leper? I tell you, they are not the cheap tricks of a magician. His healing touch and wisdom comes from our God, *Elohim*. He is only a threat to the hypocrites of this temple." Nicodemus paused while the other men shook their heads and feigned insult. Several seconds later he spoke again.

"One day a woman ran to Yeshua and fell at his feet, begging for mercy. Someone had caught her in the act of adultery and men of the village were chasing her. With the villagers gathered around Yeshua and the woman, ready to stone her, do you know what he did?"

The High Priest remained still but Annas and Matthias shook their heads.

"Yeshua held a rock out to them and said, *'Let he who is without sin cast the first stone.'* There he was, surrounded by an angry mob, most of which were probably adulterers too, but no one took the rock from him. They turned and left... And do you know what Yeshua did with the woman?"

Again, came slow shakes of the priests' heads.

"He helped her from the ground and said, *'Go and sin no more.'* That's all... *'Go and sin no more,'* then he left." Nicodemus let his gaze drift from man to man. "Does this sound like someone you must kill to save the temple? I remind you that the law requires a man be heard before being judged—and judging him is what you're doing now."

The aged man gradually rose from his chair, glanced at Caiaphas, and started toward the door. Daimyan didn't move until he observed the High Priest wave approval. At Nicodemus drawing near, the Captain of the Temple Guard opened the heavy door and held it until the old man walked out. The door closed behind him and Daimyan slid the latch back into place.

"Nicodemus doesn't understand the true threat Yeshua presents against the temple," Annas said, looking from one man to another. "If we allow Yeshua's influence to spread, the people will believe in him, not us. The next thing will be the Romans destroying both our temple and our nation."

"The Romans removed our right to carry out capital punishment so we must eliminate this false-prophet from within his circle of followers—find a weakness to exploit—someone to testify against Yeshua, then find a reason for Pilate to sentence him to death," Caiaphas said, massaging his forehead as he stared at the floor in thought.

"To break a rock, you must first find its weakest point, then hammer a wedge into it until the rock splits," Matthias remarked, looking at Caiaphas.

Daimyan lightly coughed for attention. "Sir?"

The High Priest raised his face and looked about the room. He saw Daimyan step away from the door.

"Yes, Captain?"

"Sir, I may know where to find the weak point you seek," Daimyan said, his one good eye scanning the three priests.

Stepping back from the Captain of the Guard, Abaddon stood in the shadows with his black cloak wrapped about him. He smiled as Daimyan walked to Caiaphas.

* * *

Caesarea Philippi, District of Batanea

Philip II, the Tetrarch of Batanea and one of Herod the Great's numerous sons, set his administrative capital at Paneas, once a cult center dedicated to the lecherous Greek God Pan. Priests from Paneas' pagan temple practiced their debaucheries in a cave and sacrificed newborns in the spring that gushed from it and flowed down the Hula Valley to marshes and on to the Jordan River. In 14 A.D., the Tetrarch named his capital Caesarea to honor Emperor Augustus, but later the city became Caesarea Philippi to avoid confusion with Herod the Great's Caesarea Maritima, the port on the Mediterranean coast.

Yeshua sat on the veranda with a full stomach, cross-legged on a thick wool blanket, enjoying the evening breeze as he gazed at the sunset's spectrum of colors. His twelve disciples lounged about him, content from the textile merchant's meal. Several of the men were silent while others engaged in talks about witnessing the day's miracles. Their host, Mulheim, had offered the evening meal in gratitude after Yeshua raised the daughter of Jairus, a patron of the Galilee synagogue, from the dead and healed a woman's twelve yearlong bleeding sickness.

Accepting the merchant's hospitality as they did with all offers of food, Yeshua and his followers dined on a stone veranda larger than most Hebrew homes. But Yeshua had surprised his band with one stipulation before agreeing to the dinner: "Where is the man's home? I will not enter Caesarea Philippi, but I will go near. Evil remains there." Fortunately, for Yeshua and his hungry followers the merchant's house sat far from the city walls.

Once Mulheim's servants cleared away the empty dishes, brought fresh wine and lit the veranda's oil lamps for the coming dark of night, the merchant excused himself and retired for the evening to allow them privacy. Each man rose, acknowledged his generosity and expressed their gratefulness then relaxed upon blankets to watch the fading sunset until stars flooded the sky.

Lowering his gaze from the stars, deep in thought, Yeshua slowly looked at each of the twelve men seated about him. His brown eyes were wet and glistened in the light cast from the oil lamps. One by one the disciples realized they were being watched and turned toward Yeshua.

"Is something wrong, Teacher?" Andrew asked, looking over James' shoulder to see Yeshua. Bartholomew's brows lowered in worry. He glanced at Matthew, the former tax collector from Capernaum who had given up everything in his life to be a follower. Matthew shrugged his shoulders and waited.

The other men sat still, gazing at their leader, but Peter leaned toward Yeshua, unsure of what was happening. Judas, who the disciples' thought had been a thief from Kerioth a town in Judea, sat off by himself to the side of the band, looking from man to man, his black eyes filled with curiosity. He alone was the only non-Galilean among them and always felt as if he were an outsider.

"Who do men say I am?" Yeshua asked, his tone as gentle as the night's breeze upon their faces.

Each of the disciples appeared stunned. They sat like mutes with no tongues, but gradually their voices returned.

"There are those who believe you are John the Baptist returned in flesh. Some say Elijah while others say Abraham, Jeremiah or another of the prophets," they answered, all speaking at once.

"But what about you? Who do you say I am?" Yeshua asked, brows rising, face etched with concern.

Silence fell among the twelve men as the weight of the question settled over them.

"You are the Christ, the Messiah... The Son of the living God, *Elohim*," Peter calmly replied, looking into Yeshua's eyes.

Yeshua warmly smiled. "You are blessed, Peter. This was not revealed to you by flesh and blood, but by my Father in heaven..." Letting his gaze drift over the disciples, his eyes filled with the sadness of a man who knew more than he could say at the moment. Then he warned them.

"Do not tell any man I am the Christ... The Messiah. In time I will explain."

* * *

Yeshua drew silent and looked skyward. Judas Iscariot knew this meant there would be no further discussions tonight, although questions remained. He also knew Yeshua would soon leave the group to go off to pray in seclusion.

Rising from his blanket, Judas walked out into the surrounding darkness, away from the oil lamps. He found a large rock and sat staring back at the veranda, wanting time alone to think about all that had weighed heavily upon him the past three weeks.

"You're disappointed in him, aren't you?" a voice in his head whispered.

Judas shook his head, but *Yes* rose in his mind.

"He's not the Messiah you expected to come and free the country. He's either a false prophet or has grown hesitant to lead the people against the Romans." The words swirled within Judas. "Maybe something must happen to force him into action. Maybe that's all he needs—a slight push to fight."

Judas watched Yeshua rise and leave the veranda.

"Maybe something *is* needed," Judas faintly said, gaze following the slender man until he vanished into the night.

Abaddon rose from beside Judas, glanced in Yeshua's direction then let his yellowish eyes drift back to the disgruntled disciple on the rock. An evil smile formed on his lips.

"*Maybe,*" he whispered in a voice that came like the wind moving through trees. He pulled his dark cloak about him and started toward Caesarea Philippi.

CHAPTER FIFTEEN

Jerusalem, District of Judea

On the fourth night of waiting outside the temple's south gate, Hanan wondered if his operatives had mistakenly given him wrong information. But they had remained adamant about Daimyan leaving the temple tonight. Their informant knew the man's habits well and harbored a grudge against the captain.

"His quarters are in the temple but almost every fourth night, exactly at the mid of night, he goes to a woman in the city and returns at dawn," the bribed temple guard had told Hanan's men before drawing a map in the dirt to the woman's house.

Hanan traveled the route to her meager home several times, searching for the best location along the way to kidnap the captain. At first, he assumed Daimyan's late night treks were to a prostitute or an adulteress, then later learned she was of some family relation. The woman and the visits were not important to Hanan. He wanted the captain. Yet there were questions Hanan needed answers to before killing him. That created a problem, but one resolved with a handful of coins.

Kidnapping the captain meant taking im through the city to get to the wilderness, risking a chance of rying eyes watching from surrounding houses. The maze of the d underground tunnels beneath the city solved the dilemma. A ho se along the captain's route had a door in the floor leading down i o a tunnel, and after paying the owner to assist him, all lay in waiti g for Hanan's arrival.

As his operatives believed, at midnight short door opened next to the massive south gate and a stout-fra ned, uniformed man walked out, silhouetted against the temple's interior lamp lights. Hanan hurried down the street to the area h had chosen for concealment. It appeared black as a moonless nig it between the buildings, though, once his eyes adjusted to the da , he could make out the form of the walking man.

Within three minutes Hanan heard Dair yan's sandals crunching against pebbles in the dirt. Sica knife dr wn, holding it ready, Hanan relaxed and listened to each footstep g ow louder in the still night. When the captain drew even with him, Ianan swung the hilt of the knife into his prey's forehead, smashin him with such force Daimyan's feet flew out from under his body He crashed into the dirt with dead weight. Hanan followed him to he ground, dropping onto the man to tear his helmet away. He str ck the captain's head again with the hilt of the Sica. Daimyan was lead or unconscious, but Hanan didn't wait to learn which. He grab ed the guard's wrists, wrapped a rope about them and dragged hir to the nearby house. The owner stood waiting and within five mir tes, the assassin and his captive were in the labyrinth below the hou e, and the owner had covered the trapdoor with blankets.

* * *

Daimyan's right eye partially opened, but he remained half-dazed. He winced and drew a deep breath when his bleeding head moved. A groan escaped his lips from the shooting pain in his shoulders at being bound against a wall with arms stretched wide and high. Raising his head, he blinked blood from his good eye, and looked at rough, jagged rock walls about him, trying to make sense of his whereabouts. Wavering flames from a dozen oil lamps cast contorted shadows on the stone walls and ceiling. The eerie shadows danced as a breeze drifted through what he thought to be a tunnel. He stood spread nude in the shape of an X, bound at the wrists and ankles to thick, iron rings driven into the rock. Against a far wall lay his leather coin bag, clothes, sword and armor in a pile, and as his senses returned, he realized another mound of clothes were beside his. Turning his head to the left, he saw a heavily muscled man, nude and squatting near a large oil lamp, hands extended to its flame as if warming them. On the ground by him lay a Sica dagger free of its sheath.

The man watched him with a cold stare. Devoid of emotion, he rose to his bare feet, knife in hand, muscles rippling across the massive chest, shoulders and arms as he moved. Thick brown hair fell about his face, highlighting the emerald green eyes that shined in the light from the oil lamps. Walking to the prisoner, the man halted in front of him, face and body half covered in shadows. He remained silent and watched blood trail down into Daimyan's face from the head wound.

"Why am I here? Return my clothes and release me before you create further troubles for yourself," Daimyan demanded, struggling to show courage though his body trembled. "Are you one of the Zealots? What is your name?"

Hanan raised a finger to his lips, motioning the man to be quiet. Letting his gaze drift over the captain's nude body, he grinned. "You're as hairy as a baboon I once saw in the market." He raised his Sica and laid its blade horizontally on Daimyan's forest of black chest hair. With ease Hanan slid the sharp edge of the blade downward, shaving a long, wide path clean of hair. Finishing, he tapped the blade against the captain's manhood. "Sharp, isn't it?" he casually said.

Daimyan drew in his breath as his stomach tightened. His brows rose. "Why are you doing this?" He struggled to remain still. "Why did you remove your clothes?"

"I don't want your blood all over my clothes. Now, listen, I have a question. Slow or fast? Which will it be?"

"What? Slow *what*?"

"Your death. Do you wish to die slow or fast?"

"Neither... I want my clothes and to be released."

Shaking his head, Hanan's eyes narrowed. "Those are not your options. You will die. Answer my questions and when the time comes, I'll make your death swift." He watched the white haze over the left eye move as the captain looked left and right. "Can you see out of that thing?"

Daimyan's body shivered as fear mounted within him. "Let me go and I'll pay whatever price you want. Look, over there, in my bag. There's twenty silver coins. You can have them and be on your way." He tried to nod toward the leather bag at the far wall, but a fierce pain in his head forced him to stop.

"I found it while cutting away your clothes. Stolen from the temple treasury, isn't it?"

The captain's lips formed a thin line. He looked away.

"Is it for the woman you were going to tonight?"

Daimyan's face became a mask of fury. Eyes narrowed from his rage, he glared at Hanan. "Leave my sister out of this. Kill me and steal the money but leave her alone."

The money was of no significance to Hanan, and upon hearing their relationship, his first thought was to leave the money on her doorstep. But the gratification he felt from tormenting Daimyan with lies in his final hours was exhilarating. He grinned.

"She'll receive it. After I'm through here, I'll go take my pleasure with her and when finished, leave the silver on her stomach. She will have well earned it."

The captain screamed and lunged at his captor, hands curling into knotted fists, but his restraints held fast. He fell back against the rocky wall, breathing hard with head hung down.

Wrapping his left fingers in a handful of Daimyan's hair, Hanan whipped the head back, smacking it against the wall. The guard cried out in agony.

"Shout all you wish. We are far below the city in the old tunnels. No one will ever hear you." Hanan paused then spoke again. "Did the Sadducee priest, Eleazar ben Makim, go to Caiaphas and say the rabbi Yeshua must die?"

"Eleazar is dead," gasped Daimyan.

"I know. I slit his throat. But before he died, did he say Yeshua must die? You would have heard them talk. You're always in the room to protect the High Priest."

"Yes. The Sadducees want the false prophet eliminated because he is a threat to them and the temple."

Hanan nodded. "What does Caiaphas intend to do? Has he talked to others about harming Yeshua?"

Daimyan remained silent and looked away.

The Sica's blade drove deep into the captain's left thigh and struck bone. Daimyan shuddered, mouth agape and eyes flared. He gasped for breath as sweat streamed down his face, mixing with the blood of his head wound. Hanan jerked the dagger free and stared at him.

"Answer the question."

"Yes... Yes, he talked to Matthias, Annas, and Nicodemus about *eliminating* Yeshua."

"Did they agree with him?"

"Nicodemus didn't. He said he wouldn't have any part in it and left."

Hanan nodded and stood in thought a moment. He walked to the far wall where the house owner had placed buckets of water to clean with, and a large jar of wine. Drinking his fill, he wiped his mouth on his forearm and returned to his captive.

"What does Caiaphas intend to do?"

"All he said was that Yeshua must be eliminated."

But Daimyan had answered too quickly and wouldn't look at Hanan. Something was lacking.

The Sica's blade drove deep into the captain's right thigh and struck bone. A howl of agony burst from him, carrying through the tunnel. He screamed again when Hanan yanked the dagger free.

"Try again," Hanan said in a low voice.

Daimyan briefly closed his eyes and sought to control his breathing. He looked at Hanan. "Caiaphas has the name of a follower he will pay to testify against Yeshua. The Romans will have no choice but to execute him."

Jaw muscles twitched as Hanan gritted his teeth. He squeezed the grip of his Sica until his knuckles turned white and his arm became hard as iron.

"Give me the name of the follower," Hanan said, raising his knife and pressing its tip into the captain's left forearm. He drove the dagger through until the blade touched the rock wall behind the arm, then pulled it free.

"Judas!" Daimyan shouted, tears flowing from his eyes. "Judas Iscariot... Release me now. You have the information you wanted." He wept, unable to stop himself.

"Which priest gave Caiaphas the name? Annas or Matthias?"

Shaking his head, the captive whispered in an exhausted tone. "I did."

Rage twisted Hanan's stomach into an iron knot. His mind flashed images of Yeshua being skewered by Roman swords. He glanced about the tunnel, stared at the flame of a large oil lamp then walked to the jar of wine again. Drinking in gulps, he set the jar aside and returned to Daimyan.

"If you will not release me, then kill me. Make it swift as you promised. I answered your questions. You have what you want. Do it!"

Hanan stared at his prisoner. No emotion showed as he stood before the captain.

"I lied. You will die slowly, screaming in anguish until you're hoarse, begging me to end your life because your suffering is too great." Hanan paused to watch Daimyan's terror filled face. "Do you want to know why I intend to torture you?" He didn't wait for a reply. "Because you and your men speared my uncle to death and broke his wife's arm in the market—and you gave Caiap] as a name to help kill my friend."

Daimyan pleaded for mercy, wept, and pulled at his restraints to free himself.

"Have you ever hunted a *ya'el* in the mountains, those goat antelopes the Gentiles call an ibex?" Hanan asked, brows rising. "When you kill one, it must be prepared..."

"You're insane... Possessed! Kill me now and be done with this game," Daimyan cried out.

"No, I'm a Sicarii, trained to show no mercy to my prey nor ask for any. I bear a mark of evil and will never know peace in this world or the next." Hanan held his left forearm up for Daimyan to see the long, jagged scar.

Pressing the Sica's sharp blade against his captive's right breast, Hanan sliced away a strip of skin. The bellow of anguished screams echoed throughout the tunnel, bombarding his ears, but he never stopped.

*   *   *

Hanan lost track of time. He stepped back, mind numb, gaze drifting about the tunnel. Turning away from his work, he walked to the jar of wine and drank until it was empty. He looked at his hands, arms and body, unable to recognize himself from the blood covering him. The oil lamps were burning low. Lifting the first bucket of water, he poured it over his head and let it cascade down his body, washing the gore away. He repeated it with the second bucket and poured over half of the third bucket onto himself. The remaining water was used to clean his Sica. He dressed in silence, took Daimyan's leather coin bag in his left hand, and carried an oil lamp in his right to see by as he walked along the tunnel. At the trap door he climbed the makeshift stairs, tapped lightly on the wood and waited. When the door creaked open, the owner of the house stood outlined against the dawn's glaring light.

Squinting until his eyes adjusted, Hanan left the tunnel and gave the old man the oil lamp and the bag of coins. "Dispose of the clothes and body so no trace of him will ever be found." Hanan motioned to the leather bag. "This will pay for the cleanup."

Exhausted, he turned to the front door and walked out into the crowded street to join the pedestrians, donkey-drawn carts, and shepherds taking their animals to market.

I'll send the woman a bag of coins after I've slept, he thought.

∗ ∗ ∗

The old man barred the door after Hanan and hid his money. He returned to the tunnel door and stood gazing into the black hole. Fresh oil lamp in hand, he cautiously made his way down the stairs, and once in the tunnel, followed it until light appeared from the few lamps that remained burning. Holding his lamp high, he approached the area and slowed to a halt. The light was dim, but enough for him to see the scattered water buckets, wine jar, and pile of clothes and armor. A pool of bloody water had spread across the middle of the tunnel floor. Nearby lay a small mound of bloody flesh.

He turned to his right, startled then stumbled back, almost dropping his lamp. Regaining balance, he stood wide-eyed with his mouth open, gazing at the hideous crimson creature bound to the wall's iron rings. A white-hazed eye stared at him, and little more was left to show this had once been a living man.

Nausea rose into his mouth; stomach violently churning. He spun and vomited until only dry-heaves came

In his lifetime the old man had never seen the raw meat remains of a skinned man.

CHAPTER SIXTEEN

Capernaum, District of Galilee

"By the Way of the Sea' was an ancient trade route running eastward from Egypt, along the shores of the Mediterranean, and on to Syria's Fertile Crescent. It ran parallel to, and often overlapped, the 'King's Highway,' another major trade route linking Africa to Mesopotamia. The routes followed a path through Galilee, Tiberias, Capernaum and Kinneret on the west side of a thirteen-mile-long freshwater lake. Each town claimed naming rights to it; Lake Kinneret, Lake Tiberias, and so on. But travelers referred to it by the district, the Sea of Galilee, and the designation remained.

Hanan had broken his fast and sat relaxing at the shore-side wine shop in Capernaum. An hour had passed since daybreak, and the sun on his back grew warmer by the minute, but the breeze off of the Sea of Galilee was as soothing as its view from his table.

Little wonder why Yeshua moved here from Nazareth, Hanan thought, gaze drifting across the wide expanse of blue water to the distant mountains of the far shore. The warm sun and the soft melody of gentle waves breaking on the shoreline grew hypnotic and against his will, his eyes closed as his spirit was calmed by nature's music.

Opening his eyes, he abruptly straighten d in his chair, embarrassed at finding a group of men standing befo e him that he had not heard approach. Yeshua gently smiled at him.

"I thought it was you. We were taking ou morning walk when I saw a mountain sitting upon a chair. Only n y old friend Hanan is that big, I told my disciples," he said, smile gro ving.

Glancing at Yeshua's followers, Hanan w is curious which was Judas. He stood, hugged his friend, and motic ned toward his small table. "Here, join me. Have your men sit and reak their fast. I may have a coin or two to pay for their food." Jovi l words came as they thanked him and took seats beneath the wine hop's awning.

"You've been a busy man, Yeshua, travel ng about and talking to the people," Hanan said, glancing at the me 1 as servants brought them food. He looked at Yeshua's weary expr ssion and the brown eyes that held deep worry as if a great respons bility rested upon his shoulders. His dark hair was uncombed and nung to the collar of his one-piece tunic that was in need of wasl ing. "You look tired, my friend, and you've lost weight since we last met. Is your ministry going well?"

An assortment of fruits, grilled meats, an a cup of wine was set on the table before Yeshua. Hanan watched hi 1 dip his hands into a water bowl, clean them, then give thanks in pi yer for the food.

Yeshua nodded between bites. "There's m ch to do and Passover is coming." He ate but drew solemn. His gaz rose to Hanan then drifted to his followers. "We leave tomorrow fc r Jerusalem."

Watching Yeshua devour the food as if l e hadn't eaten in two days, Hanan waited to talk and sat enjoying he morning with his friend. He glanced at the men accompanying Yeshua. They were a mixed lot, varying in build and appearances, 1eir tunics and robes all of modest make from the region. Most were engaged in light talks of no importance, laughing as traveling friends do once bonds of trust are made. To the far side of the disciples sat one man alone at a table, his dark eyes cutting to the others in glances, smiling only when spoken to. His thick, dark hair held slight curls and his hook nose and scrubby beard gave his face an elongated appearance. The man's tunic was plain, yet of a better-quality weave than his companions, and he wore his *himatia* wrapped tighter about his body. The differences told Hanan what he needed to know. An assassin tracked his prey by minute details.

"How is Miriam?" Yeshua asked, finished with his meal.

"You mean, your mother?" Hanan's brows slightly rose. He was a bit shocked at Yeshua not calling her *mother.* "She's fine. You should go visit her—and your family too. They would enjoy seeing you."

Shaking his head, Yeshua grew sullen. "Thank you for looking after her." He paused and gazed out at the lake. "All is in motion now as my Father wishes and I must continue the path he has set for me."

Glancing at the disciples, Hanan turned to Yeshua. "I need to talk with you in private. Can we go walk along the shore?"

Yeshua nodded and they rose from their chairs. He looked at his twelve followers, told them to return to Peter's home, then started toward the lake while Hanan paid the wine shop's owner.

The two friends walked thirty feet before anything was spoken between them. Hanan was the first to break their silence.

"I've learned you're considered a threat by the Sadducees, Pharisees and the Sanhedrin council. They are afraid of losing their political and religious controls and want you dead."

One hand cupped in another behind his back, Yeshua nodded and continued his ambling walk along the shore. Hanan watched his friend's face and grew frustrated at his tranquility.

"Yeshua, are you listening to me? I'm not making this up. The information is reliable. The Sanhedrin intend to have someone give false testimony so they may turn you over to Pilate for execution." Hanan halted and stood with the lake's light shoreline waves lapping onto his sandals. He gazed at Yeshua's placid expression, growing angrier by the second that his friend wasn't disturbed by the news. "Did you hear me? They plan to kill you—and the betrayal will come from one of your followers!"

Looking across the water, Yeshua inhaled deeply and gave a slight nod. "I've heard every word you've spoken, my friend, and know you speak the truth." He let his gaze drift to Hanan. "Yes, Judas will betray me. The devil has his ear and convinces him of the need to do so. The devil has followed me my entire life trying to bring harm to me and those I know. He followed me into the desert and tempted me every day. Yes, my Father has told me of these things. What has begun cannot be stopped until the prophecies are fulfilled. I am in my Father as He is within me."

Shaking his head, Hanan walked a step then angrily spun to face Yeshua. "I cannot say that I understand all of this. I can't believe *Elohim* would willingly let you go to your death like a lamb to the slaughter. Let me stop Judas from betraying you. I have men that can protect you—."

"No, Hanan, that is not *Elohim's* way. My Father sent me here for a purpose and I have accepted that fact. I am the Messiah, but I did not come to free the people and lead them to my Father through violence... The way to *Elohim* is through me, believing in me, because

I will take on everyone's sins so they may enter the house of our God, *Elohim*." Yeshua's face grew somber and he remained quiet, looking out across the lake.

"My sins are for me to bear, no other... Because of them I will never see the heaven of *Elohim*, but if anyone should, Yeshua, it should be you." Hanan's voice trailed to silence as he lowered his gaze to the water's edge. He was lost for words. His friend truly held an innocent soul. Then the words of John the Baptist, standing in the Jordan River, rose in his mind: *The Anointed One to come is the lamb of Elohim who will take away the sins of the world.*

"In time, my friend, you will be with me in my Father's house. Within you is a great battle. Darkness struggles to defeat the good in your heart. I have prayed for you since we were boys in Nazareth, but *Elohim* will not allow me to cast out the evil that has marked you. He says if your victory is ever to come, you must find it yourself in the living water. Such is the word of my Father and I must obey."

Yeshua warmly smiled and turned to walk back along the shore of the lake toward Peter's home. Emotions churning, Hanan felt as if a red-hot iron had punctured his chest. His mind became a maelstrom of sorrow. He knew the punishment Yeshua would receive at the hands of the Romans. A sense of helplessness flooded him.

* * *

It was midafternoon of the second day after visiting Yeshua when Hanan returned to his home in Nazareth. Benjamin and Elizabeth, the elderly couple that had served his uncles as long as Hanan could remember, were at their home on the estate, and the large house was quiet. They kept everything clean and orderly but Hanan didn't require them to remain at the residence while he was away. There was no need. Walking through the house, its silence grated his nerves more whenever he saw Micah and Yosef's personal effects that remained in their rooms. His thoughts wandered from them to Yeshua then to the men of the Sicari, the organization he now led, and what their future held.

Cup in hand, he found a jar of Micah's favorite Damascus wine and walked to the veranda to relax. The view was magnificent with the shadow-painted, distant purplish mountains, the rolling landscape of green olive and fruit orchards, and large expanses of open land wherever his gaze drifted. The chair he chose was next to Micah's favorite. He still couldn't bring himself to sit in it and didn't know if he ever would. Being next to it was good enough for now.

He finished his first cup of wine and leaned back against the chair, dozing when a man shouting his name jarred him awake. The urgency in the voice made Hanan rise and from habit, check the position of his Sica beneath his robe.

"Here," Hanan yelled. "I'm on the veranda."

The visitor stopped shouting. When he came around the house into view, Hanan recognized him as one of his men and waved him to the porch.

Simcha ben Mudash was a weasel of a man; almost skinny in build, short, with dark narrow eyes, a flattened nose, and a chin that protruded more than it should. He always wore a desert styled headdress, dirty tunics and oversized, ragged robes. But for a thief working the crowded markets and festivals, stealing whatever caught his eye to resell, it was easier to conceal property beneath his clothes. He bought and sold information to the highest bidder, often to opposing parties, yet Hanan was the one man he never sold information about.

Simcha knew his master would track him down if ever a suspicion of treachery arose.

"Don't you ever bathe, Simcha?" Hanan asked, shaking his head. "I could smell sheep long before you came around the corner." A friendly grin flashed to make the little man believe he was kidding, but Hanan's true thoughts were worse.

"I bathe once a month, master, whether I need to or not. In my line of work, people speak more freely around me when they believe I am nothing more than a beggar."

"Stop calling me *master*. I'm not your master or some religious teacher. Call me Hanan as everyone else does."

"Yes, master—I mean Hanan."

Hanan motioned him to wait, entered his home and returned with a cup.

"Here, have some wine. I'm sure the journey here has made you thirsty." Hanan filled his cup and motioned the man to take a chair. But when Simcha was about to lower himself into Micah's chair, Hanan brusquely grabbed it and ordered him to choose another.

The operative sat across the table from Hanan, drank half of his cup, and smiled wide at the wine's flavor and smooth taste.

"Why are you here?" Hanan bluntly asked, no longer feigning the role of a gracious host.

"Problems are rising within the organization, Mas—Hanan. There are men who say we have done little more than trim branches off a tree, and it is time we begin to chop the trunk itself, with or without you." Simcha finished his wine and set the cup on the table, sliding it toward his employer as he glanced at the jar. But Hanan made no move to refill the cup.

Hanan sat stone-faced, staring at the little man. "I'm too tired for riddles. Speak your mind. If you have news I should know, tell me. You will be paid handsomely as always."

"Sir, I do not tell you for money. This is something that threatens us all."

Leaning forward, Hanan lifted the wine jar and filled both of their cups. "Go ahead. You have my attention."

Simcha looked about the veranda as if eavesdroppers were near.

"Our numbers have grown to the size of a small army. I've been told some wish to splinter off and add men to their ranks under the name of the Sicarii. This would be in preparation for taking greater actions against the Romans and villagers who assist them in any manner. While you have been careful to ensure we vanish into the night after a mission, there are men who say we must openly initiate full attacks against our enemies and no longer conceal our names and faces."

Outwardly, Hanan appeared calm yet beneath the façade, a volcano existed on the verge of eruption. His green eyes studied Simcha for signs of deception.

"We have instilled fear in many, but what these men you speak of do not understand is open revolt now will only end in failure. Three or four hundred men warring against trained Roman legions is futile. The Empire will bring their full might against us. Do you have the names of those who are demanding greater action?"

"They are mostly young men whose fathers were Zealots killed by the Romans. They have not been in the Sicarii long, but they want revenge more than justice for our people. I was given several names but want to be sure before speaking them. I thought you needed to know before the kettle boils over and scalds us all."

Hanan drank his wine and sat in his chair gazing out at the orchards. Simcha finished his wine and motioned to the jar, waiting for approval to have more. Without glancing his way, Hanan nodded then spoke.

"Revolt is coming, but without unity and proper planning, it will be a short-lived war for us. I've been away on business, but I've heard people in towns speak of their hatred of the Gentiles, the constant rise in their taxes, and the rampant corruption in the temple. A revolt may come soon or take years to arrive, but with men recklessly wanting war now, we are doomed."

Simcha upended his cup, gulped the wine down and wiped his mouth with a dirty sleeve of his robe. "Let me see if I can identify these young leaders so there is no mistake when you wish to approach them."

He watched Hanan rise and walk into the house, then return carrying a small bag.

"You've done a great service for me, Simcha." Hanan dropped the bag on the table. It landed with a thud and clink of coins. "Learn more and tell no one except me."

"Only from my lips to your ears, Mast—I mean Hanan." The operative stood, slipped the coin bag beneath his robe, and left.

Hanan watched until Simcha was gone from sight down the road. Rubbing his face with both hands, Hanan exhaled in a hard blast and wearily shook his head.

What else can go wrong? he thought.

CHAPTER SEVENTEEN

District of Judea
Sunday, Month of Nisan, Day 9

Yeshua chose to stop near a stream for the night though they were less than two hours from Jerusalem. With dusk drawing near, camp preparations remained to be made before dark set upon them. Everyone needed to be rested for their entry into the city tomorrow.

The day's travel from Bethany had been without problems, but the day itself had been wearisome. At noon Yeshua and his disciples arrived at his deceased friend's house. The family greeted them with grief and anger. Lazarus had died three days before and buried on the fourth. Although, summoned, Yeshua hadn't come until today. Seeing the depth of their sorrow, Yeshua wept, surprising his followers for they had never known him to cry. But at the entrance of the tomb, he stood and called out for Lazarus to come forth... and he did. When they left, Martha, one of Lazarus' sisters again proclaimed: "I believe you are the Messiah, the Son of our God, *Elohim*, who is to come into the world."

Now, having finished their meager meal of bread, fruit, and water from the stream, they relaxed about a small fire. Little talk passed between them. An uneasiness gradually consumed each man the closer they drew to Jerusalem. Yeshua may be greeted by the masses with reverence for the miracles he performed or as a villain of the faithful for his declarations against the temple's Sanhedrin council. And there were his foreboding words of how the prophecies would be fulfilled.

A waxing moon climbed into the heavens among the stars; its far-left edge draped by a black crescent yet bathing the landscape in ample light to see by. Within a few days, a full moon would rise and blanket the land with enough light to travel or work by if necessary.

The disciples drew comfort from the moonlight. It kept their despondent thoughts about Jerusalem at bay and allowed them to see anyone approaching the camp, especially robbers or temple guards seeking their arrests. But they never expected the arrival of a lone shepherd boy who quietly walked to their fire and stood staring at them.

Peter saw him first and leaped to his feet. About the camp fire the other disciples quickly rose, confused as to what was amiss. Yeshua calmly remained on his blanket and watched the boy of twelve or thirteen years look about the men as if searching for someone.

"Are you lost, boy? Do you need help?" Peter asked, his gaze drifting over the young man's head for signs of robbers advancing toward them.

The slender boy remained silent then looked at Yeshua.

"My master sent me to find the Rabbi and ask him to come talk," the shepherd boy boldly said.

Yeshua slowly rose and walked to him. May I ask your master's name before I go with you?"

"A priest of the council who only wishes ɔ talk. That is all I am to say."

"It may be a trap, Teacher. Bandits may be waiting. Let us all go with you," Matthew said, his eyes glancing about the surrounding land.

Yeshua grinned and turned to his followers. "I will be safe. This young man will protect me. Won't you?" He miled and patted the shepherd boy on the shoulder. "Let us go to your master."

* * *

Yeshua followed the boy for several min tes as he led the way along the road then angled toward a row of trees by the flowing stream. Beneath the wide spread branches of an ancient olive tree sat a stooped, bearded man in the flowing ro e and headdress of a Sanhedrin priest. He sat upon a large rock, s ɪring into a campfire with hands stretched to the flames for warmth To the far side of the fire stood a donkey nibbling at stubs of grass n the rough ground. The donkey raised its head, ears perked and b ayed when its owner drew near.

The priest saw their approach and groan d as he stood.

"Thank you, Eli," the old man said, pullir ɡ the front of his robe closed for warmth against the chill of the wilder ess night. He watched the boy go rub and scratch the donkey's head hen faced Yeshua. "I appreciate you coming to talk, Rabbi. My nam is Nicodemus and as you've already been told, I'm with the temple ouncil. Please. Come sit with me. I apologize for the primitive acco nmodations and this secrecy, but once you reach the city it will be difficult for us to meet in private."

Yeshua nodded and found a comfortable position on a rock near the campfire. "I'm honored to meet you," he said, watching the priest ease himself back onto his former seat.

"The honor is mine, Rabbi. I've seen you before, but we've never formally met." Nicodemus shifted his gaze to the shepherd boy. "Eli is a trusted lad who helps me get about the area as I need. I must admit, riding a donkey from the city has left me quite sore. Even with thick blankets, a donkey's backbone is rough on an old man's backside." He smiled and extended his wrinkled hands to the fire again.

The firelight made the priest's grayish eyes shine and brightened the flowing, silver beard brushing his chest. His tunic and robes were of the finest quality and several jewels on his priestly chest plate sparkled, yet everything about Nicodemus spoke of a man who was not enamored by riches and pompous ceremony.

They talked in generalities, but Nicodemus wasted little time before directing their conversation to Yeshua's teachings.

"Rabbi, I've seen you perform miracles that can only come from *Elohim*. No one could do so if God were not with him. But my questions are centered upon your words of 'being born again' and seeing the 'kingdom of God.' Some believe you refer to a man literally being born again from their mother's womb. Truly you cannot say that a man must enter his mother's womb a second time to be born again. What is it that you do mean?"

Yeshua's brows rose. "I'm surprised a teacher would misunderstand. I do not speak of literal rebirth, but of a spiritual rebirth, one in which we cleanse our soul in the immersion of living water, be born again in believing in and accepting *Eloh m*—and through His teachings move into His kingdom, the kingdor of our God, *Elohim.*"

A wry smile appeared on Nicodemus' lip , letting Yeshua know he had well understood but only wished to h ar it from him. They talked at leisure about the Torah, the Laws of Moses, and the parables Yeshua always spoke in his teachings.

"It must be difficult for you being a Pharisee among the Sadducees of the temple, especially with the 1 arguing constantly about the Scriptures," Yeshua said, curious ho v opposing sects survived under the same temple roof.

A light laugh came from the priest. "W have a give and take relationship with them. We give and the Sadd icees take—and take. Although the chief priests and high priests ar Sadducees, the numbers of both parties are divided well enough or our seventy-member Sanhedrin supreme court council that the Sa ducees cannot freely have their way. The Essenes remain clear of t ie bickering, though. They are committed to their dietary laws, livir 3 a monastic life, and celibacy when it fits their needs. Personally, th t celibacy stuff would drive me crazy."

Yeshua grinned. He liked the aged priest nd enjoyed their talk.

Nicodemus pointed a finger skyward nd shook his head. "Pharisees believe in the resurrection of the d ad, as you do, Rabbi. We wish to reach the kingdom of God you sp ak of. The Sadducees deny the afterlife. In their belief the soul p rishes at death. We teach the existence of angels and demons in a spiritual realm while the Sadducees reject the idea of an unknow , unseen world. The Sadducees consider themselves elitist, aristo ratic, and are power hungry. They may control the temple, but we c ntrol the synagogues in this country and that disturbs them."

Letting his gaze drift to the flames of the campfire, Nicodemus' face drew somber. "The greatest difference, though, is the Sadducees are more accommodating to the Romans and their Gentile laws than we are. They're concerned more with politics and control of the people than religion. It's why they fear you. They do not want Roman attention brought upon the temple any more than what we have. And worse, there are Pharisees united with the Sadducees in that belief. I would warn you about the conspiracies against you, but you know they exist as I do."

"There will always be men who conspire against others. They do so because they are weak of heart, lack courage to do what is right, and live in fear of our God, *Elohim*," Yeshua said with a tone of sadness.

"May I offer a suggestion for tomorrow?" Nicodemus straightened his posture upon the rock and laid his wrinkled hands in his lap. The firelight danced in his gray eyes.

The Nazarene nodded with a smile.

"Rather than walk with your disciples through the city gates of Jerusalem, I suggest you enter riding a donkey. I can have Eli waiting outside the city with his donkey, and he can lead the animal through the streets while you are attentive to the crowds. There is another reason, though, why it would be prudent to do so."

Yeshua watched Nicodemus' face.

"When a king rides through the gates upon his horse, everyone sees him as an arriving conqueror. But riding upon a donkey tells all that he has come in peace. Such an arrival would announce you have come as the Prince of Peace, and with good intent."

A warm smile crossed Yeshua's lips. "Truly you are blessed with wisdom, Nicodemus." He rose and gave a slight bow of the head to the priest. He glanced at the shepherd boy. "Then I will look for you and your four-legged friend upon the road tomorrow before entering the city."

The boy looked from Yeshua to his donkey and rubbed the animal's head.

Nicodemus groaned and massaged the small of his back as he stood from the large rock.

"I will have Eli bring a thick blanket for your ride." His gray eyes shined in the firelight. A smile had formed on his lips but faded when he spoke again. "You carry a heavy weight of responsibility, one that I could never begin to bear. When you cross the city gates, know there are men who love you, but there are more who fear your arrival and wish you dead. Evil will be at every turn anxiously awaiting your downfall. I pray that our God, *Elohim*, will protect you."

"Thank you for your words of wisdom and blessing." Having spoken, Yeshua walked from the camp.

CHAPTER EIGHTEEN

Jerusalem, District of Judea
Monday, Month of Nisan, Day 10

The shepherd boy quietly sat in the shade of a tree, watching dust rise from the road, stirred by the endless stream of pilgrims walking past to enter the city. Behind him stood his donkey with eyes closed and nostrils lightly flaring at times. It was the only sign that life still existed in the animal.

At the sound of boisterous cheering, Eli glanced eastward along the road. Squinting against a glaring sun he could see the crowds gathered about a group of men as they walked from the Mount of Olives toward the city. When they drew closer Eli saw the Rabbi's crème colored headdress then recognized the men following him. The shepherd boy waited until they were near before rising from the shade.

"Are you ready, Eli?" Yeshua smiled at him as he waved to the surrounding crowd.

The roar of the cheers came in waves, making it difficult to hear, but the boy nodded in reply. Adjusting the thick blanket on his donkey's back, Eli held the lead rope while Yeshua mounted.

"We'll enter through the old wall's south ern gate. Follow the road past the Siloam Pool and pass in front o the temple gates. We won't be entering, though. That will be for another day," Yeshua shouted, laughing at how jubilant the people were. He saw the boy's lips move yet couldn't hear him, then the donkey lurched forward to follow its master.

Yeshua's disciples trailed the animal, their heads whipping left and right in amazement of the people. The joyous reception and festive atmosphere were far from what they had imagined.

Thousands of pilgrims stretched from outside of the wall, through its gate, and on into the city's interior. As Yeshua made his triumphal entry, Eli led the donkey along a narrow lane formed by the people pressing forward to see the young rabbi. Laying their cloaks and small branches of trees down before the animal to cushion the walk and welcome Yeshua, pilgrims sang, *'Blessed is He who comes in the name of the Lord. We bless you from the house of the Lord...'*

As Yeshua and his disciples made their way through the city streets, those who did not know him asked, *"Who is this you praise?"* The faithful answered, *"This is Yeshua, the prophet from Nazareth of Galilee."*

More cried out, *"Praise our God, Elohim, for the Prince of Peace has arrived! The Messiah has come for us at last!"*

But not all were pleased at his presence.

Standing along the top of the towering temple walls, twenty members of the Sanhedrin council listened to the jubilant cries of the pilgrims and sternly watched the man upon the donkey ride past in the street below. The High Priest Caiaphas scowled and lightly shook his head in contempt. Others about him followed suit, grumbling about the false-prophet and his miracle tricks. Yet to one side of the priests stood Nicodemus leaning on the wall as he watched Yeshua and the disciples. He smiled warmly at the cheers of the people, but sadness filled his eyes.

Yeshua had paused in the street. He sat on the donkey gazing at the temple then raised his eyes to the priests lining the top of the wall. They stood staring at him.

"Peter?"

"Yes, Teacher," Peter replied, moving forward to stand close.

"Do you see this great building?" Yeshua's calm voice held a prophetic tone.

Looking the length of the temple, Peter turned to face Yeshua. "I see it."

"No stone that stands here one upon another will not be thrown down... And no Judean—man, woman, or child will survive that time."

Stunned by the revelation, Peter let his gaze drift from Yeshua to the enormous temple. When he looked back at his teacher, Eli had begun to lead the donkey away.

* * *

Jerusalem, District of Judea
Tuesday, Month of Nisan, Day 11

In the morning sunlight of a cloudless sky Yeshua and his disciples walked through the city's outer wall gate on their way to the temple. Night had been spent on the Mount of Olives where Yeshua preferred during his visits to Jerusalem. There were nights, though, when they accepted invitations to stay at the homes of supporters, yet those times primarily came when he and his men needed a full meal.

Peter, the unspoken leader of the disciples, walked behind and to the right of Yeshua. The others followed as they chose, leaving Judas by himself to trail them. They walked in silence, sensing tension within Yeshua. Normally, he set their tone for the day. If he began with a morning lesson of the scriptures, the day would be upbeat with constant talk. But today, as he had every day since starting for Jerusalem, he awoke in a somber mood and said little unless spoken to. This, and his cryptic words of pending doom, kept the disciples anxious and confused.

Walking through the throngs of Passover pilgrims, Yeshua waved and greeted them with kind, encouraging words. Some within the masses surged forward, reaching out to touch his garments and plead for his blessings. He paused at an aged woman who knelt beside his path, crying as she held her hands up before her face in supplication. Leaning close he listened to her whispers in his ear. When she finished, he straightened his posture and laid his hands on her head. Eyes closed, his face rose to the sun and he spoke in a voice so low that none near him could hear his words.

"Rise and go home. The power of your faith has healed your grandson," Yeshua said, helping the elderly woman to her feet. She wept and kissed his hand before hurrying away.

Watching her leave, Peter kindly smiled and was about to speak but Yeshua had renewed his walk.

At the temple they entered the Hulda Gate and started the upward walk through a long, wide tunnel and staircase until coming out in the sunlight bathed Court of Gentiles with the colonnaded structure behind them. They were greeted by the chaotic, wavering bleat of sheep and goats, flapping dove and pigeon wings, and a din of people's chatter as crowds of pilgrims moved to and from the money-changer tables. The pungent odor of manure hung in the air.

Two Sanhedrin priests of the higher ranks, their black robes flowing as they walked, moved along a line of sheep held with ropes by their owners. The priests paused at times to inspect an animal for the slightest blemish that would bar them from being sacrificed. Upon approval, the priests arrogantly waved a hand over the creatures without a glance at their owners. But Yeshua frowned when he saw their swaying hands stop and the animal's owner laid coins in the priests' palms.

Lips pressed into a thin line, brows drawing downward, Yeshua's brows drew downward as he watched a priest's fingers curl about a coin. Peter turned to speak to Yeshua but stopped at the rage he observed burning wildly in the young rabbi's eyes.

Where the balustrade had once separated the Court of Gentiles from the wide, open courtyard leading to the Holy of Holies, tables now sat beyond that short wall for money-changers to embrace the overflow of pilgrims.

"They are nothing more than thieves," the young rabbi said in a tone of disgust.

Never having seen Yeshua so infuriated during their time together, Peter glanced back at his fellow disciples and motioned them to watch Yeshua. Confused, they stepped forward and looked about the area to see what their leader had focused on.

A stoop shouldered, elderly woman wrapped in a tattered robe stood holding two cooper coins out to a lanky, dark-skinned, dove seller dressed in a white tunic and blue robe of excellent quality. The contemptuous expression on the seller's face as he reached for a pigeon instead of a dove, drove Yeshua furious. The young rabbi's hands curled into knotted balls as he spun to face Peter.

"The poor cannot afford grander sacrifices. These robbers steal their money by selling them pigeons at the price of doves." Yeshua scowled and pointed to the robed men sitting at the money-changer tables. "They collect Greek and Roman coin here in my Father's house in exchange for Jewish coins." Spinning about, he stared at the animal-sellers who tugged at ropes to drag their sheep and goats from rickety pens to waiting buyers. Dung littered the stone floor and smeared in streaks beneath the hooves of animals struggling against the ropes. "They defile this house of prayer!"

Strong cords, three feet in length and used by the buyers to lead their purchases away, hung draped over the top railing of a nearby goat pen. Yeshua strode to the cords, grabbed a handful and tied them into a knot on one end. Holding the knotted end, he swung it once through the air like a Roman nine-tailed-whip then smashed the top rail of the goat pen, snapping it in two. The support railings fell, and the entire pen crashed to the stone floor. Frightened goats spun in circles, bleating then burst from the pen and ran into the crowds.

"You've made my Father's house a den of thieves!" Eyes wide, the veins of Yeshua's neck protruded like brass cords as he shouted. "You prey upon the poor!" Grabbing a large birdcage, he flung it to the ground. It crashed into the stone and shattered. Pigeons and doves flapped their wings to get airborne then flew in all directions.

Pilgrims ran from the madman, crying out in fear. Money-changers rose from their chairs, scraping coins from the table into their hands, but they were too slow. Yeshua ran to them and overturned their tables. Coins fell, bounced and rolled across the stone floor, kicked away by the sandals of fleeing people. One table after the next was knocked over by the furious young rabbi as he whipped people who blocked his path.

Peter swung an arm at his fellow disciples. "Help our teacher," he yelled, and the twelve men smashed bird cages, ripped open the sheep and goat pens, and flung bags of coins into the air from one end of the Court of Gentiles to the other. Mayhem broke out as women screamed and men bashed into one another trying to escape.

Sanhedrin priests raced from their temple offices to find pandemonium spreading across the entire courtyard. Yeshua whipped the money-changers away from their overturned tables, refusing to allow them to retrieve their fallen money. Bleating sheep and goats fled through the crowds, tripping people, and feathers floated through the air as doves and pigeons soared to safety.

"Stop this madness now," ordered a black-robed priest who stood pointing a finger at the rabbi. But Yeshua spun, wheeling the makeshift nine-tailed-whip through the air. He swung and struck the priest's arm, knocking coins from his hands.

"Do not speak to me of madness, you pious thief!" Yeshua shouted, his brown eyes burning wild with fury. "My Father's house will no longer be defiled by you."

A squad of temple guards rushed into the courtyard with spears at the ready, but a ranking priest standing to one side of the melee quickly raised a hand, halting their advance.

The chaos dwindled and quiet followed. Yeshua and his disciples stood throughout the Court of Gentiles, breathing heavily as they watched the guards. Smashed bird cages, cracked pieces of wood from the animal pens, bags of spilled coins, and broken tables lay scattered about them on the stone floor. Several of the money-changers laid on the floor where they had fallen from Yeshua's whip. They scurried on their hands and knees toward the temple guards, glancing over their shoulders at the band of twelve men and their madman leader who stood with his whip in hand.

The line of temple guards parted, and the slender High Priest Caiaphas stepped into view. His face remained stoic as his dark eyes swept the calamity and ruin of the courtyard. The gold trimmed, black robe fell about him, draping from his mitre and over his shoulders then down to the floor. What little that could be seen of his black tunic beneath the robe showed embroidered designs in gold thread, and a thick grayish-black beard partially covered the multi-jeweled breastplate of office that hung from about his neck.

"Rabbi," Caiaphas called out, staring at Yeshua. "By what right do you enter the temple and disrupt it as you and your men have?"

"By what *right*?" Yeshua asked in a mocking tone, tossing his whip onto the polished stone floor as he took a step forward. "It is written, my house shall be called a house of prayer, but you have made it a den of thieves."

The public affront struck the high priest harder than a slap of the face. Muscles twitched in his jaw from gritting his teeth. His nostrils flared, and his lips pressed into a thin line. He stared at the young rabbi and was about to speak when Yeshua turned and started toward the tunnel leading out of the temple. Caiaphas watched the twelve men back away, their eyes cutting to the temple guards as if expecting an attack. When they were gone, the high priest gazed at the destruction in the Court of Gentiles.

The money-changers crawled about the courtyard to retrieve coins. Animal sellers rushed forward, capturing loose sheep and goats, arguing with one another over their rightful ownership. The bird sellers waved their hands through the air, crying out about their losses. Priests stood in groups, some angry while others were stunned.

"Don't stand there running your mouths and gawking... Clean this courtyard!" the high priest yelled as he strode away.

The demon kept the cowl of his black cloak pulled over his head and moved beside Caiaphas, keeping step with him. Abaddon's long, skeletal fingers gripped the front of his cloak to keep it closed as they hurried through the courtyard.

"Now you've witnessed how truly dangerous this false-prophet is to the temple—to the faith of the people," the demon whispered only for the high priest to hear. "You know what must be done to save the faith and the temple from him. What is the life of one man when compared to saving a nation? Or would you prefer the Romans rule this temple?"

The black cloaked man abruptly stopped and watched the high priest walk on. His yellowish eyes gleamed and a contemptuous vile smile formed when Caiaphas paused to talk with the priest Matthias. The smile grew and rotted teeth appeared at hearing the high priest whisper, "Find the man Judas. Bring him here and make the offer as we discussed. One man's life to save our faith will be silver well spent."

* * *

Jerusalem, District of Judea
Thursday, Month of Nisan, Day 13

The afternoon sun baked the masses edging along the street and through the market. With each day the city grew more con-gested with pilgrims as the Passover drew close. Tomorrow after-noon the temple priests would slaughter the lambs for sacrifice to mark the festival's official opening, and each following day would bring a different ceremony.

Sitting at the last open table beneath the awning of Yosef and Sarah's wine shop, Hanan studied the people and wondered if any of his rebellious Sicarii would attempt an assassination against his orders. He had stopped several plots of men wanting to strike out on their own, but the numbers of the restless steadily grew. He knew one day it would take more than words to control his men.

A short, skinny man in a clean headdress crème tunic and robe approached his table. Hanan only recognized him by the dark, narrow eyes, flattened nose and protruding chin. Leaning forward onto the table, Hanan squinted as he let his gaze drift over his operative.

"Simcha?"

"Yes, of course it's me." Simcha ben Munash curiously looked about himself then at Hanan. "What's wrong, master?"

Hanan lightly laughed. "You bathed and are wearing clean clothes."

The operative rolled his eyes and exhaled in frustration. "May I sit with you?"

Motioning to an empty chair across the table, Hanan grinned. While Simcha eased into the chair, Hanan gestured to a shop servant for more wine. The operative gazed at the pedestrians out in the street until the wine was brought. Lifting his cup in gratitude to Hanan, Simcha drank several gulps and smiled as he wiped his mouth on the sleeve of his robe.

Hanan glanced at the wine shop patrons sitting near and when satisfied no one was eavesdropping, he nodded to the informant.

"You were right, master. I bribed a guard and was told the disciple Judas was secretly summoned to the temple. He met with three priests behind closed doors, so I don't know what they discussed, but he left with a bag of coins. The guard saw the bag and believes it was the thirty silver coins he'd earlier been ordered to take to the three priests from the treasury."

Hanan emptied his wine cup and refilled it, then poured Simcha's cup full.

"And what of the other matter I asked you to look into?"

Simcha quickly downed his wine and lightly belched. His brows pulled together as he pointed to his empty cup. "That wine tastes like the same kind I drank at your home."

"It's from my uncle's personal stock that is kept here... Now, what about the other matter?"

"I followed the rabbi as you ordered. He secured a room on the second-floor of a house for a meal with his men tonight—only tonight. It must be something special because there are no rooms available in the city with thousands of pilgrims wanting every space to be found," Simcha said in a low voice, leaning toward Hanan to emphasize his words.

Hanan gazed at the masses moving through the street, watching them yet deep in thought. He heard Simcha speaking and faced him. "What? I didn't hear you."

"I asked if you heard what the rabbi did in the temple the other day?"

Hanan shook his head and was pouring more wine for them when Simcha spoke.

"He and his followers destroyed the Court of Gentiles and—."

Wine spilled across the table as the wine jar slipped in Hanan's hands. He grabbed it and sat motionless, staring at Simcha with flared eyes. "They destroyed it? The rabbi destroyed it?"

"Yes. The story spread like wildfire after it happened last Tuesday. Naturally, everyone adds to the tale but from what I was told by a guard who witnessed it, the rabbi whipped the money-changers, and with his men, smashed cages and released all of the animals. He even told the high priest that the temple had become a den of thieves."

Hanan handed the wine jar to Simcha and sat laughing. "Yeshua whipped the money-changers—and called the temple a den of thieves!" His laughter grew so hearty that patrons about him turned to see what had occurred. When he regained control of himself, everyone returned to their own affairs.

A confused expression crossed the informant's face, but it didn't slow his drinking. He poured a cup, gulped it down, and refilled it while his master was in such good humor.

"Sorry... If you knew how peaceful that rabbi normally is, you would laugh as well at hearing he became violent." Hanan shook his head as he warmly smiled. "But I'm afraid that didn't win the rabbi any friends in the temple. If anything, he made more enemies than he already had there." The realization of the truth in Simcha's words made Hanan grow depressed.

Simcha nodded. "There is something else, master, that I'm sorry to have to bring up."

Hanan's face grew stern.

Simcha swallowed as if the words were stuck in his throat. "I had to pay highly for the information from the guard, and—."

Relieved at there being nothing further about Yeshua, Hanan reached into a bag beneath his robe. "You've done well, Simcha. Here, this should help you for a few days." He laid a handful of silver coins in front of his operative and watched the man eagerly sweep them off the table into his hand.

"Thank you, master." Simcha finished his wine. "Is there anything else I may do for you?"

Resting his muscled forearms on the table, Hanan cupped one hand into the other as he looked at the operative. "Yes. Stop calling me *master.*"

"Yes, mast—I mean, Hanan." Simcha nervously grinned.

* * *

Thursday night, Month of Nisan, Day 13

The hour had grown late and where the light of the full moon didn't fall, black shadows shrouded alleys and portions of the streets. Hanan patiently sat within a shadow, his gaze drifting to the two-story house across the street. Wavering light from oil lamps and men's silhouettes could be seen moving in its high windows. Three hours had passed and Hanan wondered if Yeshua and his disciples had decided to stay the night. He wanted to talk with his friend once more and attempt to convince him of the pending danger.

The night air of the cloudless sky held a piercing chill. Tugging his cloak tighter about him, Hanan thought of leaving. A weariness had set over him from sitting so long on a cold stone bench. But the creak of a door broke his doldrum. He looked to the stairwell on the outside of the house that led from the street to the second-floor room where the lone figure of a man stood. The man closed the door behind him and waited, framed in the moonlight as he glanced about the area. Hanan recognized him. It was Judas Iscariot.

Yeshua's betrayer started down the steps, appearing nervous as he looked up and down the street. Once off the steps he turned northward and raced away in the direction of the temple. Hanan thought of following him, catching him in some desolate area and eliminating the threat to his friend, but Yeshua had adamantly spoken against the action when it was suggested. Watching the traitor leave was difficult, but Hanan sat upon the stone seat again and chose to wait.

* * *

Less than an hour passed before the second-floor door opened again and men filed out. In the moonlight Hanan recognized Yeshua in the lead as they came down the stairs. Once together on the street, the men adjusted their cloaks and solemnly walked eastward.

Hanan listened but could not hear any words they spoke. He trailed them as they left the city, crossed the short length of the Kidron Valley then on to the Mount of Olives, a mile-long ridge paralleling the eastern part of Jerusalem. There Yeshua left his disciples to wait for his return, but told Peter, and the sons of Zebedee, James and John, to accompany him. They walked a brief distance to the Garden of Gethsemane, an ancient olive orchard where Yeshua often came for spiritual solace.

"Wait here for me. Pray that *Elohim* will give me strength for what is to come," Yeshua said. "I will be no more than a stone's throw from you." He walked between the old, gnarled trees, moonlight falling on him as he passed from one tree to another.

Hanan crept around the first group of disciples, eased past the second group then stopped when he observed Yeshua kneeling against a large boulder in a clearing. Standing behind a tree, Hanan kept watch over his friend and the area.

The bright moonlight blanketing the abandoned orchard left dark shadow circles beneath each tree. No breeze blew yet the chill in the air penetrated robes and cloaks, at times sending a fierce shiver through the body. But the sense of helplessness flooding Hanan's soul as he gazed at his praying friend left him feeling like a man adrift in a sea with mountainous waves crashing upon him. He heard faint crying and realized it came from Yeshua.

"Father, I am weak and frightened, and may fail you. My strength has left me. If it is possible, let this cup pass from me. If this cannot pass unless I drink it, let it be as you, not I, would have it so."

Yeshua drew still with head bowed then rose and walked to his waiting three disciples. They were fast asleep, and he woke them with scolding words.

"You couldn't keep watch with me for one hour?"

Returning to the clearing, Yeshua repeated his earlier prayer twice more, and upon finishing each time, went to Peter, James and John. He found them asleep.

"In my need of prayers, you fail me. Your spirits are willing, but your flesh is weak," he said, then left them. Again, they promised to stay awake and pray for him.

Hanan watched and when about to go talk to Yeshua, moonlight bathed his friend in a wide beam that grew brighter by the second. He remained behind the tree as Yeshua raised his face and spoke to someone standing on the large boulder where he knelt. But to Hanan's eyes, no one was there.

The brilliant beam of light dimmed until the moonlight returned to normal. Head bowed, Yeshua went from his agony, his shoulders visibly shaking.

The voices of arguing men carried through the orchard from where the first group of disciples had remained. Their words grew more distinct and Hanan rushed to Yeshua. Little time could be spared before the unknown men began their search of the area.

"Yeshua," he said, touching the praying man's shoulder. When Yeshua raised his face, Hanan was shocked at the stream of tears and large beads of sweat that drenched him.

"Why—why are you here?" Yeshua sluggishly rose to his feet, but at hearing the angry voices he glanced in their direction.

"I don't have time to explain. We must go. You've been betrayed. I believe those are temple guards coming to arrest you." Hanan pulled his friend's right arm to lead him away but Yeshua refused to move. "Yeshua, please, you must come with me!"

"It has begun," Yeshua said in a troubled voice. He gazed at the fiery torches near the trees where the three disciples had slept. "My betrayer is at hand."

Withdrawing the Sica from beneath his robe, Hanan spun in the direction of the torches. He held the dagger in his right hand and took a defensive stance. "Leave this place. I'll kill anyone that attempts to follow you. Go, Yeshua, run," he pleaded.

Yeshua shook his head once and gently laid a hand over Hanan's muscled forearm.

"This is not the way of my Father nor mine. Put away your dagger. You must not obstruct what will come. You are my dear friend, a true friend, and one day we will meet again.. But I must leave, and you cannot follow. Promise me you will not interfere regardless of what you witness. Promise me, my friend."

Sheathing his Sica, Hanan glanced at the fast-approaching men now less than one hundred feet away. He turned to Yeshua and gazed at him, lost for words. An intense pain stabbed his heart. Tears trailed down the cheeks of the broad-shouldered, heavily muscled man.

Yeshua stepped forward and wrapped his arms about his friend. Hanan laid his head on Yeshua's shoulder and wept.

"You there," a burly temple guard shouted. "Remain where you are." The guard began to walk faster and the armed guards, priests, Pharisees, and Yeshua's disciples were close behind.

"Leave me, my friend, and don't look back." Yeshua pushed him away, and bravely stepped in front of Hanan to partially block him from view of the approaching guards.

"Forgive me," was all Yeshua heard before his friend fled into the night.

* * *

Racing through the orchard, blending with the shadows of the trees, Hanan didn't halt until he was confident no one followed him. He moved between the trees and stopped when he found a clear line of sight to the crowd. The mob's torches lit the area with enough light to distinguish faces.

Hanan felt his heart pounding against his chest as he watched. Judas embraced Yeshua then kissed him on the cheek. The guards seized Yeshua and a scuffle broke out between the disciples and the guards. A knife blade flashed in the torch light, a man screamed and grabbed his ear. Yeshua waved his followers back then cupped his hand over the bleeding wound. The temple guards swarmed forward with spears leveled to arrest Yeshua, and tl e disciples bolted in all directions.

Consumed with rage at Judas' betrayal und the cowardice of Yeshua's men for not defending their leader, I anan readied to leave when a bullish-framed guard drove a fist deep 1to Yeshua's stomach, doubling him over. He fell to the ground and vo guards laughed as they kicked him.

Drawing his dagger, Hanan prepared 1 imself to charge the guards, but Yeshua's earlier words sounded in 1is mind: *Promise me that you will not interfere regardless of what yo witness.*

His grip on the Sica tightened until his xnuckles grew white. Nausea rose into his dry mouth and his stom ch churned. Backing from the tree that had concealed him, Hanaı wheeled and left the Garden of Gethsemane.

CHAPTER NINETEEN

Jerusalem, District of Judea
Friday, Month of Nisan, Day 14

At an hour past the mid of night Hanan strode through the city's outer wall gate, rage still fueling the inferno within him. *He's like a lamb being taken to slaughter,* he thought, recalling the way the temple guards had arrested Yeshua. The tension in his body felt like an iron fist squeezing his chest. He wished a gang of robbers would leap now from the shadows so he could release his fury upon them. But the image of Yeshua bravely awaiting his captors, rose in Hanan's mind, dispelling his thoughts, shaming him for his want of vengeance.

Pilgrims without rooms laid in clumps, sleeping next to closed businesses along the city streets. Hanan's mouth was as parched as a desert and though he found wine shops, none were open. Halting in the middle of a street, he looked about in frustration then realized where to go to quench his thirst at any hour of the day or night.

* * *

The alley was dark but Hanan knew his way. At the third door in the narrow passage, he stopped and hammered its wood several times with his fist. A man within the two-story house grumbled about the late hour, then latches clacked as they were unlocked. A stubby, scowling man in a dirty tunic and robe swung the door open but quickly smiled at recognizing his frequent patron. Hanan entered without waiting for an invitation from him.

"You are fortunate, master. The room you prefer has just been vacated," the brothel keeper said, wryly smiling as he closed the door behind Hanan. "We've been quite busy with the festival, and I'm sorry but I do not have two women available at the moment as you normally wish. I do have a young, fresh flower, though, that I've recently taken in. You will not be disappointed."

Hanan was in no mood for conversation. The moans and cries from the carnal pleasures of patrons in other rooms carried down the long hall. A scowl crossed his face. He dropped coins in the stubby man's waiting palm and started for the stairwell leading to the second floor.

"Have two of your biggest jars of wine brought to me," he said, turning his back to the keeper and walking away. "And make sure it's none of that donkey piss you sell to the Romans."

The room was the largest in the brothel, though, it could only hold an oversized wood-framed bed with woven leather straps to support the working women, a low stool, and a bowl of fresh water for patrons to wash before leaving. A three feet wide walk space lined the bed. Oil lamps at opposite ends of the room cast light throughout it, showing the dingy stone walls and the peculiar stains. The room's musty odor was strong upon walking through the door but grew bearable as the minutes passed. Only one window existed, and it was shut. Hanan shoved its wood panel away to let the night's cool air in then flung his brown cloak onto the bed

A faint knock came and a young woman with chin lowered to her chest entered the room, attempting not to jostle and spill the two jars of wine she carried in her thin arms. Observing her difficulty in setting the jars on the floor, Hanan grabbed them by their lips. He turned to the window and set them on its flat, recessed windowsill. With his back to the woman, he raised a jar and drank in deep gulps to quench his thirst. He heard the door close. Silence returned to the room. Staring out the window at the dark buildings across the street, he stood quiet, trying not to think about the suffering Yeshua may be undergoing. When he turned with jug in hand to sit on the stool, he paused, surprised by the woman still in the room.

Straightening his posture, he stood with the jar in his right hand, hanging by his side. No emotion shone on his face as his green eyes stared at the nude woman standing beside the bed. His gaze drifted over her lean body, the small mounds of her breasts, and the dirty tunic hanging from her hands to cover her womanhood. Her head was even with his chest and long, raven-black hair fell about her downturned face as she awaited his orders. At best he believed she was no older than fifteen or seventeen years but knew she would soon grow old before her time in a brothel.

"What is your name?"

"Rebekah, master," came a soft reply.

"Look at me when you speak," he ordered, more gruffly than he realized.

Rebekah's head sluggishly rose. The innocence of her simple, yet comely face, and the fear in her black pearl eyes disturbed him. Without reason, his shameful past in brothels rose in his mind.

"What do you wish me to do, master?" Her eyes cut to the bed then back to him.

"Put your clothes on—and stop calling me *master*. My name is Hanan," he said, taking a seat on the stool. He lifted the wine jar and drank as she dressed in her tattered tuni. When finished, she stayed by the bed. A glimpse of fear still shone in her eyes, but it was gradually being displaced by confusion.

Shaking his head, he motioned to the bed. "Sit. This will be an easy night for you. All I want is wine." A sad expression appeared as she sat on the edge of the bed.

Hanan cynically grinned. He reached into the money pouch beneath his robe and withdrew several coins. "Here," he said, tossing them onto the bed. "In the morning, tell the keeper you earned your money. He has no need to know otherwise."

She gathered the coins, placed them by her side and let her gaze drift to him. The mountainous man sat with the wine jar raised, drinking in loud gulps. Lowering the jar, he wiped his lips clean with the back of a hand and stared across the room with dead eyes.

"Right now, my only friend is being beaten by temple guards. He told me it was the will of *Elohim*... and that the prophecies must be fulfilled. What kind of god lets an innocent man be beaten?" Hanan's head turned to her. A dark mood painted his face. The emerald green eyes narrowed as his brows lowered. "What kind of a man abandons his friend to be beaten?" he asked in disgust.

Hanan raised the jar and drank deeply. The young prostitute watched but said nothing. One hour then two passed with him drinking and speaking in riddles that were little more than puzzling confessions of his soul. She listened and nodded at times, although, he appeared oblivious of her presence. Then silence filled the room. He sat gazing at her with the second empty wine jar resting on his lap.

Shivering, she rubbed her bare arms for warmth against the cold night air.

"Wrap yourself in my cloak. I'll not have you freeze to death and it be added to the list of my sins."

The feel of the thick wool cloak about her brought a smile to her pretty face as she eased further back on the bed and drew her slender legs up into the cloak. "Thank you," came her weak reply.

"Is Rebekah your true name?" Hanan set the empty wine jug beside him on the floor. "Are you a Jew?"

Lowering her gaze to the bed, she nodded.

"How old are you?"

"Sixteen in a few months." She raised her big round eyes and saw him staring at her with no indication of his thoughts.

"Leave this place, Rebekah. Go far away and start a new life." Hanan's voice trailed to silence. He glanced at the ceiling and let his gaze drift about the room.

"A woman with a child by her side does not go far before hunger stops their journey," she replied. Fire filled her dark eyes. "Why does every man believe that *sinners* in the brothels want this life? Who enjoys stinking, drunken pigs defiling them all day and night? I'm here so my son doesn't starve. The keeper takes most of the money I make and leaves me barely enough to buy food."

"How old is your son?"

"Two."

"And the father, is he one of the soldiers that comes here?" Hanan asked in a fiery tone.

Rebekah shook her head. "I was a servant in a Gentile's house until the master raped me. When his wife learned I carried his child, she threw me out saying I had offered myself to him to become his mistress." Her eyes momentarily grew wet, but no tears fell. "My family was ashamed and refused to let me return. But I kept my son and will do whatever I must so he may live." She defiantly stared at Hanan for several seconds then lowered her chin to her chest.

"You're brave. Not all women love their children as you do." The thought of his mother abandoning him, wanting him dead crossed his mind adding to the conflicting emotions he already had this night. "If you and your son had a place to live, would you go?"

The prostitute raised her head and studied his face. "Do not make such jokes. I may be a *sinner* as the people call us, but I still have some pride left in me."

"I am many things, Rebekah, but I do not lie. My home is in Nazareth and my servants have grown old. They are in need of help to keep my house in order and cook for me when I am there. My home is big enough for you and your son to have a room. I will give you money so you may leave in a few hours once the sun rises. Now tell me, is it *yes* or *no*?"

A smile appeared on her lips as she listened, but it began to fade.

"Cook, clean, and warm your bed when you wish? Is that what you are saying? I only want there to be no confusion about my duties."

Rage exploded within Hanan. He grabbed the empty wine jar beside him and threw it across the room as he leapt to his feet. The clay jar shattered as it loudly smashed against the stone wall.

"Did I say spreading your legs would be part of your duties?" he yelled, face flushed from anger. He stood like a furious wild beast ready to fight. "I offer safety to raise your son, and you insult me by thinking I have need of a personal whore?"

"I apologize, master. Please do not be mad. I wanted no misunderstanding between us. Please, I meant no disrespect. I believe you are a good man."

Hanan settled himself back onto the stool and looked at her. "I'm not a good man, but you will never have to fear me raping you."

"Then I wish to be your servant as you have asked, if you will still allow me."

His rage slowly diminished and he exhaled hard. He reached into his money pouch, removed five silver coins and dropped them on the bed. Motioning to the money, he said, "That is more than enough for you and your son to find passage to the estate of Micah ben Netzer in Nazareth. Tell my servants, Benjamin and Elizabeth, to let you have Yosef's room. Tell them Hanan sent you but do not speak of your time in this house. What is your son's name?"

"David."

He nodded and gave a hint of a smile as he thought a moment. "That's a good name. But when you arrive at my home, tell them your name is *Ruth*. Elizabeth will like that. Ruth was King David's grandmother."

Happiness shone in Rebekah's face.

"Has David been circumcised?"

"Yes, mast- I mean Hanan."

"Good, that is in keeping with the Laws of Moses and he will have no problem entering the Nazareth synagogue."

Shouting voices rose in the street, echoing between buildings. Hanan stood from the stool and looked out the window. The faint light of dawn was appearing on the horizon. He listened to the people's frantic words and glanced at the street below. Small groups of men and women raced along it. He heard a woman say, *'the Nazarene,'* as she passed below the window.

"Something is wrong. I must go," he said, pulling his cloak from Rebekah's body. He paused at the door. "After I leave, make the keeper believe I slept with you and give him his usual money, but don't let him see the silver. Make some reason to go home then never return here. Follow the instructions I gave you. My servants will take care of you." Hanan looked at her dirty, stained tunic and gave her more coins from his pouch. "Buy clothes for you and your son. You will need new clothes for your new life."

He started for the door, but a small hand squeezed his forearm. Rebekah stepped close, softly crying as she took hold of his large hand. She raised her face to gaze into his green eyes.

"Truly I have been blessed this night. I will be a faithful servant. May our God, *Elohim*, protect you wherever you go." Rebekah kissed his hand.

Hanan stood still, unable to speak. Her words tore at his soul. He glanced at his hand then to her but left without a reply.

CHAPTER TWENTY

Jerusalem, District of Judea
Friday, Month of Nisan, Day 14

The blush of dawn lay across the city, making the streets faintly visible without a need for torches. Hanan no longer felt a chill in the air as he half-walked and trotted to keep pace with the growing crowds that hurried through the streets. News of the young rabbi's arrest by temple guards was sweeping through the city like a sandstorm. Women wept and men argued over his innocence or guilt. The crowds followed a twisting path but Hanan felt confident they were headed to the prefect's palace, one of Herod the Great's former residences.

The praetorium, Pontius Pilate's stately home while in Jerusalem for festivals, was second in size only to the great temple complex, but first in extravagance. He and his wife Claudia had quarters if they wished in the Antonia Fortress, but Pilate refused its usage, complaining of the military conditions being an insult to his wife.

High walls and massive gates surrounded the praetorium, concealing from view the grandeur and luxuries Herod had constructed for himself. Tales were told of its lavish interior with polished white and black marble floors with intricate mosaics gold plated furniture, silver and exotic jewels embedded in walls an pillars at every turn. Many a servant had contributed to the acc nts, and few people doubted them.

Atop the walls and at every gate stood quads of Roman soldiers in russet tunics and long capes, heavily a nored, with spears in hand. The greatest number of soldiers were p sted on the inside of the iron fence and gate leading into the mass ve courtyard below a porch of the residence. Their spears were kept leveled at all times in order to advance and spear protestors throug the iron bars. It was to this gate the crowd led Hanan.

Forcibly making his way through the pe ple to reach the iron fence, he saw several of the men he had assig ed to follow Yeshua's mother, then observed her pressed against t e bars, watching the proceedings in the courtyard. The horde of cur ous pilgrims and citizens surged forward but Hanan put his muscle arms about Miriam, moved her between him and the iron fence. Sl e hugged two women close to her; one he knew as Mary Magdalene a follower of Yeshua, and the other known as Mary, the mother of t e sons of Zebedee.

Using his back and the immense strength in his arms, he forced the people back until her and her companic s could safely stand without fear of being crushed. Seeing that her protector was Hanan, she hugged and thanked him for having come. Ier eyes were red and puffy from constant crying.

"Why are you here in Jerusalem? I tho ght you were still in Nazareth," he asked.

"I knew my son would come to the Pa over and I hoped to see him. Oh, Hanan, they arrested Yeshua at n dnight and took him to a priest named Annas for questioning, the 1 to the home of the

High Priest Caiaphas for more questioning, and now he's here at the Roman prefect's home." She looked through the iron bars to the robed priests and armed temple guards that stood about Yeshua in the courtyard. His head was barely visible among them.

"Hanan," she said, raising her face to him. "He's been beaten... One of his cheeks is swollen and an eye is half-closed. There was blood coming from his mouth and—" Her words tapered off and she leaned against Hanan's massive chest and wept.

Wrapping an arm about her shoulders, he didn't know what to do except gently stroke her head. Pain clenched his soul and guilt consumed him at not having stayed to defend his friend from being arrested. He looked at the priests waiting in the courtyard then let his gaze drift to the people standing near. The one known as Peter stood by the iron fence, staring through the bars at Yeshua and the men surrounding him.

"You, disciple," Hanan yelled to get his attention.

Peter pulled his shawl over his head and tried to conceal his face.

"Aren't you one of the rabbi's disciples? One who deserted him in his time of need?"

Turning to Hanan, Peter's face was a mask of terror. His eyes flared as he adamantly shook his head. "No, no, it wasn't me. I don't know him." But at the sound of a rooster crowing in the distance, the disciple's mouth shot agape and he grew pale.

Hanan scowled as he watched Peter push his way through the mass of people to flee.

A man turned from the iron bars to Hanan. "Yeshua told Peter that before the rooster crows three times, he would deny knowing him. That was the third time. I know because I am John, one of the disciples, and was there when Peter was told. The man's eyes were wet, and the remnants of tears shone on his cheeks. "Yes, we did run, but were ordered to do so by our teacher." He looked at Hanan for several seconds then turned his attention to the governor walking out onto the porch.

"What do you want at this hour of the day, Caiaphas? The sun is not up yet?"

Hanan gazed at the porch above the courtyard. The Prefect Pontius Pilate stood with fists resting on hips, dressed in a soldier's russet tunic, and ceremonial, dark brown, chest armor with his sword, a *gladius*, hanging from the right side of a wide belt. He glared at the Sanhedrin priests below him. A servant carried a shiny chalice to him. He drank until it was empty and gave back.

With the pilgrims and citizens noisily mumbling, wailing, and whispering about him, Hanan couldn't hear what either Caiaphas or Pilate were saying.

"Quiet, you fools," he said as loud as he dared so the prefect wouldn't hear him. When he looked back to Pilate, legionnaires had walked down the steps and taken custody of Yeshua. They led him up to the porch and followed Pilate into the house.

"Why didn't the priests go with him, Hanan?" Miriam stood gazing at him.

"If the priests enter the Roman governor's palace, it will make them unclean for the festival ceremonies and they would not be able to eat the Passover meal."

"But why bring my son here to the prefect?"

A long pause passed before Hanan could find the courage to answer Miriam.

"Because they have judged him to be a criminal yet have no right to execute anyone. Only the Romans may do so—only Pilate may order his death."

* * *

"Tell me, are you the king of the Jews?" Pilate slowly walked a circle about the beaten prisoner, looking the slender man over from head to foot. His soldiers formed a wide circle about them in the massive room where the prefect conducted his daily affairs.

"Is that your own belief or have others talked to you about me?"

"Should I care? I'm a Roman. Your people and your high priest handed you over to me. What is it you have done to warrant their hate? Caiaphas said you call yourself the king of the Jews. Are you a king?" There was no hostility in Pilate's voice as he questioned the prisoner.

Yeshua looked at Pilate when the prefect halted in front of him.

"My kingdom is not of this world. If it were, my servants would have fought to prevent my arrest by the Jews. No, my kingdom is from another place—one with our God, *Elohim*."

The governor of Judea softly grinned. "You *are* a king, then," he said.

Nodding once, Yeshua gazed at him. "You are right in saying I am. It is for this reason I came into the world, to testify to the truth. All on the side of truth listen to me."

Pilate renewed his walk about the prisoner, shaking his head as he looked at the floor. When he came back around to the front of Yeshua, he stopped and let his gaze drift to the man's face.

"Truth? What is truth?" Pilate's brows rose from his bewilderment. He studied him for several minutes, waiting for an answer.

The prefect knew of the miracles Yeshua performed and his reputation, yet had never heard of the young rabbi urging rebellion. Claudia had counseled too against becoming involved in the squabble between the Sanhedrin priests and the Nazarene the people called a prophet, the *Anointed One.*

When no reply came from the prisoner, Pilate rested his right hand upon the hilt of his sword and glanced at his military aide.

"Bring him."

With Yeshua and his soldiers trailing him, Pilate returned to the porch.

* * *

"I find no basis for a charge against him," Pilate declared, staring at Caiaphas in the courtyard.

"How can you not find guilt in him? He travels throughout Judea proclaiming to be the king of the Jews. He began in Galilee and—."

"Wait," the prefect shouted, holding a hand up to stop Caiaphas. "Is he a Galilean?"

"Yes, and all of the men who follow him." Caiaphas wryly grinned as if he believed this new revelation had stirred the Roman governor to action. But it wasn't the action the high priest expected.

Pilate waved his soldiers to return Yeshua to the custody of the priests. "I know Herod Antipas is in town to observe the Passover. Take your prisoner to him. He's under Antipas' jurisdiction, not mine." Having spoken, the prefect marched away before Caiaphas could voice an objection.

* * *

Hanan heard Pilate's order and pulled Miriam and her two friends away from the gate. He knew the Romans were about to use their spears to clear the way for the priests with their prisoner and temple guards to leave. A centurion shouted an order and without hesitation, a squad of legionnaires moved forward, driving their spears between the iron bars. The crowd cried out in fear and backed far away. The gate opened long enough for the priests to pass through, then swung shut behind them. Half dragging their prisoner, Caiaphas and his entourage started toward Antipas' palace with the masses close behind.

"We should follow them," Miriam urged in a frantic tone.

"No, they will bring him back here. Yeshua has been preaching for months in the tetrarch's district. If he thought Yeshua was advocating rebellion, he would have already arrested and executed your son long before now. This will merely be a game between Antipas and Pilate with neither man wanting the political repercussions. It's best we remain here."

Seeing Simcha watching from across the street, Hanan walked to him. They spoke and the little man raced after the priests.

* * *

The sun outlined the horizon, ready to begin its ascent into the clear sky. The early morning air still held a chill but was swiftly dissipating. Crowds of pilgrims and curious citizens had stayed near the gate, but not in the numbers as before. A long hour passed as Hanan anxiously waited with Miriam. When he began to question the decision to remain, the cries and shouts of people moving toward him were heard.

Running ahead of the approaching mob Simcha stumbled to a halt before Hanan, panting in deep breaths. He tried to speak but Hanan gestured for the excited man to calm first.

"They're coming. Nothing more was done than mock and ridicule the rabbi. Antipas ordered him to perform magician's tricks, but the rabbi stood in silence. The tetrarch pulled his purple robe off and placed it on Yeshua, saying a king should be dressed like a king, then instructed the high priest to return the prisoner to Pilate."

Caiaphas led the returning horde, his glower telling of his mood. The Roman soldiers swung the gate open long enough for the priestly group to enter then closed it, taking up their stations within the interior with spears leveled. As Yeshua had passed, Miriam cried out to her son, but he was shoved on by the temple guards and never looked her way. The purple robe lightly furled about him.

Having been advised of the high priest's return, Pilate sat upon a throne-like chair on the porch, staring at the approaching men. He knew they would not enter the palace and become unclean, but he chose to make them grovel before him in the courtyard. When the high priest and his entourage halted, the prisoner wearily stood among them. His left cheek displayed a wide, horrid red mark that blended into the crimson swelling of his partially closed left eye.

Miriam moved to the iron bars and pressed her face between them to see her son. Stepping behind her for protection from the masses swarming to the fence, Hanan observed low ranking temple priests take up position near him and throughout the overflowing crowd in the street. He wasn't sure what their role was, but he didn't like their sudden presence.

The noise of mumbling men and weeping women rose, making it difficult for Hanan to hear Pilate's words to the high priest. Caiaphas swung his arms through the air as he talked, and the prefect angrily shook his head and shouted back at him. All Hanan could hear was Pilate saying *innocent* as he pointed to the prisoner. The priests in the crowd about Hanan began to yell *blasphemer* at Yeshua.

Rising from his chair, Pilate glared at the high priest and let his gaze drift to the throng of people watching the proceedings from the gate. He raised his arms into the air to bring about silence.

"By Roman custom at Passover, I may release a prisoner chosen by the Jewish people. We hold a criminal named Barabbas. Which do you want released? The murderer Barabbas or Yeshua who is called the Christ?"

Caiaphas spun toward the gate and raised his arms into the air, shouting, "Barabbas... Barabbas... Barabbas!" Immediately the priests around Hanan began to echo his words, "Barabbas... Barabbas... Barabbas." And half of the waiting mob joined the chant.

"What shall I do with Yeshua the Christ?" Pilate shouted.

A new chant came, led by Caiaphas whose face had become a mask of rage.

"Crucify him! Crucify him! Crucify him!"

Lowering himself back onto the throne, the prefect gazed in astonishment at the people.

Hanan saw Pilate's head lightly shake. It was evident he believed Yeshua was innocent.

To the far left of the porch a beautiful Roman woman in an elegant white robe with jewels about her neck and in her black hair, walked out of the palace. She handed a soldier a paper and waited while he delivered it to the prefect. Pilate read it, his lips becoming a thin line. He grimaced then glanced at her and nodded. She returned into the palace.

"What's happening, Hanan? Who is that woman and what did she send him?" Miriam asked, looking back at her protector.

"I believe she's his wife and may have warned him of being caught in a trap by the Sanhedrin. Pilate's back is against a wall. If he executes a man everyone believes is innocent, and an uprising is caused, it will displease the emperor Caesar Tiberius. He would question Pilate's ability to rule and could order his death. If Pilate doesn't execute Yeshua as the Sanhedrin want, they could petition Tiberius and say the prefect released a criminal that encouraged the people to rebel." Hanan knew the prefect had few options in the matter, although, he had tried to release Yeshua earlier.

The prefect had the prisoner brought from the courtyard up to him. He walked away from the edge of the porch so the priests below couldn't hear their conversation, but to ensure privacy he ordered legionnaires to block Caiaphas' view and stand along the edge of the porch. Once his men were in position, Pilate stepped close to Yeshua.

"Where do you come from?"

Yeshua remained silent.

"You refuse to speak to me?" The governor's eyes slowly closed as he shook his head in frustration. He looked at Yeshua again. "Don't you realize I have the power to set you free or crucify you?"

"You would have no power over me if it were not given to you from above."

"Tell me, are you the son of this god, *Elohim*, as I have heard?" In Pilate's voice came a pleading for the right answer. But none came.

The prefect ordered the soldiers away from his chair and had Yeshua stand near. Pilate stood staring at Caiaphas.

From behind the high priest someone shouted, "If you let this man go, you are no friend of Caesar. Anyone who claims to be a king opposes Caesar."

The uproar was deafening, but among the calls for crucifixion were those who cried for mercy.

* * *

Abaddon stood behind the chair, his yellowish tinted eyes within the shadow of his cloak's cowl shifting from the governor to the prisoner. Long, bony fingers curled over the back of the chair; their sharp, dirty fingernails digging light rows across its cloth. He moved unseen by all from the chair to Pilate's left side and whispered in his ear.

"Have you grown so weak that priests now tell you what must be done? Show them you are the might of Rome, the fist that wields the sword in this land. Scourge this troublemaker. Crucify him and be done with this farce. Do you not hear the people? They are on the verge of rioting. Satisfy their thirst for blood and give them the death of this menace. Bring this to an end."

Backing away, a vile smile formed on Abaddon's lips as he looked at Yeshua. But his smile faded when he realized Yeshua could see him and had been watching him all along.

* * *

Pilate ordered Barabbas to be turned over to the temple priests. When he next spoke, his words were for his aide, but he stared at Yeshua.

"Scourge him," the prefect said in a low voice.

Legionnaires grabbed Yeshua by his arms and led him down the porch stairs. Once in the courtyard they passed through a solid gate leading into an adjacent yard.

A deafening uproar of arguments rose from Caiaphas' priests, temple guards and the people outside the palace gate. While some continued to shout, *'Crucify him,'* others cried out, *'Release him.'*

* * *

Squeezing the iron bars, Miriam pressed her face between them and screamed, "No – no, he's innocent!" Her legs went weak and she slid down the bars to the ground.

Hanan gripped the fence bars over her head and used his immense strength to hold back the surging crowd from crushing her. His eyes were scrunched closed from the physical strain, and the muscles in his arms were bulged hard as iron.

"Raise her up," Hanan yelled to the disciple near her. John nodded and pulled her to her feet. He held her in his arms as she wept.

Hanan felt the pressure of the shoving masses lighten like water draining from a vast jar. He breathed easier and relaxed as he watched them move down the street to another gate where they could watch the legionnaires with Yeshua. He turned toward the porch and saw Pilate angrily swinging his hands as he argued with Caiaphas.

CHAPTER TWENTY-ONE

Jerusalem, District of Judea
Friday, Month of Nisan, Day 14

Miriam broke free of John's arms but Hanan caught her and held fast.

"I must go to him," she cried struggling against his grip. Her companions reached out to hold her and Hanan released Miriam to the two women.

"No, Miriam, you do not need to see what is happening to Yeshua." Hanan tried to keep a stern face, but the glistening in his green eyes gave him away.

She shook her head, broke from the women, and hurried toward the next gate.

Hanan's emotions swirled like a violent maelstrom within him. He felt miserable, nauseated, furious, and helpless all within the same moment. But he raced after Miriam to protect her. It was all he could do for now.

At the next gate Hanan fought his way through the masses to allow Miriam to reach the fence's iron bars. Again, he stood behind her like a wall to prevent the people from surging forward and crushing her. At the iron bars she cried out fro 1 her grief and placed her hands over her mouth when she saw her s n

* * *

Since Yeshua's midnight arrest in the moonlit Garden of Gethsemane, he'd been dragged from one pri st's house to another, taken to the temple, the prefect's palace, the te rarch's residence and back to the governor. Along the way and at e 'ery location, he was scorned, taunted and struck, but no beating ould compare to the Roman scourging he was about to receive.

The crisp morning sunlight in a clear sk bathed the soldiers' yard. Legionnaires trained in its loose, thick soil to cushion their falls, but in the middle of the yard stood a tall sturdy blood-stained post with iron rings positioned at different lev ls.

Spurius Ligustinus Magnus, the thirty five-year-old Roman centurion, squinted against the sunlight as he walked into the yard to take custody of Yeshua. He'd been summon d from his office and given the responsibility for ensuring Pilate's rders were executed without fault. A professional soldier from *Legio X Frentensis*, Magnus was battle-hardened and respected for his mi dset; obey and fulfill his orders unto death. His bravery in battle ad earned him multiple military honors, yet not as many as h s namesake, Spurius Ligustinus, who had received six *Corona Civic* s, the highest Roman award for heroism.

Four of Magnus' ten-man special squa l were Greek Syrian auxiliary troops from the *Chors I Sebasten(um* unit who hated Jews and relished inflicting pain upon them. [hey were the *lictors*; the whippers. Five of the remaining men we e Samaritan auxiliary legionnaires from Samaria, and the sixth was Roman legionnaire.

These men were known as Crucifixion Guards. They escorted condemned prisoners to Golgotha, the hill of the skull outside the city walls, where they crucified them and stood guard until death arrived for the doomed.

The Crucifixion Guards waited by a wall, jeering and watching with arms crossed. The prisoner's punishment meant nothing to them other than how long it would take to be administered. But the four *lictors* laughed as they walked about Yeshua, at times pelting him with balled fists while mockingly calling him the king of the Jews. They stripped away his clothes and the purple robe before tying him to an iron ring by his wrists which kept him partially bent over.

"Thirty-nine lashes. If you strike forty, you will wish you had never been born," Magnus ordered. The centurion knew he wasn't restricted to a specific number, but forty was the maximum lashes by Jewish law. The Jews always halted at thirty-nine to ensure the law was never violated, and Magnus chose to do the same, refusing to give anyone reason for protest to the prefect.

Removing his horsehair crested helmet, he held it under his left arm, and with his right hand raised his vine stick cudgel, the symbol of his rank. The *lictors* nodded and walked to a table to retrieve their whips.

* * *

At the iron fence citizens, gawkers, and pilgrims squeezed close to one another to watch. Hanan blocked an area where Miriam, her companions and John the disciple stood to peer through the iron bars. The constant talking, crying, and shouts of 'release him' and 'scourge him' from the crowd made it difficult to hear the legionnaires in the yard, but Hanan thought it best. Miriam didn't need to hear the verbal abuse her son was receiving. Janan leaned forward to whisper in her ear.

"Miriam, please, do not stay. You should n't see what they are going to do."

Eyes red and swollen from crying, she wiped tears from her eyes and cheeks and looked over her shoulder at the brawny man. She shook her head. "I must be here with my son."

Simcha stood near his master. He covered his mouth with a hand and averted his gaze from the soldiers' yard. "I cannot watch this. I've seen scourging before. If you have no further need of me, I will leave before they begin."

"Go down the road and wait. I may need you later... I don't blame you for wanting to leave," said the leader of the Sicarii. He watched the little man shrink back into the crowd and push his way through until free of the throng.

* * *

The first pair of Greek Syrians appeared like; their bald heads with beardless faces sat almost without necks atop tanned, barrel-chested bodies with arms as massive as slave rowers on a Roman galley. They wore sandal boots as the regular Roman soldiers did but were bare-chested with only a lower tunic to cover their thighs. The second pair of *lictors* were identical to the first two men with the exception of having close-cropped hair.

Each man chose their whips and swung them one-handed to test the balance and flexibility of the nine leather thongs that were the length of a man's arm. The thongs were tightly woven with embedded pieces of bone, jagged metal, or small iron balls attached at the tips.

The bald-headed *lictors* took their positions, one to each side of Yeshua, while the second pair of whippers awaited their turn. The Crucifixion Guards taunted and laughed at the *lictors* then ridiculed the prisoner, spat at him and called out, "All Hail the King of the Jews!"

Gritting his teeth, the first *lictor* swung his whip with might in a wide arc and lashed Yeshua's back, ripping deep wounds across his slender frame. The howl of agony that burst from the young rabbi's mouth was blood-curdling to all within hearing distance. The mob watching from outside of the iron fence angrily shouted, women cried and wailed in sorrow. Miriam screamed and pleaded for the whipping to stop.

Hanan grimaced and grabbed the iron bars, squeezing until his knuckles hurt. His fury flowed from him in a long, guttural roar. Seeing Yeshua's eyes flare and mouth go agape at his suffering, Hanan shuddered as if a fiery torch had been pressed against his chest.

When the nine thongs stuck to Yeshua's back, the *lictor* jerked them free, tearing flesh away or ripping the skin into short strips. Taking turns, the second whipper struck the prisoner's back with his whip, grunting as he exerted his strength. The thongs spread apart and laid horrid wounds and blood streaks across Yeshua's back at all parts. Blood flowed down his back and off his ribs, dripping onto the loose soil. The whippers worked at a slow pace because the jagged metal and pieces of bone kept digging into Yeshua's muscles and bones, and nearly every lash had to be jerked free.

A Samaritan soldier sitting at the yard's equipment table, kept count and marked each lash on a document, verifying it had been administered. Having lashed Yeshua fifteen times, the first two *lictors* stood blood speckled and spattered from face to chest and arms, breathing heavily, their blood drenched whips by their side. They had begun at mid-back, whipped upward to his shoulders, then downward to his buttocks and backs of his legs. The prisoner's back was awash in glistening crimson blood and abysmal wounds. There were horrid lacerations and red streaks on his ribs where thongs had wrapped about him, and one facial cheek bled where the tips of the thongs sliced him open. He had been screaming in misery and howling from his agony, but after fifteen lashes he could only weep and shudder from the intense pain of each strike. When Yeshua's legs buckled from the shock to his body, and he fell to the dirt still tied to an iron ring, the *lictors* had never ceased and lashed him where ever they could strike.

Against the wall, several of the Crucifixion Guards mimicked Yeshua's suffering and shouted, "How does it feel now to be a king of the Jews?"

Magnus stood as if carved from granite. He never spoke, flinched or averted his gaze when blood sprayed the air from each thong's impact. Once when Yeshua cried out and struggled to raise himself from the dirt, the centurion gave an almost imperceptible nod of respect for the prisoner's courage but otherwise remained motionless while the punishment was administered.

The fresh pair of *lictors* stepped into position and renewed the whipping, hideously smiling when the prisoner's body quaked in anguish and his mouth went agape.

"Nineteen... Twenty... Twenty-one," the soldier at the table called out for all to hear.

Chaos had broken out in the crowd watching from beyond the iron fence. Their cries, shouts, wails, and arguments carried through

the yard. And still the smack of the thongs as they struck the prisoner and dug deep into his flesh could be heard.

"Twenty-three... Twenty-four... Twenty-five."

The centurion let his cold gaze drift to the wailing woman sitting on the ground leaning against the iron bars. Behind her stood a
mountainous man, face contorted from watching the ruthless whipping, hands gripping the bars as if he were trying to rip them loose.

The prisoner was convulsing against the post and though his
mouth was open, cries and howls no longer came.

"Twenty-eight... Twenty-nine... Thirty..." the soldier at the
table stated.

"Halt!" Magnus ordered.

Caught up in the madness, the *lictor* to Yeshua's right side,
raised his whip as if to continue. The centurion drew his sword.
The sound of it being drawn from the sheath was enough to make
the *lictor* immediately drop his whip onto the dirt and back away.
Sheathing his sword, Magnus walked to the prisoner while easing his
helmet onto his head. He stood gazing at the bloody pulp of a man.
Ordering the four blood-spattered *lictors* to leave, Magnus motioned
the Crucifixion Guards to take custody of the prisoner.

Earlier, one of the guards had intertwined slender branches of
a thorn bush to make a barbed head-wreath. He walked to Yeshua,
laid it atop his hair, then used the hilt of his sword to press it down
onto the prisoner's head. The finger long, sharp thorns all about the
wreath pierced the skin of the head. Yeshua winced and cried out as
blood flowed from the punctures.

"Every king should have a crown," the soldier gleefully stated,
and his companions about him laughed at the torture.

The wrist bonds were cut away and Yeshua collapsed in the dirt.

The prisoner was pulled to his feet and held until he showed signs of consciousness. His breechcloth was put on him and the purple robe, Antipas' gift of royalty, was draped over his shoulder. Within seconds the robe was soaked in blood from the open wounds and once drenched, stuck to his body.

"Carry him if you must, but don't let him fall," Magnus ordered. "We're returning him to the prefect."

"Centurion, we are nine lashes short of what you ordered," said the soldier at the table as he rose with the punishment document in hand.

The officer raised his vine stick cudgel toward the slender, bloody prisoner. "My orders were to scourge him, not kill him. He's barely alive now. I halted the lashing and my command will stand."

Magnus started toward the adjacent courtyard, and Yeshua staggered forward with the Crucifixion Guards surrounding him and holding onto his arms. When they crossed through the gate, the prisoner left a trail of blood on the stone pavement of the courtyard. Magnus ordered his men to stand with Yeshua away from the high priest and his followers, but where Pilate could see the scourged man.

The centurion climbed the porch stairs and gave his report. Pilate nodded and walked to the edge of the porch to look down at Caiaphas and his priests.

Hanan rushed to the courtyard's iron fence, shoving people away to allow Miriam, her two companions and the disciple, John, to be near the iron gate. She was still crying when she turned to Hanan.

"Will they release him now?"

All the brawny man could do was despondently shake his head.

With the crowd having grown momentarily silent, Hanan heard the prefect.

"Here, look at him. He is only a man and has been punished for causing you problems." Pilate pointed to Yeshua who stood with eyes closed, viciously whipped, crimson blood dripping from him into puddles about his feet. His left cheek was ripped open and he wore a crown of thorns with the drenched purple robe hanging from his shoulders. The prisoner staggered and was kept from falling by the Crucifixion Guards to each side holding his arms.

"Scourging is not enough. We have a law, and according to that law he must die because he has claimed to be the Son of our God, *Elohim*," the high priest demanded. "He claims to be a king which is against Caesar. Only you may execute him because our right to do so was taken away by the Romans."

The prefect straightened his posture and stood erect with fists on hips. His head slowly shook; his face a mask of disgust as he stared at Caiaphas.

"Shall I crucify *your* king?" Anger filled the governor's voice.

"We have no king but Caesar," shouted the other priests surrounding Caiaphas.

The prefect looked to the door leading into the palace. Claudia was not in sight. He let his gaze drift to his aide, then nodded toward a small table and waited.

Towel draped over his forearm, the soldier lifted a large brass water bowl from the table and carried it to the governor.

The shouting dwindled while Pilate dipped his cupped hands into the water and rubbed them together. He raised them above the bowl, lightly shook them then took the towel from the aide's forearm.

"I am innocent of this man's blood," the prefect stated to Caiaphas, drying his hands on the towel. He let it fall to the polished marble floor. "It is your responsibility."

The high priest gazed at the prefect but displayed no emotion. The priests behind Caiaphas shouted, "Let his blood be on us and on our children!"

Again, priests and their followers bellowed from beyond the fence's iron bars. "Crucify the false prophet."

Pilate turned to Magnus who wore a granite expression. His words rang like iron.

"Crucify him."

The Roman commander clapped a knotted fist against his chest and started away, but after three steps, the prefect stopped him.

"Fasten a sign in bold letters to his cross that says 'Yeshua of Nazareth, The King of The Jews,'... Write it in Aramaic, Latin, and Greek so all will know."

The fierce centurion clapped his chest with a fist and left.

"Do not write such words," Caiaphas yelled in annoyance. "It will make people believe the deceiver is truly our king."

A humorless grin formed on Pilate's lips as he gazed at the high priest.

"What I have ordered will not be changed," he replied, and returned into the palace.

CHAPTER TWENTY-TWO

Friday, Month of Nisan, Day 14

Two of the soldiers with Yeshua broke away and ran to the training yard. They returned carrying a wooden beam and square board. An aide on the porch took the board and wrote words on it as the prefect had commanded. The two soldiers supporting the condemned pulled his purple robe away and dressed him in his one-piece, seamless tunic. Every movement Yeshua made, and every touch of the guards' hands upon his brutalized body evoked an intense grimace or shriek of agony.

Miriam gasped and pressed her hands tightly over her mouth when the soldiers removed the purple robe. Her son's face, arms and back, chest and the backs of his legs were an intricate patchwork of bright crimson lash stripes, glistening red strips of flesh hanging loose, and gaping wounds that trickled blood to paint his body. Her eyes slowly closed as she lowered her chin to her chest and wept.

Pulling Yeshua's mother and her companions away from the iron fence, Hanan wanted them safe from the soldiers' spears that would soon be driving people back from the gate. Having seen the commotion of soldiers and priests in the courtyard, he realized they were preparing to leave for Golgotha, the Hill f the Skull, outside of the city.

The disciple John was the last to leave tl ifence. He wiped his eyes dry and followed Hanan out into the st eet that was growing more congested with festival pilgrims and ci izens by the minute. Orders were shouted, spears drove through tl fence forcing gawkers back, and the wide iron gate swung open.

The centurion led the way at a slow wa from the courtyard with the prisoner trailing and three soldiers t each side of the condemned to push him on and keep the crowds way. Across the nape of Yeshua's neck and stretched along his arms iy the rough wooden cross beam of the cross he would be crucified (1. His arms were fully extended, and his hands held onto the beam a best he could to keep it balanced. His steps were more of a shuffle ar 1 in his beaten condition, he could barely retain his balance.

Hanan looked at the length and girth (the thick beam and estimated it was at least seventy-five pounds. I appeared bigger than Yeshua's skinny body.

Magnus cleared a path for his squad anc the prisoner through the sea of screaming, crying, shouting peop :. Once out into the street, he started along the Way of Sorrow, the Way of Grief, a winding half-mile route to Golgotha that all ( )ndemned walked to their death.

People spat at Yeshua as he painfully shui led along the dirt and stone route. While some accused him of being false prophet, others wept and pleaded for mercy for him from tl : soldiers. The chaos rose, but the centurion continued his slow tre , pausing at times for the condemned man to catch up. One of Mag ius' soldiers followed the prisoner with a regular whip of nine thon s, not one with metal and bone attached, striking him at times and shouting commands to move faster. Yeshua was gasping for air and screamed in agony when struck. The beam pressed his crown of thorns into his head, pushing the thorns deeper, releasing more blood than before to drip down his face and body. His tunic had absorbed so much blood that little of its original crème color could be seen.

Miriam cried out for her son, wanting to touch him, and Hanan hurried her further along the path to a bend in the route so she would be close enough. Yeshua fell when he reached that point. She leaped from the crowd, weeping, and laid her hands upon him, but her touch made him wince. When he turned his face to her, he appeared lost within his mind. A soldier saw her and swung his spear to club her, but Hanan stepped in to take the brunt of the blow to protect her. It was at that moment Yeshua and Hanan locked gazes. Yeshua's good eye focused and Hanan believed his friend recognized him. But that second passed, and a dull gaze returned.

The centurion forced a path clear at sword-point, then ordered his men to increase their pace. They could only go as fast as their prisoner could shuffle his steps. The route was narrow, and the escorting soldiers struggled to keep people away from their prisoner. A hundred yards further and Yeshua fell again. The beam rolled over his head, pressing his face into the stone paved road. His vision was marred by the trail of blood flowing into his right eye from his head wounds.

From the wailing crowd a young woman knelt by his side and placed her veil in his right hand. "Here, Rabbi, please wipe your face so you may see," she said, trying to speak as she wept at his misery.

Yeshua pressed the cloth against his face and was handing it back to her when a whip lashed him. Trying to rise, he fell back onto the pavement. Hanan rushed forward and li ed the beam, blocking the soldier from striking his friend aga 1. The prisoner rose and Hanan eased it onto his shoulders. At h aring Yeshua cry out from the pain of the beam's weight pressing in o his gaping wounds, Hanan could no longer hold back his tears.

The woman held the veil in her hands, an l when she glanced at the cloth, the impression of the prisoner's face as clearly on it, made by his blood. She held it to her chest and cried

Magnus shouted and the escort renewe l their walk with the condemned. Another hundred yards passed th n Yeshua fell, no longer able to carry the beam. He was whipped as le laid on the ground, but the soldier stopped and looked at a man w lking near.

"What is your name?" the soldier with t e whip asked a dark, olive-skinned, heavily muscled man

"Simon of Cyrene."

"Carry the beam for him."

The man protested but a soldier presse a spear's point into his chest. Simon lifted Yeshua off the grou d then grabbed the beam. Resting it on his shoulders as Yeshu had, Simon carried the beam and tried to support the condemne man as they walked toward Golgotha.

The march continued for several more m nutes before the prisoner and his escorts reached the top of the hi . Simon dropped the beam and slowly lowered the battered, bleedi g man to the ground between two men crucified on crosses. He h ard their moans and glanced at them. A soldier pushed him away wi h a spear and ordered him to leave.

* * *

Laying on his left side, Yeshua could see his mother and two women standing and watching, held back at spear-point by two soldiers. Crying and wailing carried to him, but shouts and arguments were no longer heard. Each breath he took seemed to shoot a wretched pain throughout him. Then came the centurion's firm voice ordering the soldiers to finish their duties.

Two soldiers stripped him of his seamless tunic and cast it off to the side. Hands cruelly threw Yeshua onto his back and dragged him by the wrists several feet before dropping him onto a beam. The rough wood against his flayed back pressed into open wounds, and again the horrid pain exploded within him. He wanted to scream but choked on blood dripping into his mouth from his face. A stout-built soldier tried to give him a bitter drink of wine mixed with myrrh but Yeshua turned his mouth away.

"Take it... It's to help with your pain." The soldier held the small jug to the prisoner's closed lips.

Still, Yeshua refused to drink.

The warm sun beat down on him from the cloudless sky, yet he shivered from the cold racing over his body at times. His right eye opened. He glanced at the sun, closed his eye and wept.

"Father," Yeshua whispered in a pleading voice, but his mouth was dry, and no more words came.

Shadows from the soldiers fell across him as they stepped over him to reach his outstretched arms on the cross beam. Turning his head to look was too painful and only made the thorns of his crown drive deeper. Strong hands gripped his arms and held fast. A burly soldier stood holding a mallet and a seven-inch-long, tapered iron spike with a thick, square shaft. He smirked as he knelt at the condemned man's left arm.

Yeshua felt the tip of the stake press against the flesh of his forearm then saw the mallet rise high into the air. The first strike drove the stake through his forearm and partially into the beam. The second and third strikes drove it deep into the wood. His tortured body shuddered from his blinding misery. Yeshua screamed in torment then gasped for air as his anguish refused to let him breathe for several seconds.

Stepping over him, the soldiers moved to his right arm and drove a stake through its forearm with three strikes. A fresh wave of pain flooded Yeshua as he cried out in agony. But when they grabbed his feet and twisted his legs to get them in alignment, fear made him tremble.

The stake drove through the top of one foot and into the other beneath it. This time it took several strikes to enter the wood. His mouth shot agape. He wanted to cry out from his suffering but couldn't. His body shook and the anguish engulfing him drove him to the edge of oblivion. Waves of agony swept throughout him.

Nine hours had passed since his arrest at midnight.

When the soldiers raised him into the air upon the cross and let its base slide to a jarring halt in a hole in the ground, he passed out.

* * *

Holding the square sign proclaiming Yeshua as the King of the Jews, a slender soldier climbed a ladder and nailed it to the top of the vertical beam.

The six soldiers kept the crowd back but let the condemned man's friends and family move to within ten feet of the cross. Using the prisoner's dried tunic to gamble on, the soldiers sat on the ground and cast lots for the seamless tunic. The granite-faced centurion stood away from his men with arms crossed over his chest armor, staring at the crucified man, studying him.

Yeshua drifted in and out of consciousness, speaking little yet groaning in pain through the morning. He awoke to find the soldiers had stripped away his breechcloth, leaving him nude with his mother and two women crying as they knelt before him. The disciple John stood beside Hanan behind Miriam. They gazed at Yeshua, almost unable to recognize him from the pitiless scourging and protruding spikes.

Seeing the soldiers argue over his tunic, Yeshua looked skyward. "Father, forgive them for they know not what they are doing."

Miriam heard him and tried to stand, crying as she gazed at her son. John clung to her so she didn't fall.

"Woman," Yeshua said, "Behold your son." He looked at John. "Behold your mother."

To each side of Yeshua were crucified men who called out for him to save himself.

"Truly I say to you, today you shall be with me in paradise." Yeshua's voice was weak, and his words were difficult to speak between the spasms of pain striking him. He grimaced and cried out in delirium, *"Eli, Eli, Lama Sabachthani?"*

Hanan wept as he gazed at his friend, then gradually lowered his chin to his chest.

The centurion's brows lowered, and he glanced about him for anyone close. Seeing Hanan, he walked to him.

"What tongue does he speak?" Magnus asked in sincerity. "What did he say?"

Never lifting his head, not wanting the Roman to see the tears upon his cheeks, Hanan spoke. "It's Aramaic. He asked God why he has been forsaken."

Magnus' gaze carried to Yeshua. The centurion nodded slowly then started away.

"I am thirsty."

The centurion heard his prisoner and abruptly halted. He looked at the slender soldier driving a spear's blade into a vinegar-soaked sponge. "Give him wine with gall and myrrh to ease his mind."

Another soldier brought the jar they had first offered to Yeshua. The sponge still dripped vinegar, but they emptied the jar over it. Raising the sponge to Yeshua's lips, he turned his face at tasting the sour wine.

* * *

At noon the sky began to grow dark as menacing clouds appeared and spread over the land as far as could be seen. Except for Yeshua's mother, her companions, the disciple and Hanan, few people remained to watch the condemned man die. The lower ranking priests that helped Caiaphas entice the masses to a murderous rage of wanting crucifixion, had returned to the temple to be with the high priest. Within three hours, at the mid of afternoon, Caiaphas would officially open the Passover Festival with the ritual slaughtering of lambs for sacrifice.

Miriam sat on the ground staring at her son on the cross. She no longer wept. She had no more tears to cry.

With the day steadily growing darker, the soldiers stood holding their spears, nervously glancing at one another. None could ever recall a day of such weather.

Yeshua spoke little more than mutters for the next three hours, and his pain-wracked groans came less. He hung on the cross, gazing out over the land.

Having edged forward to be near his friend, Hanan saw Yeshua inhale deeply then lower his face to look at Hanan.

"It is finished," Yeshua said, closing his right eye.

The hour was mid-afternoon.

* * *

Hanan was about to turn away but saw Yeshua's crimson painted ribs lightly move.

Magnus believed the prisoner died and motioned his only true Roman soldier to him.

"Longinus, bring your spear."

"Sir, do want me to break his legs to see if he's dead?" The breaking of a crucified man's legs was standard Roman procedure to check for death.

"No, break the legs of the other two, but only spear this one."

The soldier Longinus went to the prisoners and bashed their legs with an iron rod. The crack of bones came loud, making Hanan, Miriam and the others startle. The crucified men never moved. Hanan glowered as he watched.

Spear in hand, Longinus walked to Yeshua's right side and stood ready, awaiting the order from the centurion. He squinted to better see the prisoner's ribs in the swiftly dimming daylight.

"Are your eyes good enough to make a proper strike?" Magnus asked, knowing the soldier had complained of increasingly weak eyesight. The centurion saw the soldier nod. He looked up at Yeshua, hesitant to give the order. It was then he saw movement.

Yeshua's face rose to the swirling clouds that had begun to blacken.

"Father, into your hands I commit my spirit," he cried out then his head fell forward and to the left. His ribs ceased to move, and he drew motionless.

"Now, Longinus," came the order as the howling wind blew a wall of dust and dirt across the land.

Hanan grimaced as the spearhead punctured Yeshua's right side, drove deep into him, then was withdrawn. A short stream of blood and watery fluid spewed before dwindling to a wide trail that ran down Yeshua's side.

The stream struck Longinus in the face. Yelling in surprise, he jumped back but tripped and fell to his knees. He feverishly wiped blood from his face.

The black clouds twisted, churned and hid the sun. Thunder rumbled as if the end of the world had come. It became deafening. The wind blew harder and cast dirt with strength across everyone on the Hill of the Skull. Miriam was almost thrust off her feet, but the disciple John caught her and held fast. Hanan raised an arm to protect his face and Miriam's companions pulled their head shawls tight over their faces. Then the earth emitted a deep growl and the ground shook.

* * *

In the temple's courtyard before the monumental Holy of Holies sanctuary, priests held sheep for ritual sacrificing by the High Priest Caiaphas. Pilgrims waited about them, anxious for the opening ceremony of the Passover festival.

When the Romans took control of Judea and the temple, they took possession of the high priest's ritual vestments. These were kept until the first day of a festival then issued to wear until the festival concluded. To avoid staining his vestments during the sacrifices the high priest wore a white tunic and robe, then would later change. But Caiaphas knew the bright red splotches upon the white cloth provided a more dramatic appearance to the pilgrims which encouraged greater monetary offerings to the temple.

He walked out into view of the masses yet gazed at the strange clouds and dim daylight. A lower level priest laid the first sheep on the altar, but Caiaphas' attention kept returning to the sky. The ominous clouds grew darker until they were black with opaque blue and gray swathes within them, then the sun vanished. Day became a dim dusk. He tried to focus on his duties at the altar, but fear forced him to repeatedly glance at the eerie sky. Raising a dagger over his head, ready to slice the sheep's throat, he recited prayers for the sacrifice to *Elohim*, but paused when the deafening thunder rumbled.

The high priest laid the dagger aside when the courtyard shook. He lost balance several times and had to grip the altar to prevent himself from falling. But a startling noise made him spin about to look at the Holy of Holies. A massive curtain stretched across its wide opening and hung from roof to floor. The cloth ripped the entire length, down its middle, and the thick support pole snapped like a twig. The curtain descended to the polished stone pavement, furling about by the furious wind gusts. Inside the Holy of Holies could be seen the raised stone altar where the Ark of the Covenant had once sat before being stolen. Only the high priest was permitted to see the altar once per year on the Day of Atonement. Yet now all could view it.

Dropping to his knees, the high priest's eyes were wide with fear as he gazed mouth agape at the roiling bl ck clouds. He prayed aloud but the rushing wind drowned his word. Priests released their holds on the sacrificial sheep and knelt, bese hing *Elohim's* mercy as they saw Caiaphas doing. The surround g pilgrims shouted, screamed in terror, and stampeded from the t mple.

The echoing thunder settled, and the lustery wind ceased. In time the temple no longer shook, and ever one stood, nervously looking about them. Caiaphas raced to the e stern roof wall of the temple and gazed at Golgotha. The ominous bl ck clouds highlighted in blue and gray streaks continually churned l t had parted in their center, allowing a brilliant ray of sunlight to s ine through onto the Hill of the Skull. From the towering temple t e high priest saw the sunbeam upon the crucified men.

Caiaphas stared at the crosses then sta gered back from the edge of the temple wall, eyes wide, shaking h head and muttering words no one could hear.

* * *

The beam of sunlight bathing the hillto spread as the black clouds broke. The dim light across the lan brightened and the clouds dissipated. Within minutes the tempe t passed as if it had never occurred.

The battle-hardened centurion looked al out the hilltop for his men. Longinus knelt in the dirt with hands pre sed over his face. His five Samaritan legionnaires stood fifteen pace back from the cross, their faces pale with panic in their eyes. M gnus swung an arm, silently ordering them to return to him. He he rd Longinus crying.

"What's wrong?"

Lowering his hands, the Roman soldier rose from the dirt. He stared at his commander and lightly shook his head. "I can see. My eyes are healed."

Magnus gazed at him for several seconds then looked at Yeshua on the cross.

"Truly this was the Son of God."

Longinus walked to Yeshua's feet and gently laid a hand on them. "We have crucified the Christ," he whispered. Raising his head, the legionnaire gazed at Yeshua's face and the crown of thorns. "Forgive me."

"Centurion!"

Magnus turned in the direction of the voice. An aged man in priestly clothes was walking up the hill followed by several servants and another equally ancient man in the clothes of a temple priest.

"I am Joseph of Arimathea. I have permission from the prefect to take custody of the man's body so he may be buried by our laws," the elderly priest said, halting before Magnus.

The centurion knew this went against the standard orders for crucified criminals. Normally, the body was left on the cross for days to deteriorate and feed the vultures, then would be removed and left in the desert for wild animals to devour.

"Here is the signed order from Pontius Pilate," said Joseph, his breathing labored from the long walk from the governor's residence. "This is Nicodemus who has permission to accompany me."

Taking the document held out to him, Magnus inspected its seal, broke it and read the parchment. He closed the document. "Your paper is in order. My men will remove the stakes."

"He was my friend, centurion. May I help get him off the cross?"

Magnus cast a distrustful eye at the heavily muscled man who approached him. "And your name?"

"Hanan ben Netzer."

The centurion nodded in recognition. " 'ou translated earlier for me, didn't you?"

"The Aramaic words."

Without replying, Magnus stepped aside He looked at his men and swung the vine stick cudgel toward the crucified man. "Take him down."

The soldiers began their work, draping a breechcloth about Yeshua and removing the stakes while Hanan waited at the base of the cross. A long cloth was twisted into a makes lift rope and wrapped about Yeshua's body. When the last stake was removed, the soldiers lowered the body into Hanan's arms.

The thorns of the crown dug into Hanan chest and right arm, making him grimace as he shifted his friend's body for a better hold. Gaze drifting over Yeshua, he carried him to the burial cloth spread across the ground and eased him onto it. Kneeling beside Yeshua, Hanan fought back his tears. His heart ached out rage came like an inferno charring his soul. His tunic and robe were smeared with Yeshua's blood, adding fuel to the fire within him.

Miriam knelt at her son's head, her tears filling onto his face as she gently pulled at the embedded crown to remove it.

"He weighs no more than a feather," Hanan softly said, speaking his thoughts aloud as he looked at the emaciated body.

Laying the crown aside, Miriam reached out and laid a hand upon Hanan's shoulder. Exhaustion painted her face and her eyes were red and swollen. "You were always a good friend to him, Hanan. I know he loved you."

Hanan's grief grew worse at hearing her. He rose to his feet, ready to leave, unable to endure anymore tragedy. The disciple John moved to him.

"Our Master, the lamb of our God, *Elohim*, will rise again in three days. He told us so. We must have faith he will."

Gaze sweeping over Yeshua's tortured body, the horrid spear wound in his side and thorn gashes, Hanan shook his head. "No man can rise from this," he replied. Looking skyward, he closed his eyes and breathed deep, besieged with anguish. He glanced at his friend once more and left.

* * *

Abaddon canted his head left, then right, studying the two criminals that had been crucified beside Yeshua. The bodies hung slumped on their crosses. He grinned and walked to where Joseph and Nicodemus watched servants clean Yeshua's face as best they could. The demon's yellowish eyes scanned the gaping wounds and flesh ripped by the whip. Moving around the servants Abaddon saw Yeshua's punctured rib and nodded in satisfaction. He raised his gaze to Yeshua's solemn death mask.

Leaning toward the corpse, Abaddon's grin spread across his thin lips to become a cruel smile. "It took longer than I wanted, but your death finally came... Oh, and what a spectacular ending it was with everyone beating and spitting on you, mocking you. But you certainly received your comeuppance with that flogging. The *lictors* put their backs into every lash they gave you. Yes, today was a splendid day, so much pain and suffering."

The demon walked a few steps away and stretched his arms in delight. He saw the centurion marching his squad down the hill.

Letting his gaze drift, he caught sight of Hanan's wide back as the man made his way along a trail leading to the city.

Abaddon's long, bony fingers tugged at his cloak and eased its cowling over his bald head. "Oh, what a life," he said, smiling in self-satisfaction. "My work will never end."

He started after Hanan knowing wherever the man went, death followed.

CHAPTER TWENTY-THREE

Jerusalem, District of Judea
Friday, Month of Nisan, Day 14

Hanan arrived at Yosef and Sarah's wine shop an hour before dusk. At nightfall, unlike other countries and by Jewish custom, the new day began and lasted until the next day's evening. He ordered a jar of wine and sat beneath the awning, brooding as he watched passersby in the street. The shop's young servant asked if he wanted food as well, but he had no appetite except for revenge against everyone who hurt his friend.

Easing back in his chair, he wearily rubbed his face with both hands, unable to recall when he last slept. Fatigue had settled over him, but he knew if he found a bed now, he would only stare at the ceiling and relive the day.

The jar was brought, and an alabaster cup was filled. Hanan downed it and waved the young man away when he attempted to refill the cup. "I'll pour my own wine. Leave me so I may drown my misery in solitude."

His thoughts wandered to Joseph of Arimathea and Nicodemus, hopeful they were able to prepare Yeshua for entombment before the sun set. By tradition, a corpse had to be b ried the same day of death. Leaving one unburied by nightfall was thought to be sinfully disrespectful to the dead.

Pilgrims still flowed along the city stree but the crowds were thinning as everyone hurried to their homes r inns to prepare for the first night's meal of Passover. While som spoke in low voices, others were boisterous, caring little if they we overheard.

"Did you know the Romans whipped the abbi this morning?"

"The temple priest say he was nothing m re than a false prophet—a magician..."

"Where were you today when the storm truck and the earthquake came?"

"Barabbas' release was rigged. Temple pri sts stood in the crowd and ordered everyone to shout for the criminal life and to crucify the prophet..."

"Caiaphas ordered the arrest of the teache 's disciples for inciting rebellion..."

With each person walking past, Hanan h ard something about the day. He drank heavily yet no amount of wi e could stop his mind from replaying every heartrending moment. eaching for the wine jar to refill his cup, he caught sight of a slender nan slinking through the crowd, glancing about as if wary of being r cognized. But Hanan knew him. It was the traitor Judas.

Hanan tossed a coin on the table for his w ne and raced out into the congested street. He scanned the crowd v here he had last seen Judas then started along the street in the sar e direction. Pushing his way through the pilgrims he lost sight of t e traitor but saw him again moving through the market. Passing a n erchant's stall, Hanan deftly grabbed a thick rope and slid it beneatl his robe without the merchant having seen. He quickened his pace until he was within arm's reach of Judas.

"Why are you in such a hurry, my friend," Hanan said with a wide smile for the benefit of the people walking around them. He laid his right hand on the nape of Judas' neck and squeezed with might. Judas abruptly stopped, and winced, unable to move.

"It's you—*his friend?*" Judas nervously asked. Eyes wide with fear, he wet his lips with his tongue. He tried to move away, but Hanan's hand was clamped about his neck like iron. "I saw you both talking by the sea that morning. He told us later that you were almost a brother to him."

"Yes, he was my friend, and was alive until you sold him out for thirty pieces of silver."

"Who told you?"

Hanan could feel Judas tremble. He shook his head. "Does it matter? Because of your lies the priests gave him to the Romans to torture and crucify."

"No..." Judas tried to shake his head but couldn't. "No, it wasn't supposed to be like that. They told me he..." The traitor's gaze lowered. "They lied to me. I took their money back and threw it in their faces. I didn't keep the blood money." His eyes glistened from the tears building along their rims.

"Because of you he was beaten and scourged all morning, then they drove stakes into him and stabbed him with a spear." Hanan's rage made him fiercely shake Judas.

"I'm sorry... I'm sorry." Judas wept uncontrollably.

"Don't worry, though. He made me promise not to kill you. But we're going to take a nice walk outside the city."

The traitor cried and mumbled as they made their way along the street and through the eastern city gate. They took the dirt road leading to Jericho and after a mile, Hanan turned off the road and pushed Judas onto a narrow trail leading out into the wilderness.

The sun was ready to descend behind the distant mountains and Hanan knew darkness would soon be upon them. "This is far enough," the brawny man ordered as they stopped beneath a tree with a large boulder by it. He released his hold on Judas and pulled the rope out from beneath his cloak.

Judas looked at him, then to the rope, but didn't try to flee.

Tying one end about the base of the tree, Hanan flung the remaining amount of rope over a branch and held it out to Judas. "Here, I promised not to kill you, so you're going to do it yourself. Climb onto that rock and make a noose about your neck."

Hesitating, Judas looked at the rope then slowly took it.

Hanan drew the Sica from beneath his cloak and held its blade up for Judas to see. "You will hang yourself or I'll gut you and leave you alive for every animal to eat."

Rope in hand, Judas made his way onto the boulder and once balanced, adjusted the length and tied the end in a noose. He slipped it over his head.

"Pull the rope tight. I don't want it coming off." Hanan stood calmly watching, holding the Sica in his right by his side.

Judas tugged at the noose, coughed from its tension, and lowered his trembling hands to his stomach. His gaze carried to Hanan. "I never meant for him to die."

Hanan didn't speak.

"May our God, *Elohim*, forgive me," Judas said in a faint voice, tears trailing down his cheeks.

"God might, but I never will." Hanan's words were as cold as a desert night. He stepped back to wait.

Judas raised his face to the night sky, closed his eyes and stepped off the boulder. His neck stretched and his eyes bulged. He quivered and shook, legs wildly kicking the air. Grunting, gagging sounds were heard. His hands reached upward for the rope, but his thrashing body made the noose draw tighter.

Watching until Judas' body no longer shook, and he swayed slowly above the ground, Hanan slid his dagger back into its sheath beneath his cloak. He spat on the dead man and started back to the city. He was thirsty, and his appetite had returned.

* * *

In the two days following Yeshua's crucifixion, the Zealots used the opportunity to recruit and incite loyal pilgrims to harass the temple priests and Romans. Random fires were set in the streets, and angry protesters bellowed in the marketplaces about the injustices the temple condoned. Caiaphas forbid his priests to leave the temple for the remainder of the Passover week until tempers settled, fearing the assassinations would renew.

Hanan was inundated with requests from subordinate Sicarii leaders across the country to strike while the people's anger mounted, but he refused. Pilate had placed his soldiers on their highest alert, preparing them for rebellion, and Caiaphas' guards waited at every gate for an attack.

"What you want is suicide. Taking any action now will only result in our men being slaughtered. No, let the Zealots keep the Romans and priests on edge while we remain out of sight. Once this passes and Caiaphas no longer feels threatened, we will decrease the number of priests—and Romans," Hanan said n a clandestine meeting far outside of Jerusalem.

The disgruntled leaders argued with H nan but obeyed and returned to their homes to once again blend into their communities until summoned. Hanan took note of the young cubs that had grown into lions within the organization. The were not quite ready to challenge him for the right to rule the Sicii, yet he felt the day swiftly approaching.

But another thought existed in Hanan fo not wanting to retaliate so soon. It was a reason he believed an doubted within the same breath. Yeshua had said he would retur 1 on the third day to fulfill the prophecy, and Hanan was waiting There were doubters too among his friend's own followers; the on named Thomas that Simcha had spoken of. Armed with that knc vledge, Hanan's conscience was eased.

* * *

By the end of the third day word spre d amongst believers throughout the city that the Christ had risen Whether it was fact or rumor was unknown, but Hanan paid a he d of street urchins to search for Simcha. If anyone knew the story, th little man would. He had befriended the disciples and assisted in f nding a house where they could safely hide from both the temple g ards and priests who searched for them.

The evening breeze gently flowed throt gh the streets, a fine balance between the day's warmth and the nigl 's coming chill. Dusk was a peaceful time with everyone setting tl eir day's trepidations aside until dawn.

At his usual table, Hanan sat with Sarah reminiscing about his uncle Yosef and how the man enjoyed relating history while the young Hanan sweated and toiled at carrying large rocks. She smiled at the tale, held the sling on her left arm which was slow to heal, and gazed with a hint of sadness at the darkening sky.

"I was twelve when I first came to Jerusalem. My fondest memory is of strolling about the city with Yosef, talking while Micah busied himself with the affairs of trade," he said, kindly smiling. He found no reason to state the journey's true purpose.

"I believe you have your own business to attend to," Sarah remarked, motioning to the stair-stepped children tugging a short man along with them as they strode toward the wine shop.

A dirty-faced boy of no more than eight years halted beside Hanan. "Here he is, master."

"What have I done wrong, Hanan?" Simcha asked with a wry grin, glancing at his escorts. "These ruffians fell upon me and demanded I come with them if I valued my life."

The gang of children proudly smiled, many displaying missing teeth.

Bearing a solemn expression, the muscled man nodded sternly. "You've all done well and earned your money. Tell me, is there anyone among you who is hungry?"

Their eyes shot wide and heads eagerly bobbed. Several of the children raised hands to ensure they were seen.

"Sarah, I'd liked to buy all the leftover loaves of bread you may have so my trusty companions may fill their stomachs after a hard day's labor," he said, trying not to laugh.

She rose from her chair and warmly smiled. "Your money is no good in this wine shop, Hanan. I have a dozen loaves they may have." Motioning them to follow, she led the way into the shop.

When the last child was gone from sight, Hanan carried his gaze to Simcha who wore the ragged tunic and robe of a beggar. His stained headdress hung past his shoulders.

"At least you don't smell like sheep." Hanan shook his head. "But why the role of a beggar today?" He pointed to a chair across from him.

Taking a seat, Simcha glanced about their table to note who was close and may be listening. "There are still many pilgrims in the city and Passover week makes them quite generous to the underprivileged." He held his robe out for Hanan to see the bulging leather pouch tied to his rope belt.

Hanan ordered a jar of wine and saw a gleam in Simcha's eyes.

"Tell me about Yeshua. People say he's risen, but I haven't seen him. We were close friends and I thought, surely of all people, he would show himself to me. Has anyone seen him or is that another useless rumor?"

The jar was brought, and the shop servant filled their cups. Simcha immediately took a drink and sighed in delight. Servants carried oil lamps from the shop and placed them about the terrace where patrons sat. The little man shook his head as he leaned toward Hanan.

"It's no rumor, sir. The woman with Yeshua's mother the other day, Mary Magdalene... She went to his tomb this morning. The heavy stone sealing the entrance had been rolled away. She entered and found his burial shroud, but not his body. A man appeared outside of the tomb, dressed in pure white with a bright light about him and asked why she was looking for the living among the dead. It was—*him!* They talked. She said it *was* Yeshua."

Hanan sat back in his chair, stunned by the revelation. Yeshua's body had been tortured and lifeless when he last held him in his arms but hearing that his friend had risen from the dead was too much to fathom. He had wanted to believe Yeshua would return yet doubted its truth.

"Do you think the disciples stole his body during the night?"

Simcha barely shook his head. "No, they are in hiding, afraid to go out of their house. Caiaphas had pleaded with Pilate for Roman soldiers to guard the tomb so the body couldn't be stolen. From what I've heard, the soldiers are saying they fell under a spell and woke to find the tomb empty. They have probably been executed by now. Romans do not take kindly to failures of duty."

Hanan emptied his cup and set it on the table, toying with it as he thought. Without waiting for permission, Simcha poured and drank two more cups of wine quickly while Hanan stared at the table's top.

"Maybe I'll see him tonight or tomorrow. I'm sure he will seek me out," Hanan said as if speaking his thoughts aloud. Disappointment hung heavy in his voice. His gaze never rose from the table.

"Did you know one of the disciples, the one they call Judas, is missing?" Simcha watched Hanan closely for a reaction.

The leader of the Sicarii raised his eyes and locked gazes with Simcha. "I'm sure he'll be found. He's probably hanging around somewhere." A smile slowly formed then vanished.

* * *

The third day led to the fourth, then the fifth, and the sixth. Soon Hanan lost track of the days that Yeshua had not appeared to him. Frustration set over him. Despondency came, followed by a heart wrenching hurt that evolved into anger. Whenever Hanan heard of a sighting, he raced to its location to find his friend, but Yeshua was already gone.

Hanan sent food to the disciples through Simcha so the little man would stay in their good graces and they would speak freely. Mary Magdalene had seen and talked with Yeshua at the tomb. He had visited the disciples at their house, told them to pray for the arrival of the Holy Spirit, and even let the doubting follower named Thomas touch his spear wound and brush fingertips over the stake holes in his arms. There were reports of seeing the Messiah on the road to Emmaus and crowds listening to him preach on a hillside. But where ever Yeshua appeared, Hanan could not find him.

The High Priest Caiaphas kept his guards searching for the disciples, but Yeshua's thousands of followers refused to speak of them. Saul of Tarsus, a half Roman, half Jew devote to the temple had become their persecutor. Through force and intimidation, backed by Caiaphas' money and brutal temple guards, Saul became a relentless hunter of Yeshua's believers and disciples. The day after the Holy Spirit came upon the disciples, empowering them with truth and abilities to heal and lead others to the way of *Elohim*, the disciples had no choice but to flee Jerusalem or face arrest. Word had come that Saul was closing in on them.

"Have they already left the city, Simcha?" Hanan stood in the street looking north as if expecting to see the disciples.

"Two days ago, sir. The one called John thought they were going to Damascus and once there, each would go a different direction to preach their master's teachings."

"Then I will follow them. If they are leaving Jerusalem it may mean Yeshua will never return here. My best chance to see him again may be where ever they are."

Simcha sadly shook his head. He had been looking at the ground but let his gaze drift to Hanan's face. "Saul left yesterday for Damascus to apprehend them. But there's something else you should know."

Turning to face the little man, Hanan's brow lowered. He didn't speak and only waited.

"Sir, you may never see Yeshua again. The disciples told me that he has ascended. Even they will not see him again."

"Ascended? I don't understand."

"He's gone, Hanan. *Yeshua is gone.* He went to sit at the right hand of our God, *Elohim.* Forty days after his resurrection, he talked to his disciples and vanished into a cloud with a bright light about him. No one has seen him since that day." Simcha paused and stepped closer to his leader. "Sir, you've been waiting two months to see him. He's gone, master. I hate seeing you so troubled. I'm sure he had good reasons for not coming to you."

The days of frustrated hope and anguish at everyone but himself seeing Yeshua, at last reached a boiling point within Hanan. He reached out with the speed of a striking cobra and jerked Simcha to him by the robe. "But I was his friend... He told his disciples that I was almost like a brother to him. Why would he forget me? Why would he turn away from me?" There was more pleading than anger in Hanan's tone.

Simcha looked into Hanan's green eyes and observed something he'd never seen before in this cold-blooded man; deep, emotional hurt.

"Sir... I don't know." Simcha's reply came in a gentle voice that tapered off to silence.

Hanan opened his fingers and released his hold on Simcha's clothes, allowing him to step back. Muddled thoughts spun in his mind. He needed a reason why his friend had abandoned him. Then Yeshua's words as they walked along the shore of the Sea of Galilee, came with clarity.

... I have prayed for you since we were boys in Nazareth, but Elohim will not allow me to cast out the evil that has marked you. He says if your victory is ever to come, you must find it yourself in the living water. Such is the word of my Father and I must obey....

"Maybe *Elohim* told him to stay away from me." Anger filled Hanan's eyes as he looked at Simcha. He raised his left forearm and gazed at the long scar. "If evil brought me into this world, then I'm destined to die with it." The Sicarii leader spoke his thoughts aloud.

"I... I don't understand." Simcha's head canted and his brow lowered.

"It doesn't matter. You were right. Yeshua is gone and I will not see him again." Hanan motioned Simcha to follow and they started toward the wine shop. "I've wasted two months and there is much work to do. My men have grown restless and thirst for action. Now I will overflow their cups."

* * *

The order was dispatched across the land and they responded, arriving at all hours in varying sized groups. Within days the assassins numbered almost four-hundred, and their tents and camp-fires carpeted the land. Men came who had not been requested, but for most, this would be their first time to see the warrior who led the Sicarii; the man who had become legendary for his skills and number of kills.

Their encampment sat in a secluded region northeast of Jericho near the Jordan River where canyons and rolling hills protected them from sight and afforded privacy. Escape would be simple if Roman soldiers attacked, but patrols rarely ventured into this land and lookouts watched from surrounding hilltops.

Hanan let Simcha remain by his side, not in a leadership role, but as his additional eyes and ears. The little man had proved his worth in Jerusalem and would be valuable again where many among the ranks were unknown to Hanan yet vouched for by their commanders.

"When do you intend to talk to them?" Simcha asked, his gaze drifting across the camp as they walked.

"Tomorrow morning. I've had word passed that we leave after I have spoken to them. We risk too much attention remaining here any longer than necessary." The Sicarii leader glanced at the men sitting around small campfires, talking with one another or suspiciously eyeing others that moved about them. "Even now among their peers some keep watchful eyes, distrusting the openness of our meeting."

Glancing at the setting sun, Simcha grinned as he looked at the stone-faced expressions of the hardcore assassins. "I believe it would be safe to say that most of these men have slept more with their knives than they have with women."

Hanan laughed. "It might be safer to sleep with their knives considering the type of women they bed." He clapped Simcha's back in good humor. The little man flew forward several steps before catching his balance.

* * *

At sunrise men waited in groups, anxious for Hanan to appear. The campfires had been doused and the ash s spread. Tents were struck, ready for departure. Lookouts signaled all was clear then the wide-shouldered, heavily muscled leader walk d out of the morning shadows. He found a wide boulder, climbed on to it, and stood silent, letting the men gaze at him. Commanders of the cells ringed the boulder, looking up at Hanan while their subordinates edged closer behind them to better hear.

"In twenty-five days the Sicarii will strike in a unified attack from one end of this country to the other." Hanan drew his Sica from beneath his robe and held it in his right hand high above his head. Men began to shout approval, but their leader raised his left hand to quiet them. "We will strike as we always have; with stealth and steel then return to the shadows leaving fear to spread like a plague when the dead are found. We are not ready yet for formal battles with the legionnaires. That will come in time, trust me."

Glancing at the sullen faces among his younger commanders, Hanan knew it wasn't the orders they had hoped for, but enough blood would be spilled to satisfy them for now.

"In this last year you have gathered names of corrupt priests, sadistic soldiers, sympathizers, collaborators, and those who have turned traitor against our people. You were told to plan their deaths and wait until the order came to strike... Now you may execute those plans." Hanan slowly turned to let his gaze drift across the grinning, smiling men encircling him. They nodded and shook knotted fists in the air. Some began to shout but others hushed them so Hanan could be heard.

Simcha stood away from Hanan, watching the young lion commanders as he had been instructed. To eyes trained to note every minute detail of a person, the little man knew their true thoughts would eventually be displayed. The three sons of Ezekias the Zealot leader, Menahem, Judah, and an unknown son, stood near Eleazar ben Jair; each man scowling and frowning. But Menahem was the worst. Fire raged in his eyes from the want of retribution for his father's death by one of Herod the Great's sons. Many in the Sicarii believed Menahem was as fanatical as his father had been, willing to slaughter and torture at a whim.

Hanan spoke for another hour and chose thirty of the best men for a mission in Jerusalem. After talking with his commanders to approve their individual plans, Hanan stood tall on the boulder, preparing to close the meeting.

"If you undergo a mission and are about to be arrested, do not be taken alive. It is better to kill yourself than be brutally interrogated by Roman soldiers. If anyone among us is heard speaking our names to the Romans, take them into the desert and kill them. You will be paid twenty-five silver coins. If anyone among us is heard speaking my name to the authorities, come tell me. You will be rewarded fifty silver coins then I will personally seek out the traitor." The muscles in Hanan's arms rippled as he crossed them over his massive chest. His iron gaze at several of the men made them swallow hard and lower their heads. "This is why I do not fear showing my face to you. There is a bounty on anyone who turns traitor within our organization."

"Commanders, twenty-five days from now execute your plans as you have told me then blend into your towns. Consider this training for what will come in time." Hanan gazed at them for several seconds then jumped off the boulder. As the small army dispersed, he could hear their contented words and the high-spirits in their voices as they talked among themselves.

Simcha approached and waited for the majority of the Sicarii operatives to leave before speaking.

"You've thrown raw meat to the lions, but that will only appease them so long."

Watching Menahem in the distance, Hanan nodded, never taking his eyes off the man.

CHAPTER TWENTY-FOUR

From dawn of the twenty-fifth day until long after dusk, targeted men and women fell to Sicarii assassins from as far north as Capernaum and Caesarea Philippi to Hebron and Arabah in the south. Few clouds passed over the land and the blood spilled in pools across the land glistened in the intense sunlight.

Jewish mistresses of Gentile officials died in their kept homes. Tax collectors were discovered with throats slit, draped over their desks with coins still clutched in hand. Children found collaborators hung from walls, many viciously mutilated. Corrupt priests were gutted like fish, and two six-man patrols of auxiliary Samaritan soldiers vanished outside of Caesarea, their bodies, equipment and horses never to be seen again. Yet the highest death toll resided in Jerusalem. With each corpse or remains found, some connection to Yeshua's crucifixion could be established.

Hanan had properly timed the country-wide attacks for the Sanhedrin council's nerves to settle and temple priests to be permitted to once again freely come and go. The two months of Hanan's search for Yeshua, in addition to the Sicarii's twenty-five day wait, had adequately returned complacency to the daily habits of the priesthood and the Romans.

At Hanan's request, Simcha identified at least seven of the low-ranking priests that had stood outside the prefect's gates, shouting for Yeshua's crucifixion. Throughout the day as they left the temple, one of Hanan's hand-picked, thirty-m n team fell in behind them. By nightfall, none of the priests returne .

Of the six soldiers in the Crucifixion Gua d, Hanan gave orders that only one was to live—Longinus, the Roma legionnaire. His eyesight had been healed by Yeshua's blood and in Hanan's warped logic, his friend had shown mercy upon the Roman and Hanan would do no less. The remaining five Samaritan soldier were trailed to their favorite brothel. There well-paid *sinners* lured them to undress and wait in the beds of separate rooms. Wine woul be fetched, and their pleasures would begin. But the only pleasures nyone received came at the hands of Sicarii operatives and Damasci s steel.

The four Greek Syrian *lictors*, though, received no swift end. They were captured separately in darkened are s of the city, knocked unconscious, gagged and loaded into donk y carts. When they awoke, they were in the wilderness, stripped naked with hands tied high above their heads to branches of trees. Moonlight silhouetted the men around the *lictors*, but clearly shone n a wide-shouldered, half-naked, muscled man. He stood like a sta e carved from stone with a whip hanging from his right hand. He raised it for them to see. The nine thongs with embedded broken sheep bone and pieces of jagged metal swayed before their flared eye .

Hanan stepped back, held the whip ou to measure his distance then with the greatest strength he cou 1 muster, swung and laid the first *lictor's* back open in gaping woun s and bloody streaks. The bones and metal buried themselves deep into the *lictor's* body. Hanan's back and arm muscles rippled as he to e the thongs free. His fury rose and with each driving strike of flesh, he recalled their glee while whipping Yeshua. The *lictor's* screams became Yeshua's cries of agony. Hanan could still hear their mocking voices as his friend wept and endured their torture. Then Hanan whipped the man harder, purging himself of the anger at Yeshua for turning away from him.

His white-knuckled grip upon the whip's handle tightened as insanity took control of him. He swung until his massive arms grew heavy.

"Hanan... Hanan!" an assassin shouted. He waved his arms trying to get the crazed man's attention.

The Sicarii leader halted and stood breathing heavily to fill his lungs. His mouth was agape, and his eyes were wide with a wild, glazed stare. He glanced at his chest and saw it glimmering in the moonlight from the *lictor's* blood.

"Hanan, he's dead."

Gazing at the bloody pulp of meat hanging by its hands, Hanan handed the whip to one of his men standing near. "Scourge the other three until they are dead. And while you whip them, remember how many Jews they've flogged."

He turned and walked several paces out into the wilderness, gaze drifting across the moonlit landscape as he stoically listened to the screams of the *lictors*.

* * *

In the hour after sunrise, the morning air still held enough chill for Sarah to wrap herself with a thick shawl. She stood at the doorway of her home and watched a shepherd walk past with his flock on the way to the market.

"I'm sorry to see you go, Hanan, but I understand you've been away from your home too long. You've helped me through my grief, and for that I will always be indebted to you." Sarah turned and stood gazing at the hard-muscled man. Her eyes were wet, but she did not cry.

Sarah's young servant girl, Jamila, carried a large water bag to Hanan, its weight forcing her to walk leaning forward. Hanan grinned. He reached out and took the bag with one hand and eased its strap over his left shoulder. The servant sighed in relief and stepped to Sarah.

"All should be in order now. You have a home, the wine shop and good servants to assist you. I've secured money in your name so that your needs will be met." Hanan lightly smiled and walked to her. "It may be long before I return to Jerusalem, but one day I may surprise you with a visit."

Sarah moved forward and kissed his cheek. "You've been so kind to me. Yosef would be proud of you. Half of the profits from the wine shop will be set aside for you. It is only right that I do so."

Shaking his head, Hanan laughed. "No, I have no need for more money. After I sold the different trade businesses, it left me with more than I will ever spend. Keep your profits and live a full, happy life." Having spoken, he warmly smiled at Sarah then nodded to Jamila. "Look after my aunt. She is the only remaining family I have," Hanan said. Without waiting for a reply, he turned away and left.

* * *

The old woman's cane tapped lightly on the stone floor as she made her way through the house. She glanced left and right, nodding at times in approval of its cleanliness. Her wrinkled hands brushed the tops of furniture then she looked at her fingertips. She smiled at not seeing dust on them.

Ruth walked into the room, broom in hand. She abruptly halted and looked at Elizabeth with a questioning gaze. Her two-year-old son, David, trailed her closely, one hand holding onto her tunic. The child peeked around his mother to see the old woman, his wide round eyes a picture of innocence.

Touching thumb to fingertips, Elizabeth barely shook her head. "You keep our master's home so clean that I have yet to find dust upon anything."

Bowing her head in embarrassment, the young woman smiled. "I want our master to be pleased whenever he returns."

Walking stoop-shouldered in measured steps, Benjamin leaned inside the door from the front porch and motioned the two women to him. He turned back to face the road leading to the stately home. When his wife and Ruth stood beside him, he pointed toward the road.

"A man is coming. Do you see him?" he asked, squinting against the glare of the noon sun. The figure of a wide-shouldered, strong man drew closer.

"It's Hanan!" Ruth immediately brushed her tunic clean and ran fingers through her long black hair. She smiled and moved off to one side of the elderly servants as they anxiously waited to greet their master. The child stood beside her, never more than an arm's length away.

"He looks tired. See how slow he walks." Elizabeth adjusted her shawl about her head.

Ruth watched his approach. "He walks like a man with a great worry."

They stood waiting for him and bowe 1 as he climbed the porch steps.

"It has been too long since we last saw ɔu, Hanan. Welcome home," said Elizabeth.

Hanan wearily rolled his head on his sh ulders and stretched his back. "The walk from Jerusalem grows l ɔnger each time. I'm glad to be home." He handed his empty water bag to Benjamin and glanced at everyone. His gaze stopped when l ː looked at the young woman with a child by her side. His brow lc vered in momentary confusion then he relaxed when he remember d her.

"My name is Ruth, sir. You employed me a Jerusalem to be one of your servants," the young woman quickly aid. A pleasant smile formed on her lips. "And this is my son, Davic ." She urged the child forward, but he leaned against her as if afraid f the giant.

"You made a wise choice in her. Ruth l ɛeps your home well and does the work of three people. I could n t have chosen a better person myself for your household," Elizabe h remarked, tenderly laying a hand on Ruth's shoulder.

Lowering chin to chest, Hanan looked dc vn at the curly haired, wide-eyed child that had moved to behind his mother. "And you are David, right?"

The boy leaned out and canted his head ack to look up at the giant. He leaped back behind his mother to hi e.

"He will not be a bother to you, sir. I will ensure he stays out of your way," Ruth stated with urgency.

"He's an excellent child, Hanan. Rarely do we hear him talk and he's shown himself to be quite intelligent. Elizabeth laughed. "I believe he's better mannered and smarter than Benjamin."

The old man snorted and shook his head in feigned anger. "Oh, sir, I'm glad you are back. This woman is driving me mad. The older she gets, the meaner she becomes."

Hanan laughed and winked at Elizabeth. "I find that hard to believe, Benjamin."

Removing his robe and rope belt from his tunic, he gave them to his head housekeeper and stretched his arms. "Would someone bring me wine? I've tasted nothing but dust for days and would like to sit on the veranda."

Elizabeth looked to Ruth, but the young girl was already entering the house to go for a wine jar and a cup. "She has been a breath of fresh air for us here, helping where ever needed. Such a nice girl. Thank you for choosing her."

Leaning forward, Hanan patted Benjamin's shoulder then kissed Elizabeth's forehead. He straightened his posture and a seriousness painted his face. "You have both been loyal and I am most appreciative of your service." He paused and drew a deep breath. "I'm sorry to tell you, but my uncle Yosef was killed in Jerusalem by temple guards."

The old woman's wrinkled hands rose and covered her mouth. She stood shocked and shook her head in disbelief. Benjamin wrapped an arm about her shoulders to console her. Tears appeared in Elizabeth's eyes and a single tear trailed down her cheek.

"We'll talk more later, but for now, I want to go relax and have a cup of wine." Hanan walked away, not wanting to revive hurtful memories.

* * *

The breeze blew softly through the veranda. Shaded from the sun by the veranda's roof, Hanan felt what little energy he still had vanish as he settled into his chair beside Micah's. He reached over and pushed on its arm to make it rock then watched somberly until it slowed to a halt.

"Here, sir." Ruth walked out of the house with his wine. She poured him a cup and waited. The boy peeked out from behind her tunic then eased back until only one of his eye could be seen.

Hanan saw him, chuckled, and drank his wine. The boy walked around his mother and stepped toward Micah's chair. When he reached out and touched it, Hanan immediately turned. "No... Not this chair." His tone was harsher than he meant it to be.

The young mother grabbed the boy, her eyes wide with fear. "I'm sorry, sir. He meant no harm. I'll make sure he never touches it again."

Staring at the child, Hanan shook his head in frustration. "I'm sorry. I know... It's just... Never mind."

With the boy in tow, Ruth walked into the house. She returned shortly carrying a wide, deep bowl of water. Setting it at Hanan's feet, she reached for his sandals.

"What are you doing?" He tried to straighten in his chair but her hold on his right foot kept him leaning back.

"Washing your feet, sir." The young woman never stopped as she spoke. Holding his right foot over the bowl, she dipped a cloth into the water and began to wash him.

At first he was taken back, but the soothing feel of the water flowing over his foot made him relax. He moaned lightly as she gently rubbed and massaged his foot. Once finished with the right, she lifted the left foot and rubbed. Again, he moaned in pleasure.

He sat gazing at her, realizing how different she now looked compared to when he first saw her in the brothel. Eating regularly had taken away the look of starvation and filled her cheeks and body with life. She was bathed and her comely face was no longer dirt stained. Her wide round eyes shined like black pearls and the long, raven-black hair about her head and face was thick and full. Against his will his gaze flowed over the contour of her body. When her eyes rose to look at him, he averted his gaze like a boy caught looking where he shouldn't.

She removed the water bowl and let his feet rest on the veranda's stone floor.

"Thank you, Ruth. That wasn't necessary, but it did feel good."

A soft smile crossed her lips. She carried the bowl back into the house. Again, against his will, his eyes followed the movement of her tunic as she walked. He turned and watched her enter the door then saw the child standing in the doorway, staring at him. Hanan nodded curtly and the child spun, racing after his mother.

Exhaling in a hard blast, Hanan settled back into his chair, refilled his wine cup and shook his head in exasperation. *Sending her here may not have been a good idea,* he thought, gaze drifting to the distant mountains.

* * *

Weeks became months and Hanan filled the majority of his days on the veranda, reading Micah's collection of books again or walking through the orchards. The men in the watchtowers grew accustomed to his daily presence and always knew he could be found at a favorite olive tree. When the Sicarii leader grew restless and sullen, he worked in the fields of his estate, clearing them of the largest boulders he could carry. Exhausted by he end of the day, he returned home feeling better yet never fully ric of the bleak thoughts that haunted him.

The child, David, reached his third year (f birth and though he rarely talked when Hanan was about, the bo; would silently stand half-hidden behind a door or his mother's tun : to stare at the giant. Sensing he was being watched, Hanan often t rned to find the boy gazing at him. But when Hanan nodded to hi; i, the child fled. Ruth attempted to keep David away from her mast(;, yet the boy seemed drawn to him.

When bored, Hanan ventured into Na; ireth to sit at Uriah's wine shop and listen to the latest political go; iip. The day after the Sicarii unleashed their coordinated attacks a :ross the nation, the prefect had ordered mass arrests in retaliatio; for his auxiliary soldiers and local officials having been slain. Pil; e had to squelch any uprisings and prove his worth to the emperor. he majority of arrests were Zealots, blamed for the assassinations, ye none of Hanan's men were ever apprehended. The Sanhedrin cou cil offered a reward for information about whomever had killed t eir priests, although, the Sicarii were suspected. But no one stepp d forward to collect the money.

Every third month or so Simcha bei Mudash arrived in Nazareth to brief Hanan on recent news and ; :port the activities of the Sicarii's young commanders. Incidents ha(occurred of collaborators being killed which bore the signs of Sic; ii assassinations. But Simcha was never able to confirm the rebelli us commanders had issued the orders without Hanan's approval.

"Tensions are rising over rumors that Rc ne will increase taxes again to pay for its indebtedness. There is even talk of Pilate possibly taking funds from the temple treasury," Simcha advised one after-noon while drinking wine with his leader.

Such talk greatly disturbed Hanan. He could see the storm building on the horizon, and when the tempest struck, it would be the opportunity for his young lions to incite war from one end of the country to the other.

CHAPTER TWENTY-FIVE

The kitchen was hot from baking all morning, but Ruth wanted to surprise everyone with special breads and pastries for their evening meal. It had been difficult at times, keeping the oven coals at the right heat while kneading and preparing the doughs between quick runs through the house to finish other duties. She smiled inwardly at her accomplishments and leaned back to wait for the last batch of pastries to finish baking.

Ruth glanced at the corner of the kitchen where David enjoyed playing while she worked. She straightened and anxiously looked about the room. Her stomach tightened and fear engulfed her.

"David?" Ruth bent to look under a table. "Sweetheart, where are you?" With quick steps she moved from room to room, checking every place her son might hide. She began speaking in a slightly raised voice, not wanting to disturb anyone in the house. But now she loudly called his name where ever she walked, not caring who she bothered.

Elizabeth rushed to her from another room, eyes narrowed in question. "What's wrong?"

"David's gone. He was with me in the kitchen while I was working then vanished."

"He can't be far. I'll find Hanan and Benjamin to help search." Elizabeth hurried to the front door as fast as her cane allowed.

Ruth made a quick round through different rooms, searching under furniture while she called out his name. When the boy wasn't found she burst toward the front door, afraid he wandered off and was lost. She took three steps out of the house and almost ran into the back of the elderly woman.

"Oh, no!" she gasped, eyes spread wide in terror.

"Silence... and be still," Elizabeth urgently whispered, holding her left arm out to prevent Ruth from moving past her.

Looking over Elizabeth's shoulder she observed Hanan standing thirty feet ahead with his wide back to them. His left arm was out and held behind him, gently motioning for them to wait and not move. Ten feet in front of Hanan, Ruth saw David's back as he stood motionless with arms by his side staring at something in front of him that she couldn't see.

* * *

Hanan's attention was focused on the boy. He crept forward, moving up behind the child in painstakingly slow steps. The last thing Hanan wanted was to startle the boy and have him bolt in fear, making the coiled, black desert cobra strike.

Sweat ran down Hanan's face and stung his eyes, but he forced them to remain open to watch the snake's every movement. He eased out to David's right, still behind him and stopped when the boy no longer stood between him and the hissing, venomous cobra. The snake laid coiled three feet in front of the boy.

Black desert cobras were different from other cobras of the land. They seldom raised their heads to produce a hood before striking and preferred to remain coiled with head down while loudly emitting a hissing, huffing sound.

From the size of the coiled mound Hanan knew the black cobra was an adult at least three feet or more in length with enough lethal venom to kill David within minutes. The snake's hissing grew louder as it repeatedly swelled its body and forced the air out. As it moved, the black glossy scales along its thick body shimmered in the intense sunlight. The hypnotic effect of the shining scales held the child's attention but Hanan feared the boy would move any moment.

* * *

Ruth stood with Elizabeth's left arm about her shoulders; her right-hand holding Ruth's right arm, forcing her to remain still.

She watched her son and prayed he would be safe yet still unaware of the snake because David and Hanan had blocked her view. But as Hanan moved to the right, her worst fears rose, and she wanted to scream.

"Hush, girl, and be still. I see the snake in front of your boy," the elderly woman whispered.

Ruth saw Hanan's right arm move. The back of his robe swayed, and she realized he was removing something from the small of his back. Moving slow, his right hand rose even with his head.

One moment Hanan appeared still then the next, his actions came as a blur. A glint of steel flashed. The big man spun to his left, aiming low, sweeping the boy up into his muscled right arm as he leaped away from the snake. When he stood safely away, he turned with David in his arm to see the cobra. The glossy black, coiled mound writhed about the large dagger driven into its center. Hurrying as best he could, Benjamin came around the house with a hoe in hand and finished what Hanan had started. Eventually, the cobra's body drew to a halt.

Terrified from the ordeal, Ruth raced to take her son from Hanan, but the boy refused to leave the safety of the giant's arms, tightly hugging his neck as he cried in fright.

She watched Hanan hold David in his right arm and gently rub the boy's back.

"You're okay now. Don't cry. There's nothing to be afraid of... You were very brave," Hanan whispered in the child's ear.

Ruth wept, unable to control herself. She stood with arms extended. Eventually, the boy leaned out and went to his mother's arms.

"Thank you," she said to Hanan, choking from her emotions.

The big man nodded, glanced at her and the boy and walked away as if nothing had happened.

Ruth gazed at him, warmly smiled, then left for the house.

* * *

"That's a big snake," Benjamin said, looking at the four feet long cobra he had stretched along the ground. His gaze drifted to the Sica laying nearby. "And that's a big dagger."

Hanan remained silent and carefully lifted the Sica by its handle. Venom might be on the dagger and needed to be washed away.

"I've heard of men who carry such weapons," the old man said. He leaned on his hoe and cast a wary eye at Hanan, then poked the cobra with his hoe. He grinned. "A man can't believe all the stories he hears."

"It's been years since we've had a snake : o close to the house." Hanan let his gaze drift about the area. "The)dd part is that these cobras are nocturnal and rarely come out duri g the day."

Hooking the snake's body with the hoe, Benjamin grunted as he lifted it to waist level. "Heavy thing. I'll get id of it, sir."

"Bury the head if you don't mind. I don want the boy to find it and accidentally scratch himself with the angs." Hanan patted the old man on the shoulder. With a final glai :e across the land, he walked into the house, disturbed without reas n.

* * *

The demon sat in the shade beneath tl ; limbs of a tree, his yellowish eyes squinting against the glare of t e afternoon sun. The scowl on his leathery face added wrinkles to th ones already present about his eyes and along his cheeks. His top li curled and several of his rotted teeth came into view. He slowly sho k his head in disgust as he watched Hanan enter the house.

"Oh, Hanan, you trouble me." Abaddo rose to his feet and adjusted the cowling of his robe. "One day yo 're a fine, butcherous animal, skinning a man alive without guilt, th n the next you're killing my pets, worried about some little bastai child... I had hopes that your friend's scourging would finally brin you over to me, but I misjudged. I suppose it's time to step up my g ne."

Staring at the door Hanan had entered, t ie demon spat on the ground and started for the road.

* * *

Ruth laid the pastries and bread on the ible next to the other food she had prepared. By Hanan's order, eve yone sat at the same table for their meals rather than separate master and servant tables. Elizabeth and Benjamin stood glancing about the room, eager to eat but waiting on Hanan and David's arrival.

"I will get them. Hanan said they would be on the veranda." Ruth wiped her hands clean on a cloth and left.

Walking through the house, drawing near the veranda, she expected to hear the man and boy talking. The silence puzzled her. Rather than call out their names, she slowed her pace and eased to the veranda door. The sight she saw made her gasp yet stirred her heart.

The big man laid back in his chair, head tilted back, mouth agape, lightly snoring with arms crossed over his chest and legs fully extended with ankles crossed. But in Micha's chair next to Hanan sat David, fast asleep, leaning on the chair's arm with his head resting upon his arm. She swallowed the lump of joyful emotions that formed in her throat. Wiping tears from her eyes, she quietly walked around the chairs to stand in front of them.

She was about to speak when Hanan's eyelids slightly opened.

"I'm sorry, master. I will talk to my son about getting into the chair."

Hanan stretched his arms, sat up properly and rubbed his face to wipe the sleep from him.

"No. It's only a chair, not an altar. The boy did nothing wrong. He may sit there anytime he wishes." Carrying his gaze to David, a fragment of a smile formed on his lips, then vanished.

"I've been thinking. If you have no objections, and since I have nothing else to do around here, I would like to begin teaching David how to write. As he grows, I could teach him to read and speak other languages as I was taught."

Covering her mouth with her hands, Ruth happily nodded. Her eyes grew wet and she slid her hands over her face to conceal her tears.

Hanan's brow lowered as he canted his head to gaze at her face. "I didn't mean to upset you. I won't do anything if that is what you wish."

She lowered her hands and shook her head, smiling wide. "I would appreciate you teaching him to read and write. Please, do so." Ruth swept her long black hair away from her face and wiped her eyes. "When he's older, if you wish, you could show him how to clear rocks from a field." Her smile brought a glow to her cheeks.

"Who told you about the rocks?"

"Elizabeth... She saw you the other day in the field and told me how Yosef trained you to become so strong."

Rising from the chair, Hanan glanced about the veranda. "The old woman talks too much." He walked around Ruth but paused at the gentle fragrance of baked bread in her hair. He inhaled deeply before moving on. "We better go eat. I don't want Elizabeth and Benjamin to die of starvation." His voice held a tender tone.

Ruth lowered her gaze to the stone floor, embarrassed at her thoughts when he slowed behind her. "Yes," she replied in almost a whisper. "I'll wake David and be there shortly."

She raised her face to watch him leave, but he stood staring at her with an engaging gaze.

He slowly turned away, and as he did, she thought she saw his lips form a piece of a smile.

* * *

Hanan kept his word and began to teach the boy whatever he could grasp. Learning Greek was made a game, though, David only mumbled his words in the beginning. Writing was taught by using small sticks to scribble in the dirt. When David grew frustrated at not being able to form his letters, the big man would snap the sticks in half, roar like a lion and chase the boy about the area.

The first time they walked to a field, David lifted rocks no bigger than his palm and cast them away. Although they only flew less than five feet, Hanan applauded and encouraged him to throw more. "Soon, we will find bigger rocks to carry from the field," Hanan proudly said.

They were returning to the house one evening when David reached up with his right hand to take hold of the little finger of Hanan's left hand. Hanan's first instinct was to pull away, but his heart surprised him and enjoyed the boy's touch. They walked to the house for their evening meal and Hanan regretted the moment would soon end.

"One day I must tell you a story my uncle Yosef used to tell me about the Spartans. Have you ever heard of the Spartans?" he asked, grinning as he looked down at his little friend.

Curly hair flying as the boy shook his head, he gazed up at the giant with innocent large, round eyes.

Hanan's grin spread into a wide smile.

From within the house Ruth watched their approach. Her bottom lip curled inward, and she swiped at her eyes, not wanting Hanan to see her tears of happiness.

* * *

After the evening meal, everyone sat on the veranda enjoying the cool breeze. Hanan drank wine and few words were spoken as they relaxed and gazed at the moonlit landscape. When Elizabeth went for oil lamps, Hanan asked if she would wait before lighting them. He wanted to relish the gentle light of the moon and gaze at the painted land.

Benjamin sat beside his wife and rocked in his chair, affectionately patting her hand. Ruth watched them and fondly smiled. She let her gaze drift to her son in Micha's chair beside Hanan. The boy turned a small wooden horse, a gift from Hanan, in his hands. But when she glanced at Hanan, she found him quietly watching her. Again, as he often did, he appeared to briefly smile before turning his head.

An hour passed then the elderly couple rose from their chairs. They wished peace upon everyone for the night and left for their nearby home. Ruth stood as well and walked to her son.

"Time for bed, my little man," she said lifting him from the chair. He wanted to stay with Hanan and lightly struggled in her arms, but she turned to leave.

"Your mother is right, David. It is time for bed. Your body grows strong when you get a good night's sleep." Hanan smiled at the boy and nodded. As if by magic, David settled against his mother's shoulder and closed his eyes, the wooden horse clutched in his right hand.

When quiet returned to the veranda, Hanan sat drinking his favorite Damascus wine as he savored the night. It was one of the few times his thoughts didn't travel to the past and leave him frustrated and angry. An hour later he stood, stretched his muscled body, and walked to his room.

He left the window open for the breeze to blow through. Moonlight filled the room in a soft glow yet not bright enough to hinder his sleep. Laying on his back, naked upon the thick blankets of his mat, he rested his right arm behind his head and closed his eyes. His fingertips brushed the hilt of the Sica dagger and soon he was asleep.

He awoke to a light noise he couldn't place. Unsure of how long he had slept, he realized he was laying on his right side and the dagger was behind him. Without turning his head, he slowly opened his eyes. In the moonlit room he could see a slender, nude form moving toward him but felt no danger when he recognized the woman. No weapons were in her hands. He rolled onto his back and looked up at Ruth.

"This is not one of your duties," he said in a low voice.

"I know... It's of my own will if you'll have me," came the reply as comforting as the night's breeze.

His hand rose and she laid her fingers in his open palm. She knelt onto his mat, settling her body next to him.

CHAPTER TWENTY-SIX

33 A.D.
Nazareth, District of Galilee

In the three years passage of time after Yeshua's resurrection and sightings Hanan lost hope of ever seeing his friend again. He accepted the fact that his abhorrent life as a Sicarii had been the reason *Elohim* kept Yeshua away. After all, how could the Son of their God, *Elohim*, be expected to befriend a murderous animal as Hanan had become. But neither did Hanan lay blame upon Micha for making him a professional killer. He bore the mark of the demon, and for that, would be forever damned.

Each year Rome demanded tax increases across its empire, some slight while others proved to be major. The Prefect Pontius Pilate ensured the emperor always received Judea's full payments. But, before Rome grew rich with his tax payments, Pilate spent a portion of the collected funds for construction projects such as the twenty-four-mile-long aqueduct to bring water to Jerusalem's Solomon's Pool. To replenish those diverted funds, Pilate took money from the temple's treasury. Caiaphas walked a deceitful line by blaming Pilate for the treasury's loss, but quietly took credit for the much-needed water brought to the city. With the prefect's history of an iron-fisted rule, no one cared to see through the corrupt priest's lies for the truth.

But of all, it was the young lions of the Sicarii that wore heavily on the mind of the thirty-eight years old leader of the assassins.

* * *

The Nazareth wine shop was Simcha's favorite site to meet his leader. Always arriving early, he ate and drank, then told Uriah to place it on Hanan's account believing the rich man would never know. Yet Hanan did, and paid the debts, but permitted it because of the detailed intelligence reports the little man provided.

At midmorning on the third day of the week, Simcha finished his second cup of wine and glanced down the dirt street. He observed a well-muscled man walking with a young woman half his height, and boy of no more than five or six years. When the attractive, dark-haired woman and boy turned toward the city market, Simcha watched Hanan continue to the wine shop.

"What news do you have for me today?" the Sicarii leader asked, grinning as he took a seat across the table from his operative.

A wicked smile crossed Simcha's lips as his gaze followed the young woman. He watched the sway of her walk and was still smiling when he turned to face Hanan. But his smile melted when he observed the fury in his leader's eyes.

"Speak the wrong words now and you will never speak again. Look at her once more in such a vile way and your eyes will never see the sun again."

Simcha swallowed the lump in his throat and tried to nod yet it came in jerky motions.

The shop keeper brought Hanan a small jar of wine and filled his cup. Observing Hanan's stern stare at Simcha, Uriah kept quiet and slipped away.

"The times are growing worse in Jerusalem by the day," the informant nervously said. "Tension is always in the air wherever you go. The arguments between the Romans and the Sanhedrin only increase and draw us closer to conflict. The Sadducees keep petitioning Tiberius to remove Pilate because of his cruelties. Pilate's problem, though, is that he no longer has any support in Rome to protect him since Sejanus was tried and executed for tyranny two years ago."

Hanan slowly drank his wine and remained stone-faced. "I've heard Pilate has executed Jews without trial. The roads leading into Jerusalem are often lined with crucified men. Is that true?"

A nod came in reply. "They are mostly Zealots stupid enough to be caught after setting fires in the streets to protest against the Romans."

"Have any of our men been arrested?"

"One that I know. He was innocent and happened to be in an area when a fire was set." Simcha glanced at Hanan. "The soldiers were not able to actually arrest him because he committed suicide with his Sica before they could capture him."

"Sounds like he did what was best. The soldiers would have whipped him until he confessed to anything, especially our organization."

Nodding agreement, Simcha displayed a sickened expression at the mention of the whip.

"What about Menahem and the other commanders? Anything I should know?"

The little man's gaze gradually rose to Hanan. "The majority of your commanders remain loyal, understanding how our stealth and secrecy have protected us. But from what I've been told, Menahem continues to secretly gather men to do his bidding. They believe they are Sicarii working under your authority and he tells them no different." Simcha wet his bottom lip with his tongue then drank a sip of wine. His eyes narrowed as he leaned toward Hanan. "To finance his actions, Menahem has begun to kidnap officials and wealthy men. He ransoms their freedom for a hefty purse."

Rubbing his forehead as if it ached, Hanan briefly closed his eyes and sighed. He raised his face again and shook his head. "If he's done that then there's more we haven't heard about."

"There is, sir. I've heard about them. He's raided villages, killed, stolen shepherds' flocks as punishment for any help they gave the Romans, and beaten wives and children of suspected sympathizers as a warning." The operative finished his wine and dejectedly sat back in his chair. "The people in the southern villages no longer rejoice when they hear the name 'Sicarii.'"

"I feel he's trying to push the Romans into a war that will only end with our people's annihilation," Hanan replied, scraping the table's top with his fingertips. He glanced about the street.

The noon sun reached its zenith and the heat of the day grew worse by the hour. Little breeze blew and the air felt as if it flowed from a baker's oven.

"What ever happened to the disciples that followed Yeshua? Last I heard they were going to Damascus."

Simcha nodded with apprehension. Hanan had not spoken of Yeshua and his followers for years, and the Sicarii leader never asked questions unless he had reason.

"They went to Damascus, but once the e they separated and went to the four winds, each man to a differ nt country to spread Yeshua's teachings. Some of the disciples have een killed."

"And what of the man who persecu ted them?" Hanan's brow lowered.

"Do you mean Paul? The one that was originally called Saul of Tarsus?"

Hanan nodded.

"Saul was on the road to Damascus w en—." Simcha drew silent, not wanting to bring up a bad memory or Hanan.

"When *what*?"

"When Yeshua appeared to him, blind d him, then let him travel on to Damascus." Simcha's voice lower d. "Once there a follower of Yeshua found Saul and said the teac er had ordered Saul's eyesight to be cured. On that day Saul beca e a believer and has been spreading the teachings of Yeshua ever s nce. But he is no longer called Saul. Now he's known as Paul."

"Yeshua blinded him? I remember when Yeshua destroyed the money-changers' tables in the temple. Now y u say he blinded this Saul or Paul, or whatever the man is called. I never have believed he would do such things." Hanan slowly shoc his head once as he lowered his gaze to the table's top and stared, l st in thought. Several minutes passed then he rose from his chair to eave.

"Do you remember the centurion from the day of the crucifixion?" Simcha asked, looking up at Hanan. "Before the disciples left for Damascus, he sent soldiers to find Pe er and escort him to his house. Peter thought he was being arrest d, but the centurion wanted to be baptized by him."

"The centurion?" The disbelief in Hanan's voice was thick. He let his gaze drift to the ground as he turned to leave.

"There's more you need to know, mas-I mean Hanan." Simcha spoke with a tone of remorse.

The big man groaned as he took his seat in the chair again.

"Why do I have the feeling this will not be good?" Hanan rested his forearms on the table's top and leaned forward.

The odd scar on his leader's forearm came into view. Simcha paused and stared, his thoughts distracted by it.

"Simcha? What were you going to say?"

The operative raised his gaze to meet Hanan's eyes, momentarily lost for words.

"I—I was told Menahem is considering an attack on the town of En Gedi."

"An *attack*?"

"No, not *just* an attack, but a slaughter. Kill all seven hundred men, women, and children there."

Hanan stared with mouth slightly agape. "That's ridiculous. Why would he do that?"

"From what my source said, in Menahem's warped logic, he believes the entire village has become puppets to the Romans because they treat the soldiers well when they pass through on their way to Masada."

"But they treat everyone good who passes through the town. It's an oasis in the wilderness with a waterfall and palm trees. The people make their living from selling food, wine and supplies to travelers that stop to rest for the night. They're not sympathizers." Hanan shook his head. Menahem's insanity was beyond comprehension.

Travelers referred to En Gedi as the 'cit of palm trees.' With its Hebrew name translating to the 'spring of 1e goat-kid,' travelers found 'palm trees' to be more favorable to spe k of as a place to rest. Thirty miles southeast of Jerusalem and wes of the Dead Sea, En Gedi was along the route to Herod the Great's mountaintop fortress of Masada where the Romans kept a garrison. ')avid's Waterfall' cascaded down a mountain, fed from a spring fa up its side. Solomon had often spoke of the fertile soil and viney rds with fine grapes. David had taken refuge in one of its many cave when King Saul pursued him with three thousand men. Although a beautiful place surrounded by desolate land, En Gedi had a vio nt history of ancient battles—and Menahem now wanted to add hi own to its record.

"I've never doubted your reports befor , but I must ask... Is your informant reliable?" Hanan's brow rose a he looked at Simcha.

"Yes. A *sinner* woman that slept with him old me he was drunk and bragging about leading his men against 1 town of traitors. It took all night and several jars of wine, but he f 1ally said the name— En Gedi."

Glancing down the street, Hanan obse ved Ruth and David standing in the shade of a building, patientl waiting for him. He rose from his chair and nodded to Simcha.

"I must go but meet me here tomorrow morning." He tossed coins on the table. "Those are for the inforn tion." He dropped a coin atop the others. "And that is for you to 1y for your food and wine." A wry grin formed on his lips. "Stop utting your wine on my account."

Simcha had smiled when he first saw tl coins but grew pale when he realized Hanan had known about the bill all along.

The leader of the Sicarii walked four steps before Simcha called out, making him stop. Hanan turned to face him and waited.

"I remembered what I was going to tell you earlier. That scar on your forearm. I've seen it before." Simcha raised his left forearm and ran a finger over it.

"Where?" Hanan's face drew cold and hard.

"Menahem. On his left arm."

Hanan stared at his operative for several seconds, gravely nodded and walked away.

* * *

The walk home had been long; not because of its distance but from Hanan's moody silence. Gazing at the ground or staring off at the horizon, his thoughts appeared to be everywhere other than with Ruth and her six years old son.

Once home Hanan walked to the veranda and settled in his chair, eyes focused on the distant mountains. Elizabeth glanced at Ruth and raised her brows in question, but the young woman shrugged in reply and carried a cup of wine to him. His gaze drifted to her and she heard a mumbled *'thank you.'*

David raced past her to sit in Micha's chair. She reached out to catch him but Hanan waved her away.

"He's fine."

Ten minutes later, Hanan finished his wine and stood. He looked at the dark-haired boy. "I'm going for a walk. Do you wish to stay or go?"

The boy slid from the chair. "Can I throw rocks?"

Hanan faintly smiled. "Of course, and I may throw some with you."

They found David's mother in the kitchen and asked permission for the boy to go.

"Are you sure, Hanan? You look troubled."

The big man softly nodded. "I'm only going to the orchards. He won't be a bother."

* * *

Every fifteen feet along the road the boy found a new rock to throw. At times Hanan tossed a rock to land near David's, making the boy laugh.

"My mother can throw better than you," David said, smiling wide as he craned his neck back to look up at Hanan.

Waving to the men in the watchtower, Hanan walked along the orchard rows and stopped at his favorite gnarled olive tree. He gazed at it several seconds before sitting in the shade of its limbs.

The sun was lowering on the horizon as he glanced at the drifting clouds overhead. The air was changing, losing its extreme heat and becoming pleasant. Scraping a handful of dirt into his right hand, he mindlessly let it sift through his fingers then wiped his palm clean. Twenty feet away David walked along, studying the ground for the best rocks. When found, he reared his right arm back and cast the rock with as much strength as he could muster. He watched it sail through the air then bounce across the ground to a halt.

Depending upon the quality of each throw Hanan applauded or laughed. But his thoughts kept returning to Menahem, and what must be done.

"Stay where I can see you," he called out when the boy kept edging further away along the orchard row.

Leaning his head back against the bark of the tree, Hanan stared at the passing clouds outlined with a golden orange by the setting sun.

"Where are you, Yeshua? If you came back, why didn't you show yourself to me as well? Am I so bad that *Elohim* forbade it? I thought of you as a friend, my only friend. Why have you turned away?" He spoke to the sky, hoping that Yeshua was listening, yet no response came. The ache sweeping through him was like none he'd ever known or could explain to anyone.

"Are you all right?" David's gentle voice held worry.

Hanan let his gaze drift to the boy standing near. "I was talking to an old friend."

Looking up at the sky, David turned back. "But you're crying..." He raised a hand and pointed a finger at Hanan's cheek.

Swiping fingertips over his right cheek, Hanan was surprised when he felt a tear. "I must have gotten something in my eye." He wiped his eyes and inhaled deeply.

Hanan rose from beneath the tree and stepped to David. He pressed the boy against him and stroked his head.

"I'm going away for a while on business. Will you take care of your mother, Elizabeth and Benjamin until I return?"

"Yes, sir. Will you be gone a long time?"

"I hope not. But while I'm gone, I expect you to continue with your studies. Read the Torah like we've been doing together." Hanan let his gaze carry across the orchard. "I'm going to miss this place."

He patted David's shoulders. "We better go home before it gets dark and your mother starts to worry."

* * *

The hour had reached mid of night whe Hanan heard a light tapping against the door frame. He turned f m Micha's desk and the papers before him to see Ruth standing b efooted in her sleeping tunic.

"Are you hungry?" Worry filled her eyes "You've been here all evening and haven't had anything to eat. I col ld prepare a plate for you and bring it if you wish."

"No, I don't have much appetite this eve ing," he replied, covering several documents, although, he knew e couldn't read. "I'm almost finished for the night."

The light in the room had grown dim a: the oil lamps burned down. Only the one by his desk still glowed b ight. He gazed at the innocence of her comely face and the glistenin in her dark eyes. The wavering flames of the lamps made the bluis streak in her raven-black hair faintly dance. He couldn't help but notice the contour of her body, and where small mounds once had een, now full breasts filled her tunic. They had laid together many ni hts, yet never spoken of love or a future together. He knew that was l s fault. She suspected what he was, what he did, yet never asked. Tl ey were content with their lives on the estate, away from the outside world of troubles. He knew neither of them wanted it to change anc so they allowed each day to come and go. But it was about to chan e, and for that he felt ridden with guilt.

"I'll leave you alone. I only wanted to s e if you were hungry before I went to bed."

He thanked her, but she stood a mom t longer as if something weighed upon her mind. Waiting, he r dded to her, yet she remained silent and left.

* * *

Only one oil lamp remained burning. He blew its flickering flame out and left his office. At his room he closed its door behind him, tossed his clothes aside and made his way through the dark to his mat. Ruth lay waiting for him.

* * *

The last few hours had been filled with a passion she'd never known from Hanan. He'd been tender and loving yet within the blink of an eye, became a wild animal, devouring her as if it were their last night together. Little talk had passed between them. She sensed something was wrong, as if he were afraid to speak and let slip a secret. But she kept a secret as well, and each time she was about to share it, they became impassioned again.

While Hanan slept, she stared at the ceiling. The faint light of dawn had begun to fill the room. She wondered if she should tell him before she returned to her room and David.

No, I'll tell him tomorrow that I am with child, she thought.

* * *

Two hours after sunrise Hanan walked into the cooking room. Everyone had broken their fast and his plate of meat strips, assorted fruits, and a bowl of lentil soup sat on the table. They were all in the room, waiting, worried over the morose mood he'd been in last night. But they grew more concerned at the sight of him wearing traveling clothes and carrying a shoulder pouch and water bag.

"Where is David?" he asked, glancing about as he set the water bag on the stone floor.

"On the veranda reading," Ruth replied. " Ie told us you wanted him to do his lessons while you were gone. Ar you leaving us?"

Laying his shoulder pouch on the table he ate several pieces of meat and withdrew a folded document fr m the pouch. It was sealed and bore his name stamp. After eatin a date, he looked at his servants.

"I must go to Jericho. If I'm not back in thirty days, everyone must abandon this house. Our country is no lo ger safe. War is coming and it would be best for you to move to one of the Jewish colonies in Crete. If I return, we will all go together."

"Crete?" Ruth stood stunned.

Elizabeth leaned forward on her cane, nouth slightly agape and eyes wide staring at Hanan. Her husbar l, Benjamin, blinked several times and reached out to steady himse on a chair.

Once the shock wore off, all three showe ed Hanan with questions. He waited several seconds before rais ig a hand to silence them and kept his voice calm when he spoke.

"I can't explain everything. There are m: lmen presently planning to force the Romans into war. It may be his year, next year or ten years from now, but it's coming. When it oes, the Romans will have no mercy for any Jew, man, woman or hild, throughout the country." Hanan gazed at them and hoped his ords would sink into their minds.

"In my room, beneath the floor where my sleeping mat has been, is a stone that covers a hole. Move the s ne and you will find forty bags of silver. Take one bag and split its c ins amongst the men of the watchtowers. They've been loyal for m ny years and deserve it. As for the remainder of the money, take so le silver to carry with you for expenses but disguise the rest in you personal belongings.

Don't let anyone know you have that much silver. There are men who will kill you for a single coin."

He paused, scanned their faces and continued. "Keep this document safe. When you leave here, go north to Tyre and buy passage to Crete. In Tyre find the Greek money-changer named Lycus. The man will help you find a ship. He deals only with wealthy clients and has kept my money in investments for years." Hanan slid the sealed document across the table to Ruth. "Give him this. It's written in Greek, but it says that half of my money goes to David ben Netzer and the other half to you, my wife. I know David isn't my son, and we are not married, but tell Lycus we are. Elizabeth and Benjamin are to live with you until their end of days, so care for them as I always have. You are all my family, and no one is to want for anything."

Ruth covered her face with her hands and wept. Reaching out, Elizabeth rubbed Ruth's shoulders as she tried to steady herself on the cane. Benjamin still sat in his chair, stunned and blinking his eyes.

"David and I can't go without you," Ruth said, trying to talk as she cried. She rushed to him, pressing herself to his chest. "Crete is too far. You would never find us if you came later. We'll go to Tyre. I'll have this man Lycus find us a safe home. When you come he will know where we are."

The elderly couple nodded in unison. "Benjamin and I might be able to make it to Tyre, but we would surely die on such a long voyage to Crete. Let us go to Tyre as Ruth suggests," Elizabeth said.

Exasperated, Hanan rubbed a hand over his face as he stared at the floor. He needed them out of the country. If they thought the journey to Crete was too perilous for them, at least Tyre would be clear of the coming war to some degree. Jerusalem would be the main focus of the conflict.

"Very well, go to Tyre. With the money Lycus is holding for me, it will buy your safety and allow you to live well." Hanan pulled Ruth away from him to look into her eyes. "Promise me that David will be educated. Let Lycus safeguard the boy's money. The Greek has a network of money-changers that will carry on his business even if he dies. Don't worry. Micah and Yosef trusted him, and he has done well for me all of these years, so you may trust him."

Ruth tried to speak but her crying stopped her. She hugged him again and managed to speak. "Come with us now. We can all leave together."

Hanan lovingly held her head. "A man is making plans that will draw the wrath of the Roman empire down on everyone. I can't let that happen." He wrapped his arms about her and lightly squeezed. "As long as I know each of you are safe, I can do what is needed. When I return, we will be married."

She cried harder, shoulders shaking from her sobs. Hanan bent and kissed her cheek.

"I've come to love you and David. Take care of him and tell him I said goodbye. One day he will be a fine man.

Ruth grabbed his neck with both of her hands and pulled his face to hers. She kissed him as if it would be the last time then slowly broke away. "May our God, *Elohim*, protect you and return you safely to us."

Hanan remained silent. He thought it best not to tell her that *Elohim* didn't care what happened to him. Instead, he nodded, retrieved his shoulder pouch and water bag, and left.

CHAPTER TWENTY-SEVEN

S imcha stood leaning against the wall of the wine shop, glancing from one end of the street to the other. He saw Hanan and waited for his arrival before walking to a table. Uriah had seen Simcha waiting, believed Hanan would soon be along, and had wine and cups ready for them.

"When does Menahem intend to strike En Gedi?"

"If he has enough men, I've heard two or three weeks. It will be a nighttime strike to create the most confusion."

The Sicarii leader sat holding his wine cup as he stared at the table in thought. Simcha shifted in his chair, nervous at Hanan's silence. The big man raised his gaze.

"Where is he staging his men for the attack?"

"South of Cyprus on the west side of the Jordan River. He can sweep down to En Gedi, attack, and escape into the Judean mountains."

Hanan held a granite expression. "Is this information from your source?"

Simcha nodded, then grinned. "She has *experience* at getting men to give up their deepest secrets."

Straightening in his chair, Hanan glanced about the street before returning his attention to his operative. He appeared at peace with his thoughts.

"How many men do you want to take with you to Cyprus?" Simcha asked. "I can gather them and—."

"None."

Eyes widening, Simcha stared in disbelief. "Are you serious? You will be walking into the lion's den, alone like Daniel. But at least Daniel had *Elohim* to protect him."

Hanan exhaled in a long breath. "I'll have my Sica." He smiled but the humor never reached his eyes. "Listen, there's one more thing you must consider. Menahem's informants will know you supplied me with information. He'll be coming for you then probably the woman."

"I've thought about it and will be prepared. As for the woman, she knows the risks of selling information."

"Very well. Watch your back." Hanan stood and stretched. He slipped the straps of his water bag and leather pouch onto his shoulders before pulling a bag of coins from within his robe. Gently setting it in front of Simcha, he looked at his operative.

"You will hear of the outcome. If I am successful, we will meet in Jerusalem. You can buy the wine."

Laying a hand over the coin bag, Simcha gazed at Hanan and weakly smiled. "I look forward to it, master." His voice came soft with a respectful tone.

* * *

Following shepherd trails between mountains, dusty roads, rivers and dry creek beds, Hanan made good time in traveling the sixty miles to Jericho. After days of rugged terrain, he rested at a small inn to clear his mind of everything except his mission: kill Menahem. The plan was simple. Enter Menahem's camp, engage him in conversation, then stab him. As for escape, that would be determined by how the rogue Sicarii men accepted Menahem's assassination.

The winding Jordan River flowed from north of the Sea of Galilee, through it and onward to the Dead Sea, wide in spots, narrow in others with depths ranging from knee height to over a man's head. The river gave life to the land and its people along the meandering route and tributaries. From this Hanan knew that Menahem's large encampment needed water and only the river could supply such volume. Walking parallel with the river, Hanan discovered the deep footprints of at least twenty water carriers burdened with heavy bags. He left his water bag, shoulder pouch and coin bag hidden in a brushy area and tracked the footprints inland to the camp. Alert for lookouts, he found concealment upon a hillside providing the best view of the assembled men. He rested through the day, waiting for nightfall but spent the hours memorizing the terrain for his escape.

Two hours after dusk Hanan made his way down the hill and started toward the encampment. In the dim light of a half-moon the outlying guards didn't see his approach until he called out and waved a hand. They startled, drew their captured Roman swords, and stood ready though their hands shook at the sight of the muscled man.

"I am Hanan, leader of the Sicarii," he said, halting mere feet from them. "I'm here to talk with my captain, Menahem."

The two guards were shabbily dressed in crème tunics and blemished, grimy robes. Their headdresses were little more than wide cloths spread over their heads and bound with thin ropes at the forehead and around. Hawk-nosed with beards that grew untamed, their skin wasn't dark enough to be considere Egyptian. They held their swords ready but only in a defensive posture. A foul stench from their bodily odors permeated the air an when they escorted Hanan into camp, he tried not to breathe too deeply.

Counting heads as he passed campfires, he stopped at a hundred. There was no need to count further. An equally large number of closely erected tents and men could be see about the area from the light cast off their campfires.

He has his manpower. There's nothing holding him back now, Hanan thought.

The guards stopped at the edge of a twenty-foot circle of men centered around a blazing fire pit. Hanan accepted them as being Menahem's war council.

Before the guards could announce the visitor, Menahem rose from the ground with an ashen face, mouth opening as his eyes widened. Hanan ben Netzer was the last person he expected to walk into his camp.

Fifteen men sat about the circle with knives, swords and Roman spears laying across their laps. Raising their heads, they eyed the stranger with a mixture of curiosity, contempt and barbarity. Hanan met their gazes with a granite stare. He knew them; not by name or person, but by the type of animals they were—bandits, rapists, thieves and murderers who were bought for a coin. He would never have chosen them to be Sicarii. They didn't fight for a cause; only for wealth, bloodshed, and the gratification from brutality.

"What do you want? To join our ranks? Menahem threw his head back and cynically laughed yet remained on the opposite side of the campfire from Hanan.

The rogue leader stood inches shorter than Hanan, stoutly framed with thick arms and legs. He appeared to have known hard labor in his lifetime but wasn't as heavily muscled and defined as Hanan. Rough faced with bushy black eyebrows, long thick hair, and an unkempt beard, Menahem's dark eyes displayed his insanity.

Standing with fists on hips, Hanan let his gaze drift across the small army surrounding him. "I came to stop you from attacking En Gedi."

"You no longer give orders. They follow me now. We are the *new* Sicarii; men willing to take on the Roman *dogs* and drive them from our land." Menahem let his robe slip off his arms and drop onto the dirt beside the campfire. He stood in his tunic and spread his arms wide. The scar on his left forearm could be seen in the light of the campfire's flames.

"En Gedi is filled with traitors," he shouted. "We will make them examples of what happens when Jews choose Romans over their own people."

"Then go to your deaths with my blessings. Become worthless martyrs. But the legionnaires are waiting for you," Hanan yelled to the men gathering from across the camp to stand near the circle and listen. He knew his words were lies, but worth the chance if he could change their minds.

"Menahem's own mouth let his plans slip out in Jerusalem for eavesdroppers to hear. How do you think I learned of En Gedi and where to find this camp? The Romans have spies too. Two *cohorts* have been dispatched from the Tenth Legion headquarters in Syria to put down your rebellion. They may decide to come here, but they will surely be waiting for you at En Gedi. You've seen legionnaires gut their enemies like sheep. Those of you that re not killed in battle will be crucified along the sides of roads for al to see."

Hanan glanced at the shock on the faces bout him. His words had struck home. Heads shook as stunned m 1 argued over deserting with their lives. They may have been coura ous when Menahem said En Gedi would be a swift victory with w nen to rape and gold and silver to loot, but they lacked the nerve to onfront sixteen-hundred well-armed and trained legionnaires fro two *cohorts*.

"Disband," Hanan yelled. "Disband t ight or be slaughtered tomorrow."

Small groups hurriedly broke away, tal ng about the legionnaires as they left, but others remained to lis n though confusion and fear painted their faces. About the circle everal of Menahem's steadfast followers rose to their feet, gazing at eir rogue leader with doubt in their eyes.

Among them a leathery faced man wi 1 yellowish eyes and cowling pulled over his bald head, scowled 1d displayed his rotted teeth.

"Kill him, you idiot, before you lose all o your men! He's lying. Can't you tell?" the demon said in a growl g, hissing voice. He moved about the circle of men to Menahem, inseen by their eyes. "He's lying!"

The swaying flames of the campfire we no more than three feet high yet cast bright light throughout the ircle. Hanan glanced at the surrounding thieves and cutthroats, smi ng inwardly at seeing so many begin to leave. A furious bellow cam . Hanan spun to find Menahem bursting through the flames, the bl le of his short Roman sword reflecting firelight.

Hanan shifted to the right, yet not enough. The sword scraped and sliced down his robe's left sleeve leaving blood trails from two wounds. He flung the robe off, swirled and snapped it like a whip in Menahem's face, releasing his hold as the sword sliced through the air and knocked part of the robe into the flames.

The rogue leader swung in a wild horizontal strike and Hanan's Sica swept below the sword and across Menahem's stomach. A glistening crimson line appeared but Menahem had remained back enough for the blow to not be deadly. They moved about in an odd dance of death, cutting and stabbing one another wherever could be reached. Though Menahem was short and stoutly built, he moved with speed and agility. His sword's length gave him an advantage over the Sica's short blade, but his attack was undisciplined and Hanan used it to his advantage. Hanan swept the Sica diagonally, horizontally, then vertically, each time leaving long open gashes to bleed, yet never deep enough to be mortal wounds.

Moving around the campfire, Hanan kicked Menahem's robe toward the fire to keep from tripping over it. A portion of the robe caught fire, though not fully into the flames. Again, Hanan advanced, stabbing and slicing at Menahem's side and left thigh. Cries of pain poured from the rogue leader then Hanan head-butted him, momentarily dazing him. It was the opportunity Hanan wanted. Ready to step in and drive the Sica's blade deep into Menahem's stomach, agony shot through Hanan's back. Someone behind him had driven a sword into his lower right side.

Hanan bawled like a wounded bull as the blade withdrew. He spun and slashed the face of a Menahem follower. Another man leaned forward and ran a sword deep into Hanan's right shoulder. Reaching up, Hanan grabbed the sword and yanked the blade free.

He readied to stab his attacker, but an unknow n man standing near slit the attacker's throat in defense of Hanan.

Hanan stumbled back in agony. Menahe n regained his senses and drove his sword through Hanan's left leg making him drop to his knees. Both men were swathed in a sheer of crimson, bleeding heavily from their bodily wounds. Menahe 1 rushed forward as Hanan rose to his feet. A bellowing war cry ca 1e and Hanan slashed at his opponent's rib cage, feeling the Sica bla le drag across bones. Menahem spun away screaming as he moved a ound the campfire to avoid Hanan's attack.

Their thick, heavy robes lay on the grou 1d, half consumed in flames. Hanan grabbed one, then the other an threw them over the heads of the men toward the encampment. he balled robes flew like launched fireballs and landed as frantic me 1 shoved one another aside to be clear.

Hanan felt his immense strength drainin from him. He looked about for Menahem and saw men carrying iim away. The rogue leader's tunic was saturated in blood but no c fferent than Hanan's. Unsure whether Menahem would live or die Hanan looked about the circle for more attackers. The majority o the men had left. A few stood staring at Hanan, but three of Me 1ahem's loyal follow-ers advanced toward him with swords at the ready. They abruptly stopped and gazed over Hanan's head. He gl nced back and saw a wall of wavering flames and roiling smoke risir ; and sweeping across the encampment. The robes had landed near a ent. Once ablaze, the night's breeze caught the embers and spread t em among the sea of tents like cast seeds.

Weaving on his feet, he gripped his Sica and faced his attack-ers, but they raced past him into the camp o save their meager

possessions. He grimaced from the anguish of his wounds and staggered from the camp, gasping for breath with each step. The night
shrouded him once he was away from the wavering wall of fire.

* * *

Making his way to the river, Hanan turned north, stumbling
and dragging his left leg yet never stopping until he found sufficient
tall reeds and thick brush to conceal him. He wasn't sure if he was
being followed but held the Sica to his chest; a wounded animal,
ready to fight to the death.

His gaze rose to the distant orange flickering glow in the sky
above the encampment. He listened for men talking as they searched
for him, yet only the splash and trickles of the river flowing about
rocks broke the silence of the night. For now, he was safe and could
dress his wounds.

Every movement spread searing pain throughout his body. In
the faint light of the half-moon he removed his tunic and remained
only in breechcloth and sandals. Slicing the tunic into long strips of
cloth, he began to bind his wounds. He clenched his jaws to keep
from screaming when he pulled and tied a strip taut about his left
thigh. The exertion of strength with his right arm made a fiery pain
shoot through the shoulder wound where the sword had been driven.
Wrapping a wide strip about his right shoulder, he bit one end of
the cloth and pulled with his left hand. The pressure on the wound
slowed the bleeding but spread a throbbing ache across his chest and
through his head. Yet it was the deep wound in his back on the lower
right side that worried him the most. No matter how he moved, he
couldn't get relief from its burning agony. The sword had penetrated
deep, too deep, slicing internal organs and muscle as it traveled in

and out of him. The wound bled in a steady fl w, and without a fire to heat his Sica and cauterize the wound, it wc ild continue.

Maybe when dawn comes, he thought, v rapping himself with his last long bandage. Tightening the cloth b))ught greater misery. His right shoulder shot a jolt of agony through)ut him, and his body shuddered as streaks of pain gripped him. He lenched his jaws and groaned in a long, guttural breath. After the cnot was tied on the makeshift bandage, he fell back onto the groui 1, winced and gasped as waves of misery flooded him. The remai ing smaller wounds would have to wait.

Hanan looked at the star filled heaven hen the night faded to black.

CHAPTER TWENTY-EIGHT

The sun broke the horizon to climb into a clear sky. Hanan's eyes eased opened then squinted hard against the harsh morning light. He tried to raise a hand to cover his eyes, but the movement shot fierce pain through him. The struggle to rise from his back to his feet left him exhausted and breathing heavily, grimacing from the agony of his injuries. He glanced at his left leg then his right shoulder. The bandages were wet and dark from his seeping blood. Touching fingertips to his back, they came away from the bandage saturated and red.

A fierce shiver of cold raced through him. He staggered northward along the bank of the Jordan River, hoping to find a shepherd that might give him aid. Every twenty feet his suffering forced him to rest and catch his breath. He used the time to survey the surrounding land for Menahem's men. None were heard or seen.

A wisp of a smile formed on his lips. *Maybe En Gedi is safe now,* he thought.

His head throbbed with a dull ache. Each passing minute became harder for him to clearly think. Growing weaker he knew he needed to keep moving and started northward again.

The warmth of the sun felt good on his body and helped keep his shivers at bay. The pain within his right side became an iron fist, squeezing and twisting, making him lean and favor it as he moved. There was nothing more he could do except force himself to take one more step toward civilization.

Hobbling into a clearing along the river bank, his side wound shot piercing pain throughout him and became paralyzing. He halted then his legs crumbled. The flowing river was five feet away when he dropped to his knees. Face raised to the sky, he opened his palms and let his arms hang out from him. His injuries were agonizing, yet it was heartache that now forced tears from his eyes.

"I always believed in you, Yeshua... I never told you, but I believed." Hanan grimaced from the pulsating misery within him. "You are the Christ, the Messiah. Please, don't turn away from me like *Elohim* has..."

The searing pain in Hanan's side made him bend and grab his abdomen. He cried out as he fell face down into the dirt. Breathing heavily, he laid still a moment then dug his fingers into the soil and began to crawl to the river.

The demon cast the cowl of his black robe back and knelt beside Hanan. Gaze drifting over the muscled man's body, Abaddon paused to watch the crimson blood trailing to the ground from the wrapped wound on Hanan's back. Rotted teeth appeared as his malicious smile spread.

"If you hadn't interfered, I would have had seven hundred dead to choose from tonight. Oh, you cut Menahem quite well, but he's still alive—barely, yet alive. I'll see that he survives though. I have need of him in the future. As for you, Hanan, you're dying. The sword sliced too many of your internal organs. I'm surprised you made it this far." Abaddon grinned and glanced about the barren land. He sighed. "You're going to die alone, Hanan, with no one caring—just like your whore mother wanted you to die in the wilderness the night you were born. What a befitting end."

Hanan's fingers curled and clawed through the soil as he inched his way into the river.

Abaddon stood, smiled and walked beside him. The demon heard Hanan mumble and cupped a hand over his ear as he bent to the dying man.

"What did you say? I couldn't hear you because you're dying." The demon's laughter carried across the river.

"Yeshua... the living water... baptize me—."

Hanan kept crawling out into the river. The cold water rushing over his body seemed to wash away his agony and cleanse him. He struggled to hold his head up but couldn't, then began to choke. Blood from his wounds spread across the water's surface, formed eerie pools about him and became streaks flowing with the river's current.

Palm trees, reeds and brush along the river bank swayed as a breeze gusted then settled.

Rather than stand rejoicing at Hanan's misery, Abaddon's brows drew sharply downward. He hissed like a cornered feral cat and backed away while watching a glowing figure appear by the drowning man.

"Neither my Father nor I have forsaken you, Hanan. You have found victory as He wished. Now, join me in my Father's house." Yeshua lowered his hands and raised Hanan from the river.

Abaddon scowled and whipped the robe's cowl over his head. Spinning away, he vanished within three steps.

Hanan rose from the water, holding onto Yeshua, confused, yet at peace. He glanced at his left forearm. The demon's scar was gone. Weeping without shame, he looked at Yeshua then to the riverbank. His Sica laid half buried in the dirt. But turning to the river he saw his body, face down with arms outstretched, drifting downstream.

* * *

Ruth stood at the front door with David by her side, watching the dirt road that led to the house. Forty days had passed; ten more than Hanan had instructed her to wait. Stroking her son's thick hair, she glanced over her shoulder into the vacant house. Her eyes were wet though she tried not to cry.

"It's time to go," she whispered, more to herself than to David.

Walking to the donkey cart loaded with their possessions, she motioned David to sit on the cart's seat with Elizabeth and Benjamin.

"Hold this, please." The boy handed her a carefully wrapped scroll before he began to climb. It was the Torah Hanan had given to David on his sixth birthday.

After the boy settled himself on the seat, she gently laid the scroll in his lap and walked to the donkey. Adjusting her shawl over her head, she refused to look back at the house. It would only make her cry more.

Tugging the donkey's reins, Ruth started for Tyre.

EPILOGUE

Those who believed Yeshua was *The Christ* and followed his teachings became known as *Christians* though they had remained in obeyance of Judaism from birth. Christianity overlapped Judaism but years later events came about to distinguish one from the other.

A new follower replaced Judas as one of Yeshua's twelve disciples, numbered after the Twelve Tribes of Israel. Empowered with the Holy Spirit, the disciples traveled separate paths to distant lands to baptize and spread the teachings. Paul, once known as Saul of Tarsus, spent his remaining years bringing Yeshua's teachings to the Gentiles in Rome and abroad.

The disciples preached the love of God, *Elohim*, yet all except one met violent ends. They were crucified, beheaded, speared, tortured, burned and clubbed to death. Only John, who had looked after Yeshua's mother, died of natural causes, and that came on a Roman penal colony island.

Hanan's premonition of the violence to come proved truthful. Small at first, uprisings spread across the land and into neighboring countries where multitudes of Jewish communities existed. Zealots were blamed, though, many of the violent riots and bloody attacks on Roman administrators, soldiers, and citize s were carried out by the Sicarii.

Numerous complaints by Jewish facti ns had been lodged against the Prefect Pontius Pilate for bringing busts of the emperor on military standards and shields into Jerusale n and seizing Temple treasury funds for the completion of an aqued ct. After ten years as prefect, he was removed from office in 36 A.] over quelling a suspected Samaritan insurrection by executing tl ir leaders.

Pilate was recalled to Rome by Vitellius the Roman legate of Syria, to answer to Emperor Tiberius for the xecutions. To Pilate's good fortune Tiberius died and the matter w dropped. Tales exist of Pilate's exile, his ordered suicide, and eve of his conversion to Christianity, yet no one knows what became o him.

Upon relieving Pilate, Vitellius traveled Jerusalem. There he removed Caiaphas, the High Priest of the San edrin Council, from office and replaced him with Jonathan, Cai phas' brother-in-law. Caiaphas had been in office ten years the sa e as Pilate. Jonathan was later assassinated by the Sicarii.

Gaius 'Caligula' Caesar rose to power 37 A.D. before his twenty-fifth birthday. At first, he was thougl to be a noble ruler. After an illness he believed had been a poison g attempt on his life, he became merciless and sexually perverted wi a craving for absurd extravagances. By his second year of reign, R ne was in a financial downfall. To slow the demise, Caligula raised t es across the empire. He compounded the Roman problems with e Jewish population by ordering a statue of himself to be erected in the Second Temple.

In 39 A.D., Herod Agrippa accused Herc l Antipas, tetrarch of Galilee and Perea, of planning a rebellion aga nst the empire. After Antipas confessed, Caligula banished him a d his wife Herodias,

Agrippa's sister, to Gaul. Antipas died in this year and Agrippa received all of his properties. Whether the emperor ordered Antipas' death has never been confirmed.

By 41 A.D., everyone believed Caligula to be insane and Rome teetered on the verge of financial collapse. His Praetorian Guard ended the insanity of his reign by stabbing him to death.

Throughout the empire Jews were revolting against the tyrannical control and ever-increasing taxation from the emperors. The clashes commenced small and centralized then spread. Through 45 to 46 A.D., famine struck Judea. The following year Judah, son of Ezekias the Zealot leader, captured the Roman garrison at Sepphoris. Legionnaires later crucified two of his sons.

The Zealots claimed the Sicarii were a splinter group of their organization while the Sicarii declared otherwise. Both wanted freedom from Roman rule and fought their oppressors at every turn. Unfortunately, they lacked the leadership and discipline to unite in a collaborative effort. Eleazar ben Simon argued with John of Giscala, and Simon bar Giora argued with Eleazar ben Ananias. The names of leaders changed, quarrels grew, and all while combatting the Romans.

Menahem, a blood-thirsty man, claimed leadership of the Sicarii after Hanan ben Netzer's body was discovered floating down the Jordan River. While the Zealots attacked legionnaires, Menahem unleashed his murderous wrath upon Jews, Gentiles and Romans.

The Council of Jerusalem met between 48-50 A.D., establishing the differences between Judaism and Christianity. Circumcision was heavily debated, although, the practice was abhorred in other lands. Should Gentile followers of Yeshua be required to undergo the ritual; and without circumcision, would they still be one of God's people? The Council addressed other problem s as well; sexual sins, blood sacrifices, idolatry, and how the Laws of loses applied to non-Jews. But in the eyes of the Roman empire, Je s and Christian Jews were one in the same.

At the age of sixteen, Nero Claudi s Caesar Augustus Germanicus became emperor in 54 A.D. Five y ars later he murdered his domineering mother. His construction pro grams and enjoyment of a cultural life brought increased taxes and f rther anger from the people. Nero acted upon whims and grew mur erous. The Great Fire of Rome erupted and destroyed a majority of t e city. Panic-stricken citizens accused him of setting the fires, and i turn, he accused the Jews and Christians of the city. Mass arrests ; id executions began. Thousands of innocent people were sent to t e arena to be fed to wild animals, crucified and burned alive. Hi persecution of Jews and Christians then spread across the entire e pire.

In Nero's twelfth year of reign, the First J wish Revolt, years in the making, erupted in Judea. The Prefect Ges us Florus confiscated the Second Temple's treasury money on beha of the emperor, then arrested anyone who protested. It was in thi year too that James the Just, Yeshua's brother, was killed by the or er of the High Priest Ananus ben Ananus.

Plots against Nero's life, as well as the n mber of his enemies, grew so great that he fled Rome. Rather tha be murdered, Nero chose to commit suicide but lacked the cour ge to do so. His private secretary had to complete the act. Before ying in 68 A.D., Nero gave his general Vespasian orders to crush he Judean rebellion. Vespasian in turn placed his son, Titus, as se ond-in-command to lead the legions.

Romans escaped from Jerusalem as rebels overran military garrisons across Judea. The Roman legate of Syria, Cestius Gallus, ordered the reinforced Syrian Legion XII *Fulminata* to bring an end to the revolt. But the hunted turned hunter, and Jewish rebels ambushed and slaughtered 6,000 soldiers. In the defeat the legion's *aquila*, their eagle, the prominent symbol of a Roman legion, was lost—an insult of the highest degree to Rome.

With Jerusalem under rebel control, a Judean Provisional government was formed but immediately its leaders, priests, Zealots and Sicarii, set upon one another for the rulership. One of the rebels' first acts was to burn the money-changers' debt records kept in the temple. Discovery of the records only confirmed suspicions of the temple priests working with the wealthy money-changers to exploit the poor and steal their lands.

Menahem's Sicarii stormed the fortress of Masada and slew its 700 garrisoned legionnaires to the last man. In Jerusalem at the Antonia fortress, Zealots led by Eleazar ben Ananias forced the garrison to flee. Following Eleazar, Menahem's Sicarii entered Antonia and slaughtered the injured Romans that had been left behind.

Without proper leadership the Zealots fought amongst themselves. The Sicarii argued for the right to govern the city, and upon proclaiming himself the Messiah, Menahem demanded command of both factions. Knowing Menahem was a madman, Eleazar led his men against the Sicarii and drove them from Jerusalem. Menahem, the butcherous leader, was later captured and tortured to death.

Jerusalem became a refuge for thousands of Jews fleeing their homes due to the country-wide rebellion. Along with the refugees came pilgrims from other lands, arriving to celebrate the coming Passover. To make the city dwellers more willing to battle the oncoming Roman army, the Zealots destroyed large quantities of their food stocks. They also believed that *Elohim* would miraculously save them from the legions. Factions within the Zealots argued, fought and murdered one another while three Roman legions under Titus' command swept across the land and marched toward Jerusalem.

By 68 A.D. Titus' 70,000 soldiers had conquered the regions north of Judea. A fourth legion joined Titus, and he turned to Jerusalem, the rebels' major stronghold.

Three legions positioned themselves on Jerusalem's west side while a fourth waited to the east on the Mount of Olives. Titus allowed pilgrims to enter the crowded city to celebrate Passover but refused to let them leave. The inhabitants were nearing starvation, and the increased number only further drained the remaining supplies. Outside the city deserters were captured, crucified, and left for the city dwellers to see. After several attempts by Titus to negotiate Jerusalem's surrender, the rebels continued to refuse his terms. Frustrated by the delays, the Roman leader ordered the attack.

The walls of the Antonia fortress and temple gates were breached. Soldiers set fire to the upper and lower city, and the Second Temple, then came Titus' command for total destruction. Although the number of slaughtered men, women, and children was exaggerated to be over a million, in truth, hundreds of thousands died. 97,000 of the city's inhabitants were captured and sent to Rome. There they were sold as household slaves; became gladiators for the entertainment of the citizens; slave labor for construction projects, and the more youthful prisoners were placed in brothels. The city's rebel leaders were sent to Rome to undergo humiliation, trial and execution. After the legions ransacked and destroyed Jerusalem, the Second Temple laid in ruin.

Yeshua's forewarning as he had stood in front of the temple on the day of his Jerusalem entry came true. *"No stone that stands here one upon another will not be thrown down... And no Judean—man, woman, or child will survive that time."*

The Sanhedrin Council lost their authority and control and were expelled to Yavne in the southern coastal plain, south of Jaffa. The Pharisees, rather than the Sadducees, became the governing sect. Their practice of Judaism was followed, and the Sadducees and Essenes fell to the wayside.

After the massacre of the Roman garrison on Masada, the Sicarii retained it as their base camp from which to raid surrounding villages. As the madman Menahem had wanted years before, the Sicarii attacked the Jewish settlement of En Gedi. Over seven hundred of its inhabitants were slain and the 'city of palm trees' was left in ruin.

Once forced from Jerusalem by the Zealots, the Sicarii chose to make the mountaintop fortress of Masada their family refuge. When Jerusalem fell to Titus, Eleazar ben Yair and 960 people remained there with no place else to go.

In 72 A.D. the Roman governor Lucius Flavius Silva was ordered to destroy the Sicarii fortress. His 15,000 men of the Legion X *Fretensis*, auxiliary units and slave labor laid siege to Masada. Though the mountain defied direct assaults, Silva chose to build a ramp to reach its top. But when the soldiers finally entered the stronghold, they were met with silence. The inhabitants of Masada had chosen to die by having their throats slit, choosing suicide over Roman slavery. Only a man, woman, and several children were found alive.

The persecution of Jews throughout the empire persisted for years to come. Insurrections rose wherever Jew sh colonies remained, and their revolt in 115 A.D. was called Kitos War.

Hadrian came to power as emperor 1 117 A.D. Leaving Roman boundaries as they were, he chose o unite the empire's diverse people and encourage building alor g with military preparedness. He distrusted written reports and personally inspected his empire's provinces.

While visiting Jerusalem in 130 A.D. Hadrian considered reconstructing for the Jews, but a Samaritan riest, based upon his people's hatred of Jews dating back hundreds of years, discouraged the idea. Accepting the priest's reasoning, Had an ordered Jerusalem to be rebuilt as a Roman colony along with th erection of two temples to honor Roman gods. A Temple to Jup er was ordered built atop where the Second Temple had stood, and a Temple to Venus to be erected atop Golgotha and the rock cave to b of Yeshua's burial.

More decrees came from Hadrian. Jerusa m was to be renamed 'Aelia Capitolina,' and the Jewish religious pra tice of circumcision, considered mutilation, was to be abolished. B t in Rome, the tradition of Romans castrating their slaves was still permitted.

In 132 A.D., the Bar Kokhba Revolt e upted. Although the Kitos War was never declared as the Secon Jewish War, Simon bar Kokhba's rebellion received that distinc ion. Roman oppression, abolishment of circumcision, the renami g of the Holy City of Jerusalem, and the erection of pagan temples ver Jewish hallowed ground became only a few of the reasonings f the war.

From his fortress in Betar, Simon bar I khba and his rebels withstood a three-and-a-half-year siege by th might of the Roman Empire's legions. Enraged by the troubles v th Judaism and the

Jewish people, Hadrian decided to obliterate the religion from the country. The legions crushed the revolt with violent force, slaughtering over a half-million men, women, and children. The number of enslaved persons was believed to be several hundred thousand, but that number cannot be verified.

Renaming the Judean Province to Syria Palaestina, Hadrian expelled all Jews and Christian Jews from Aelia Capitolina, the former city of Jerusalem. Upon penalty of death, they were never to enter the city except for one day each year—the holiday of Tisha B'Av.

And for the next one hundred fifty years, the city remained a pagan Roman town.

ABOUT THE AUTHOR

G lenn Starkey is an award-winning author living in Texas with his family. He served in the Marine Corps; is a Vietnam veteran; worked in Texas law enforcement; was security manager over petrochemical facilities, and security director of a major Gulf Coast port. For the past eleven years Glenn has volunteered as a reading mentor to elementary school children. He has been baptized in the Jordan River.

Feel free to contact Glenn through GStarkeyBooks@aol.com and browse his website, https://www.glennstarkey.net . His novels are available from all major booksellers.